"An enchantment worth the price of admission."

— *New York Times Book Review*

"*Carnival for the Gods* is an artful, curious book, adventuresome and compelling."

— *The Chicago Tribune*

"Much of the beauty of Gladys Swan's fiction is her skill at balancing earthiness with cosmic vision."

— *The Sewanee Review*

"Swan has once again shown her mastery of the short story. Perhaps with five volumes of short stories she should be celebrated with other masters such as Katherine Ann Porter or Chekhov."

— *Southern Humanities Review*

"In these times of so much 'throwaway' fiction Swan's collections shine with the timeless luster that comes from well-polished prose and a true ken for storytelling."

— *Kansas City Star*

"Swan claims the reader's attention in these vigorous renderings of human experience."

— *Publisher's Weekly*

"Swan's fiction emphasizes humanity's need, desire and ability to construct personal meaning from experience. Seeking self-affirmation and the strength to persevere, each of swan's characters is involved in a crisis and on the verge of a revelation."

— *Contemporary Literary Criticism*, Vol. 69

A Dark Gamble

Gladys Swan

SERVING HOUSE BOOKS

A Dark Gamble

ISBN: 978-0-9913281-9-2

Cover art: "Hangover," painted by Gladys Swan, photographed by Monte Nevins

Serving House Books logo by Barry Lereng Wilmont

Published by Serving House Books
Copenhagen, Denmark and Florham Park, NJ
www.servinghousebooks.com

Member of The Independent Book Publishers Association

First Serving House Books Edition 2015

"The Flood" was first published in *The Southern California Anthology*

For the town of Silver City, where the journey first began

Books by Gladys Swan

NOVELS
Carnival for the Gods
Ghost Dance: A Play of Voices
The World of Carnival (selections)

SHORT FICTION
On the Edge of the Desert
Of Memory and Desire
Do you Believe in Cabeza de Vaca?
A Visit to Strangers
News from the Volcano
A Garden Amid Fires
The Tiger's Eye: New & Selected Stories

Every journey has a secret destination of which the traveler is unaware.

—Martin Buber

I. The Flood

Only imagine it—the town rising up into existence out of the wilderness. Struggling up without an idea of itself, from all that strikes the mind as chaos. Gold! Discovered in the hills. And everybody's running to get there, like dogs after a bitch in heat. Seized by the fever dream. The madness of desire: gold—that will transform your life, transport you beyond the aching moment, the pile of hollow bones you've left behind. No more sweat and tiredness. You'll be taken out of all that, lifted up to float in the bliss of accomplished desires. Ah, sweet radiance. A dream that breaks apart all sad resignation, throws all the traps out the window—good sense, habit, home ties, the gleanings of the closet—lets it all go— the past broken beyond mending. And lets in the new, all fresh and sweet, like the air after a rain. You're out of the doldrums. Out of the pious dullness. You've heard the cry: Gold! and you're awake. There's something you've always wanted, always hankered after— you suddenly remember. You're on your feet and set in motion— caught in the whirlwind. You'll make your fortune this time round. Something's out there for you yet.

You can't help it—how well I know. Whatever goaded you into this world has never let up. That plaguing impulse. The moment I hit the ground, I was ready to be off in the next wind. No help for it. Once you're bitten by destiny, even if you don't know what teeth are ripping into your hide, there's nothing for it but to throw yourself into all the chances—no escaping them back there in that savage place among the adventurers. Imagine them flocking there, feeling the lure like a call to the blood: Gold. Nuggets as big as walnuts! Whatever gold is—whatever promise it holds of the improbable second chance. And all those who seek it. I'm hoping they'll tell me a thing or two.

Forget Columbus, forget Coronado. All the conquerors who took us into a new world, and the rest who took us farther yet—till we're left standing in the corrupt and corroded middle of things. The energy—where has it gone? Into shopping malls and showplace ranches, and re-enactments of the Old West for the tourists, and gambling casinos where the Indians have a chance for revenge on those who did them the dirty. All the rawness smoothed away except for new forms of violence that keep breaking the crust. And what is there left to discover? Maybe that was the question that burned in me, set me going, trying to imagine how it was before the kiss of the future drew us in. The golden future, that lovely vision, all in gauzy blue, beckoning, pressing her lips forward in that kiss of promise and fatality.

Oh, the awakening of that first lust. There's been a strike, and the rumors have come flying. A vein that goes deep as promise in a pure, shining ribbon, just waiting to be lifted out. Strike out for the territory, shove in with your elbows, grab your share while the grabbing's good. And me—I can see myself in the middle of it all, caught in the moment. Trying to make my claim upon the future like everybody else, heedless of what it might hold.

There they are, the slim beginnings. I'm walking toward the miners' shacks springing up out of whatever boards they can scrounge up, cut, hammer together. Dirt floor. A couple of iron skillets hanging on the wall. Cot. Stove. Mine is there among them. I go out on my mule with pick and shovel, lying out in all kinds of weather, bring back samples, take them to be assayed in the little corner of the express office set up for it. The assayer's office got there just about as quick as the saloon and the general store. Drink and victuals and harness—if you had any sense you'd make your fortune off them alone and leave go the rest. But who has that kind of sense? Not me—I've got too restless a spirit.

More people coming. Entertainment. Room for the poker game. The whores moving in. Every day a new set of faces, a new spread of rumor—who's found what and where to go get it. Life on the edge: each new day pulling you on to strike the vein of the future.

Gambling one day's expectations against the next— All one big gamble. How hard it is: living out on that wild land with the fleas and the lice, coming back with weeks of grime ground into your skin and spending a night in what passes for a hotel, sleeping with the bedbugs and half a dozen other snoring men—getting drunk, paying for a woman, and just barely missing getting shot in a brawl, over nothing. For your life isn't worth a nickel. But you drive on. A new set of supplies to take you back into the dirt and the cold, with you hoping against fever and the bears you'll make it back one more time. Always having to dodge the man who might kill you for your claims, not to mention the Indians marauding in the territory. And for all that, you maybe dying with only a pocket full of scraps, claims on paper. That's what happened to one fellow. I wasn't there when they went through his pockets. But I heard the tale—how some of those little slips were worth a fortune. Only he wasn't around to claim it or to appreciate the irony.

You've seen it a hundred times. Prospectors rushing out, the town rising up: all of it done now on a Hollywood set. All congealed into the familiar. If you want any of it, you have to go back and dig it all out and look at it again. Because something happened.... If it happened that way.... One moment you're convinced. But then a little set of facts rises up that doesn't fit the picture. And you've got to count through it all again, all the fragments in your hands, trying to make them take a shape. Like those chunks of rock they mined, melting them down, refining them into gold pieces they could tally. Because what really happened—that's the teaser. You keep getting the story again. Over and over—and it's never done. It pulls you back. Only now I'm the one who's got to get hold of it. If it is a story... Maybe it's on account of all the rumors and anecdotes I've heard, the tales I've read, all piling up, pulling at me, till I got taken up, trying to imagine that life once again, entering into the experience, living it. And once you get into it, you can't get out again until you've given it its due.

It happens like this: there's an old tintype of the Pioneer Saloon, and I'm back there standing at the bar. I can feel the whiskey glass in my hand, and the smooth polished sheen of the wood of the counter top I run my other hand along. Somebody/s telling me how the fellow operating the new stamping mill has taken to buying land. Don't know him, who is he? Englishman, they tell me—say his family has got dukes and earls back aways. Right smart he is. And then I'm the one in the assayer's office looking at the scales, waiting for the verdict. A shake of the head. Nothing much this round. It's again into the hills. I'm thinking, maybe the placer should be set a little higher along the creek. I've seen the glint in the bottom of the pan. Something's coming down; there's got to be more where that came from.

I've roved those hills ever since I was a boy. Now I give them back to the time when only the Indians and a few settlers were the hunters—herds of elk and antelope moving through the glens, and the grizzlies with their menace—all that land full of animals and birds, their color and movement and noise, their roving and preying and feeding. The edges of photos dissolve as if they were only a local border around time.

And the time I was born rises like a hill above the past while I sink down into what lies below. Now let the eye wander into an inward space   where I forget time and myself. Over and over it happens. Another piece of change and enterprise. Every time you come back to the town from wherever you've been roving—you've forgotten how long, the days slipping away as into a pile of tailings— it's there waiting for you: a new house, a new saloon or store, a boarding house newly become so by virtue of a sign.

This time it's the new hotel. I stare before the fact. It's impressive. A hotel with polished doors and cast iron balconies intricately wrought. And on the top, a fancy cupola all painted blue and gray, so anybody needing a breath of pure air can climb to the roof and look out over the town to the Burro Mountains. A marvel, as in those stories where somebody commands a genie to bring him a palace and wakes up the next morning and finds it right outside the bedroom window, all bedecked with gems and gold. I couldn't believe my eyes. Standing right there: a real piece of civilization—

out of the frenzy of building that just barely keeps up with all that's going on. The makeshift trying to shift into the permanent. A sawmill cutting timber from the pines and oaks for the mines and the miners' shacks. A brickyard turning out brick made from good local clay, a great find. From the East, a woman coming with a load of plate glass. Carpenters and bricklayers building real houses with porches and bay windows. Carving out a place in the nest of the mountains.

They're here now, all those assembled by chance, and it looks like they're going to stay, maybe never go back to where they came from. And more keep coming. A town. Finding itself a name: Destiny. A place on the map. Now a main street taking its direction down through a row of big cottonwoods that have been there forever. Stores on both sides, the trees arching above the enterprises of that dirt street teamed up with newly civilizing ambitions. Taking away the rawness as they blend with the solid shapes winning the ground from the mesquite and the lizards chasing through.

You can hardly see the dirt of the main street any more, it's so covered over with playing cards thrown from out from the saloons. "A new deck," somebody yells And there goes the old one, fanning out into the middle of the street. From sixteen saloons that's a lot of cards. You've got a wide choice as to where to go to lose your loot, your luck, or your life, whatever you were aiming to do. I stand there over that swirl of kings and queens and numbers, the flung figures of chance and luck, till they seize hold of my brain, whirling into a dance of numbers and possibilities.

From the very beginning that street became a trough of dirty water every time it rained. Something had to be done about it, so they built a bridge over the mud and trouble, over all the scattered cards, so folks wouldn't get their shoes dirty. You see how it is, that play of ingenuity, one thing leading to another, into a new habit, landing you conveniently into the midst of a new piece of reality. For now there were ladies in the town, and the notion of a family and a settled life. And you had a way to get across a street, where, before, there wasn't any. And pretty soon the notion of elegance was born from the presence of the local brick factory and the freight coming in with imported furniture, to create a handsome town with fine houses in the Victorian style, and a main street with mercantile stores and a stables. I've never known a creature yet that didn't seize the chance to elevate its standard of living. That's how it was—all before the turn of the century. (Though don't forget the saloons.)

Up on one hill lived the Mexicans, who came to work the mines, now operated by companies, and down below the town were the gardens worked by the Chinaman who gave the town fresh vegetables. A Jew who'd crossed the world from Poland and another from the Ukraine, having left the lower East Side, came to try their fortunes in the clothing business—in the West. And the Buffalo Soldiers, former slaves mustered out from military duty, turned to cowboying and prospecting, one becoming a Justice of the Peace.

The telegraph came, and then the railroad. The whole town was there to greet the first train at the newly built depot, and plant a silver spike made by the jeweler from local silver. The engine, all festooned with flowers and ribbons, made its way into the station with a military band marching alongside. The mayor gave a grandiloquent speech. Here was a moment of history, one that babes in arms would have cause to remember. Now the town would be linked to the rest of continent, all in the spirit of Manifest Destiny. And look what was here: no mean town of half–finished shacks. No piece of raw beginnings, isolated, beyond reach of all but the most intrepid. "Look around you." Maybe you recall when the first brick house was built by our worthy judge. And how the number of handsome dwellings has multiplied. They carry a message: *We've come here, and we mean to stay.*"

The civilizing hand had been at work, the ladies of the town coming together to sponsor a hospital and a school for their young ones. The new generation coming on, who would inherit the town. The Mexicans had built a massive–walled church of adobe right near the center of town, its newly forged bell striking out a summons to the believer. From wood and brick the Methodists and Presbyterians had each created a shape for their worship, their preachers coming all the way from the East to take up the condition of souls teetering on the edge of perdition. A fertile field. First the miners and the whores and the soldiers, the wild nights in the saloons. Abandon and the thin excuse for killing. Then the taming hand and the pious word. And after the soldiers had come to rout the Apaches, pushing them into the reservations, chasing Geronimo from here to Mexico, capturing him finally and holding him prisoner in the basement of the Fleming house, then the ranches and the roads would be safe— so they thought.

It had come—the right moment for the hotel. A place for the wayfarer. Hospitality in the wild, and for the citizens, a local palace. Wagonload after wagonload of brick carted in. The foundation laid of stone, walls going up. One story, then two. The whole trimmed in gleaming white wood. In every room a brass bed and a velvet carpet, lace curtains at the windows. And what awaited you when you walked in: a spacious lobby, the dining room on your right hand; to the left, a game room with billiards and card tables for the gentlemen; and for all the guests and visitors, a ballroom with crystal chandeliers and a grand piano. A piano that had to be ordered special and cost a thousand dollars plus the freight.

Thomas Weston was going to have himself a showplace, he being the younger son of English nobility, who'd come to this remote spot to build his fortune. He boasted that no finer hotel could be found either in Chicago or San Francisco. He'd been to those cities and seen for himself. The offspring of his ambition he called Weston House.

Then the flood came.

Who'd have thought? No one paid any mind to the dark-bellied clouds gathering over the mountains with the gray streaks trailing down. It had rained before. How often they'd watched the main street turn into a trough of mud and water. They'd built their bridge, then a dam to hold back the water. The state of boots and shoes had been given ample consideration. Even after the rain started pelting down, no one paid any heed. Sooner or later it would stop. But the rain didn't let up, and somewhere back in the mountains, the water began to wash down the slopes, gullies filling, overflowing, the water gathering force. Water roaring through arroyos, making its own path. Muddy and full of fury. Breaking out, some said, against sheer human blunder. All the trees that had been felled for the mining operations, all the livestock sent out to crop the grass— mules and horses and cattle: the hand of man making a place for himself, brushing against the scheme of things, bringing on disaster.

Maybe there's a price to pay when you tear something out of the land—a few thought that.

But others claimed it was punishment for all the rioting and whoring and gambling and killing that had gone on ever since they struck those veins of ore.

All that sheer force. Water tearing loose everything in its path, uprooting trees and tearing away rocks. Think of it coming toward you all unknowing. A billion and a half gallons, so the newspaper attested. Enough anyway that you couldn't keep any account of it in your head, but had to wait for science to do the arithmetic. The flood snatched out fifteen hundred feet of railroad track and a couple of bridges, then came on, greedy for more. Struck the planing mill, borrowed the timbers and swirled them around to dash them against the trees of an orchard all hung with peaches the Indians had planted. The fruit came raining down, bobbing in the flood, scattering to the winds.

That flood was discovering itself, like a kid turned loose with rocks to throw, all gleeful in its power. And more. Water wouldn't take all the glory. Wind joined in. Howled around like a mad thing. And lightning cracked the sky. It could have been the end of the world. Seemed like it. Or at least the end of the town. And as they met the daylight, the citizens knew terror.

The water came on, discovering caprice. Struck a warehouse and floated away the whiskey, case after case of it, and went on with its drunken battery. Hit the livery stable, picked up saddle horses and moved on with its collection of livestock and saddles and sheds. Now the flood came on all sides, sweeping onto houses and stores, tearing away the great noble cottonwoods lining both sides of the street, flicking out the bridge over the main thoroughfare, the Mayor having crossed only five minutes before. Flushing away the playing cards lining it, the combined efforts of myriad players of those sixteen saloons. The flood struck upon medicine and law. Took off seven hundred dollars' worth of books and instruments from Dr. Ernest Healy and spoiled the fine law library Judge Hanson McCowan had brought from the East, giving him jurisdiction over a mass of waterlogged pulp. It struck hardware store and general store, set afloat kegs of nails and cans of kerosene and tubs of lard and sacks of beans and potatoes, and ruined the bacon and the flour.

Quickly and by odd turns, the town woke to its condition: Adam Kunz, a butcher, in his room at the rear of the saloon, lay deep in Sunday sleep. Water floated his bed around for a while, then turned it over. The cold astonished him, sent him fleeing in his nightclothes. The Chinese laundryman Ying Lee, trapped in his washhouse, was crying out at the top of his lungs as the water continued to rise. He was rescued just before the shed was carried away. A traveling auditor for the Atchison, Topeka, and Santa Fe, and the local agent, marooned in the station house surrounded by the rising waters, climbed to the attic and were left for a time to audit their lives before they thought to break a hole in the ceiling with an ax and clamber to the roof.

They watched the big iron safe from the Post Office float past and saw that a conductor on the other side of the rail yards had climbed a tree to wait for the waters to subside. He would cling there a goodly while. Morley Fulton, struck with terror for his family, got his wife and children to the roof, and his neighbor from across the street threw them a rope. Mrs. Amos Potter, who'd just escaped from a cyclone in Baxter Springs, Kansas, managed to survive this disaster as well. The most memorable events of her life, perhaps, had come one on the heels of the other. She died in her sleep in her eighty-second year, which meant she'd seen a couple of world wars before it was all over.

And a little boy, who'd gone under twice, and felt himself slipping out of the world for good, was plucked up by Frank McBride, a carter, and set down to live his life and die another death.

In their various ways they clambered to safety, helping each other. All but one. One casualty when the flood came to the hotel. Breathless and frantic, the telegrapher burst in, the danger at his heels. Tom Weston was behind his desk, while his wife, who took charge of the dining room, was in the kitchen. Their young son was playing in their rooms at the back. Rousted out, the guests, all and sundry, in various states of dress and undress, fled to the second story ahead of the water invading the lobby and dining room. Submerging the carpets and sinking the beds with their promise of comfort, it mounted toward the ceiling.

"Head for the roof," a tall, bearded man yelled out, taking charge.

A babble of voices rose from the guests, men and women, some with their kids, frantic to gain the roof, some snatching up valises and their money.

"Stay calm," the bearded man ordered, "and leave your traps behind."

So they did, some racing up the stairs, the men helping the rest to make their way out through the windows of the cupola to stand on the roof.

"Fetch a rope!" A command flung out to anyone who'd pick up the end.

"Tom, what are you doing?" Mrs. Weston called to her husband. He'd been just behind her, but now he raced back into the corridor, while she went forward, holding the boy by the hand.

"The rope," he yelled. "We've got to have a rope. Julio!"

Julio came running. Julio, the boy who ran errands and helped the cook in the kitchen and shined the boots and shoes left out in the hallway, came running with a coil of rope.

"Tom," Mrs. Weston yelled as she turned toward the stairs. "Hurry, Tom."

But Tom Weston did not follow. He took the coil of rope and called for Julio to assist him. The piano. It had to be saved, the piano that cost a thousand dollars plus the freight.

"Papa," called his son.

"Don't worry," he assured them. He and Julio would save the piano. Surely the water would not rise above the mezzanine where the ballroom was. And it didn't. But it came with such force it ripped off the back wall and the floor began to tilt. A cry from above as the lodgers retreated as far as they could from the yawning gap.

"Tom," his wife shrieked. Her voice, their son's voice, all the voices, were drowned by the wind.

"We've got her," Tom Weston yelled to Julio. "Hold her."

Julio groaned in protest. The time for music had passed, and he was certain it would never come again. No, the town was doomed. He prayed hastily to the Virgin of Guadalupe, as the piano began to slide across the tilting floor. It was time to let go of music, if not his soul, and he flung himself in the direction of the opposite wall, crawled toward a window, the top part shattered, fumbled it open, and clung to the window ledge for all he was worth.

"You can't, you can't." Tom Weston yelled at the piano taking its leave. Then it pitched into the flood.

Above on the roof, the boy, Gilbert, witnessed a moment of frenzied dance, as though the instrument accompanying his father had given him a musical motion. He was too astonished to cry out as he watched that black shiny object, in its former place immovable as stone, bobbing and floating. And his father like a bit of stick pulled along behind. Then both he and his mother were shrieking together. For a moment his father was swept up against the black wood, and the boy expected him to pull himself up on top, but in the next his father was wrenched away and disappeared under the surface, the piano bobbling along like a toy.

Days later it was found several miles below the town, dashed to pieces. Thadeus Walton collected several of the keys, which he kept in a box till, over the years, they turned dry and yellow: "Nature playing its tune," he'd say when he showed these curiosities.

The flood has been in my memory ever since I can remember. Like a stain in a fabric or a germ running in the blood. A piece of inheritance. And all the rest—a story that refuses to die. You always run into somebody who once knew so-and-so and claims to have got things straight from the horse's mouth. You can look in the newspaper files for the events, add a few facts to swell gossip and speculation. I remember Fletch Griffith once making some remark about Tom Weston when I was listening to the men sitting around at the drug store counter drinking coffee, my grandfather among them. "Well, he wasn't nearly as crazy as his son." he remarked.

"No," my grandfather said. "Poor Tom got cut off in that flood—maybe he was lucky, considering. His boy took up where he left off. Gil—I knew him."

"Some folks live to suffer," Fletch said, as though it was a matter of their own contriving.

"He had a restless heart," my grandfather said, not saying whether he agreed. "Not a man to be appeased."

Maybe that's what got me. The curiosity that catches you at the crux of what matters to you. Sets you up to be haunted by ghosts. I think some of it has come to me those nights I've sat staring into the fire, trying to see a man who lived here once and left such an imprint on the town, he'll never be forgotten. An inescapable memory. It may be I saw him so clearly I had to take him on, as though he were my own, a brother.

Only it's not all that easy. The edges get blurred as you start looking for the straight scoop. There are holes and gaps you have to fill in. For when a man refuses to die, he becomes richer and stranger than any man you know. That's where the haunting is. A half-breathing impulse from beyond the grave beckoning you towards the unspoken, taking its ghost shape in your mind until it begins to stir again. Maybe it chooses you, so it can enter into story. Gil Weston's not a man to lie down tamely under an epitaph. It's been a long time since he lived here. But it could have been yesterday as well.

I've come back countless times to this town transformed by its many changes, dragging its past as it strains toward the new. I hardly recognize it anymore. The neighborhood where I grew up lies buried in a suburb. New developments all around. The spittoons are gone from in front of the city hall, where the old men used to stand around spitting and passing the time of day. The whorehouse, once the home of a worthy judge built before he and all his family were killed by the Apaches, has been demolished and the new Post Office now stands in its place.

A broad highway, cars rushing past, connects the traveler to Arizona and points west. I've visited those bits of life still buried there under everything that's happened since. No end of things still happening out of those raw beginnings. The water still rushes down the gulch that was once the main street. The story of the town continues beyond me as I try to get what I know, what I've heard, and what I imagine all to lie down on a page. Just when I think I've got it straight, it goes snaking through my hands. Something else to be discovered, to be dipped up out of the flood. It's like trying to capture an image that lingers at the corner of your eye. It keeps changing. But that's not the half of it—I can't account for myself either.

Without a by-your-leave, I've landed here alive and kicking, in the middle of things. I'll take my part if I can discover what it is. Who knows where things will end up—it's a question.Anyway, the flood turned the main street of the town, where all the mercantile stores and saloons and stables were, into a ditch thirty feet deep. After the water had subsided and the wreckage cleared away and Thomas Weston laid to rest, the owners repaired their walls and opened up the other entrances of their shops, turned their backs to the flood and their doors to the future and went about their business. Safe enough now. But always to be reminded when it rained, the ditch swirling with muddy water, the town's inheritance in the changing moment. The flood that left a solitary widow to grieve over her husband and a son to grow up without a father.

II. The Aftermath

Nina Weston was a small woman, petite, as they say, and you could tell she had good breeding the way she spoke to everybody and didn't treat even the old codger who roamed the town, skittery and lunatic, as if it was somehow beneath her dignity to bid him good morning. Just looking at her made you feel called upon for equanimity, seeing as how she'd stuck it out in this rough place, naught but her own resources to keep her going. For there was a sadness in her eyes that floated behind everything she did: she'd doted on Tom Weston, who'd wooed and won her, lured her away from her family back East and all the life she knew, when she was but seventeen, and ten years younger than he. He was a handsome man, an educated man, and whenever he walked into a room, the eyes not only of the women turned in his direction. He had stature, and he had charm. But he had a head on his shoulders to boot. He was all up on the latest science, and if you betrayed the slightest interest, he'd talk your ear off about what they were doing in the world with steam engines and all the experiments that had led to the invention of the telegraph and what counted for the future. Eloquent—he had a way of speaking that lifted your mind right off the foundations: all that science making a new world. Expanding the horizons beyond a raw little town lost in the hills beyond hell and gone. For he'd lured her away to a place where nobody knew yet what they were living. And maybe she was sore at him, too, for leaving her alone and unprotected.

That was old Angus' view of things, who'd been in the town forever. Came from pioneer stock, an old ranching family who'd come early into the territory, grown prosperous and seen it all fall away. Claimed he knew Billy the Kid before he'd got that name, when he was accused only of robbing a Chinese laundryman and was thrown into the pokey for the first time; just a boy, but a wily one, who managed to escape by shinnying up through a chimney hole in the roof. And his mother, too, who ran a boarding house, a widow trying to keep up her two boys, but dying of TB despite her best efforts to get them grown, leaving them to fend for themselves.

Nobody ever argued with old Angus that he was born thirty years too late for any of that. Maybe he did know Nina Weston. Or maybe his life and his father's and grandfather's, who'd practically raised him when his mother took off with a fireman on the Denver & Rio Grande, had all run together and become one life, and he couldn't put down a hook and line without pulling up a whole string of incident lifted out of time as one long memory.

I'd begun hearing his anecdotes for the first time as a boy, and over the years they kept coming back again, sometimes embellished, sometimes with voices chiming in to argue and put in their own version. That left me kicking around the common legend. For the principals, as they say, were long since dead. And the wildest surmise competed with the rest. The voices would work around in my head for a while, fretting me with questions and bits of detail that wouldn't altogether jibe, never quite connect. Then I'd come back to Angus with the questions that'd been brewing. Angus would nod his head, look at me, a long slow smile forming that left a little sunken shadow in his cheeks. I liked to watch it coming on. It meant something was gathering. For a moment he wouldn't say anything, as though it all had to come flowing back like some dense but glowing liquid. Then he'd find it, or it would find him, and he'd begin, as though he'd happened on one more tributary of a larger river.

First there was the question of why Nina Weston didn't pick up and take her boy back East where her family was. Angus shrugged— it wasn't important. Maybe her life was here, and her suffering connected to it, which, in an odd way, allowed her to continue to live, even though she'd lost a major reason for doing so. Fortunately, she wasn't left high and dry. The flood had undermined the foundation of the hotel, so there was no rebuilding it. They tore it down, left the land empty. The two other hotels in town, far more modest, went on with their business. And it would be a nearly half a century before anybody would think the town worthy of something more grandiose. Then it would have all the look and feel of a commercial enterprise, bright and modern, with no pretense of Tom Weston's effort at a civilizing presence.

But Tom Weston had land as well, a ranch of around twenty thousand acres. A modest ranch as ranches go, but the land was good for cattle, part of it bordering on the Gila. So he had good water, not always easy to come by in these parts. Cattle enough for Nina Weston to get a decent living. The foreman and hands had been well-treated, and they were content enough to go on serving the wife—at least for a time. She left them to do the work, branding the calves in the spring, mending fences, taking care of the horses, rounding up the cattle to be shipped east to the fattening pens near Kansas City.

Meanwhile she threw herself into the education of the young. She'd come from a family of professors, and her father had seen to it she had an education. And though she never held an official position, she became a kind of patron to the town. They took her advice, looked to her for help and money. She helped plan for the first high school and got them a teacher for Latin and English. She had a special feeling for the Mexican children, when nobody considered they were more than a set of hands and backs. And she insisted they had to have their chance for learning, too. Not everybody agreed, but she wore them down, finally won their consent—though they had to go to a separate school.

After folks got wind of all she was doing, she got a reputation for being a public benefactor. And they sent her letters and messages desperate with their troubles—usually the women—pleading for help after a spell of drought or illness. She never let anybody go a-begging; she'd send them money to help tide them over till they got back on their feet. A soft touch, some people said, and figured she'd get cheated in the end.

Then she did something, a small thing, like throwing a stone and hitting a target you didn't intend. Raising consequences. The congregation was soliciting funds for a walkway of paving stones in front of the Methodist church, and they asked her if they could put her name down for a donation: she said she'd match Jack Cameron dollar for dollar for whatever he gave. By then Cameron was a local legend. He'd long since quit the stamping mill, where he'd started out and was on his way to a fortune in land and cattle. Those who asked her wondered at her—what impulse possessed her? She wasn't the sort to lead them on or spare herself a penny. Not that Cameron was tightfisted, but he had a well-known contempt for piety. When Cameron heard about it, he threw back his head and roared with laughter. Then he sat down and wrote out a check for five hundred dollars. Naturally, she had to match it. They got their paving stones, with enough left over to convert a few more aborigines in darkest Africa.

Maybe that was the spark that ignited the fire and aroused the blood between them. But that's only my speculation after the fact, for she had land that would have caught Cameron's attention in any case, a choice parcel. That's what Jack was after. Not that he wouldn't keep an eye out for the gleam of precious ore all the rest hankered after, but for Jack Cameron, land was the solid ground of fortune.

During that time the boy Gil was growing up on the ranch, under the care of women. Martina, who'd worked in the kitchen in the hotel, came to take charge of the household, and when Nina Weston was off to town on errands of social benefit, the boy was left to Martina and a young girl, a niece or cousin, who helped out. He must have been a handful, that boy, from all that was said about him—a kid who'd kick and pinch and throw tantrums when he was thwarted. A willful boy who couldn't keep still but had to be doing something every minute.

"If his mother was a civilizing force," old Angus used to say, "the son was there to undo it." He would laugh ruefully.

In town the ladies feared for their furniture and china when he and his mother came to visit. On the ranch there were other fears. He'd be after the hands to teach him how to ride, and they were fearful more for the horses than for him, the way he'd whip them into a gallop, riding them till their necks were lathered and their bodies steamed.

He seemed dazzled by danger, I would say courting it, making off to the woods, exploring caves and climbing along ledges, ripping his clothes, falling into the mud of creeks. Fortunately, the stretch of territory was big enough to hold him. By the time he was eleven or twelve he knew it better than the hands who worked it. Often he'd disappear without telling anyone. A great distress to his mother. "Gil," she would scold him after one of his forays, "it's dangerous your going off on your own. What if you got hurt—how would we find you?" If Martina refused to fix food for him to take, thinking to keep him in reasonable bounds, he'd save up bits of his dinner or even head off without food, taking his fishing gear, and prepare to make a meal off the river. Once he failed to come home by dark, and Nina was beside herself, ready to call together her neighbors to hunt for him. Next morning he appeared, bedraggled and repentant— he'd been exploring a cave, been overtaken by darkness. It was the only time she struck him—hit him hard across the face, then wept over it afterwards.

In school he balked at following directions or commands, never doing what he was bidden, but only what suited him. Unruly, but full of curiosity. He'd go off to a corner to read whatever had caught his fancy. He read in all directions—tales of exploration and adventure and histories of ancient cities and various wars and conquests: the Greeks' defeat of the Persians, the conquest of Mexico, and feats of daring during the Civil War and the settlement of the West. He liked to read books about Indians, and he knew more about them than most of the folks in the town. He said he'd have been an Indian if it were left up to him. I'm sure some folks would have found that pure oneriness.

He was always into fights. Maybe at first the bigger kids picked on him, but later on other kids called him a bully and sometimes ganged up on him. He was strong and utterly fearless, and much of the time his attackers got the worst of it. Miss Booth, who ran the one-room school in the valley, said he needed a man to whip some of the devil out of him and made him sit in the corner at least once a week. At first there were muted complaints about the boy, for the parents didn't like to cause the mother grief over her son, the only legacy that really mattered to her. And he adored her. Finally, she took him out of school and, till he got too much even for her, she kept him home and tutored him herself.

"He knows more than I do," she'd say, as though admitting to one more way he was going beyond her, and when circumstances made it crucial, it must have been a relief to let him go. She sent him to a military academy back East, where one moment he excelled in sports and learning, inspiring the admiration of both his teachers and his classmates, and in the next, threw it all up to go his own erratic way. He grew proud and imperious. A sulky boy, they said, though one or two defenders called him a natural born leader. He kept his attitude: when he came back, he'd show folks a thing or two. But that was later. Long before that, Cameron had imprinted his shape on Gil's boyhood.

"You can't really know anything about Gil Weston—if that's what you're aiming for—" Angus said, "until you know about Jack Cameron. They became each other's fate, got drawn into it." He sat musing over that awhile.

"Is that the way things happen?" I said. Even walking into the idea seemed dangerous. How did you look out for yourself? I wondered at the time.

"Yes," he said. "That's what I think. If Jack hadn't existed, Gil would have created him. He had to have something to take on, huge enough to fit his more than ambitious soul and to make him suffer. Aiming for the sky, suffering deep as earth. Yes," he said, confirming it for himself, "that's what he had to do. Some men have to have that much or life would have betrayed them. They have to be use themselves up, all their fire."

They found each other early. It was maybe Gil's losing his father in the flood that left the space empty for Jack Cameron: his father's place. So it must have looked to Jack. But in Gil's eyes, a dark shadow was left hovering over that place. It wasn't altogether strange the way Jack came into Nina's life. There weren't all that many single women in the town, and Cameron had need of a wife to replace the one he'd used up, so to speak. Small wonder he came courting.

Once Angus had started on Jack Cameron, he took his time to divulge what he knew, relishing the telling of it. "There's lots to tell about Jack Cameron," he would say, whetting my curiosity. "All this you're clamoring to know," he said once when I came around.

"You think you're ready to take him in, are you?" he said, cocking his head. He sized me up, gawky adolescent that I was, and gave a little laugh. I think I halfway amused him, the way I came pestering around. "One of these days you're going to know too much," he joshed me. "More than you can use."

I had the impression he'd been holding back, letting out a little at a time, playing me on the line. Even then it made me wonder, as though I were standing in front of a mystery I had no clue about. Now I think he was a man who'd sounded his own depths and ruminated over the facts and speculated beyond them. And they let him see things his own way. I wanted a way to see them too.

I'd already gotten an image of the boy before he was sent away. I could see him lying awake at night grinding his teeth, wanting to strike out at anybody who put claims on his mother's attention. Trying to think of ways to prove himself, make people take notice, keep off anybody foolhardy enough to be a suitor. She belonged to him. He told Martina once of a snake that lived inside his kneecap, insisted it would come out and bite Jack and poison him. Even when he was away from home, his brain must have festered with the thought of the man, knowing his mother was alone and maybe couldn't fend him off. Then afterwards caught in the very trap he'd laid for himself, after all his wariness, his mother's resistance. And having to wait until Hombre came along. I was in a fever to know more.

"Back for the local history, eh?" Angus said. "The stuff you can't read in the news clippings. Well and good."

28

For I'd gone through the library files of the old newspapers now defunct, *The Golden Era, The Pioneer, The Mining Enterprise*, collecting enough of those teasing facts that never satisfy for long. I'd gone to see Angus when he was bound up with sciatica, alone and in need of entertainment. I sat there in his living room, while he reclined in the platform rocker, a crocheted afghan around his legs. He was sipping whiskey to hold off the pain in his backside and leg, and because he had a mighty liking for the stuff.

"Yes, old Cameron," he said, easing himself back in the chair, wincing. "Yes, it's time to get down to the nitty-gritty. He was English, too, like Weston, though I doubt he and Weston ever ran in the same circles back in their old stamping grounds. Cameron claimed to have some pedigree, was the younger son of a lord, he liked to tell people, though I wouldn't put it past him to have invented his connections. Maybe he was one of them bastards those kings and nobles and such are always begetting. Lord knows the world's full of them." He gave a faint smile. "Once he saw how easy it was to impress the yokels, he went at it. He liked notoriety, liked to thumb his nose at people he felt were beneath him."

Whiskey and the pleasure of telling were making him expansive. He looked at me a time or two to see how I was taking it in. He'd hooked me, as he always did,.

"At first Cameron didn't attract any special notice. Lots of people were coming to these parts, now that the mines were a going thing. Some of them prospectors, but the rest taking whatever work they could find. Some folks made money, but a lot more went bust. But this was a fellow good with mechanics, though how he learned them, what with the mighty station he claimed for himself, I'll leave you figure out. But he had his eye out, on the ready to make his own luck.

"He worked at the town's first stamping mill, repairing parts. Then, a couple of years later, he'd become manager of the operation. He was smart—none smarter. Capable, respected by the men. Along the way, he got some shares in a mine—of course anybody could do that—and then here comes the news some company wants to buy him and the others out. He sold his share for $50,000. Think of that amount of money back then! That raised a few eyebrows, let me tell you. Because he'd kept things close to the vest. Didn't brag about what he was going to do or what he had or what he was going to get. Not like some of your loudmouths carousing in the bars. People hadn't looked to him as an upstart, the sort who'd climb to the top."

He paused to wet his throat. "Takes a special talent. I've never done it, even though I've come from a line of those souls tough enough to hack out a place here in these parts. No, I never had the incentive, and likely you don't either. Not to pull yourself up by whatever it takes to get you there, even if you have to knock a few off the cliff. That's ambition, boy. Real ambition. Only it's got a sharp edge." Then he added, "On both sides." But he went on before I could ask him if he was referring to Gil Weston as well.

"Handsome man, Cameron—you know that if you've seen his picture. But you'd know the hardness in him just reading his expression. Determined as a hawk. And as he got older, leaner, harder, that nose, that hawk's beaked face was trimmed to its original fierceness. With eyes to match. The eye for prey. Whatever he'd grabbed onto, it was like he had to hold it tighter and fight his way up to the next notch. Sometimes when you passed him in the street, you'd wonder what new scheme was turning in his head. A man of infinite calculation. You could see the wheels grinding out the chances. And it was always a shock when his face broke into a big grin that left him looking almost boyish. No, you didn't expect it. Or that he loved a boy's good time. Loved having company around him, and something to celebrate. Loved music, loved giving parties. Could waltz with the best; waltz a woman around till she was giddy with pleasure. And he loved to have a fiddle to start up and to grab hold of a woman and pull her out into a square dance. Great square dancer. Out there making his way through those intricate figures, never missing a call."

Could I believe all that? Or was he making it up as he went along, just because I'd come with my hankering, and he was going to satisfy me, a sucker for a story, or else push me to where I'd have to satisfy myself. I'm still none the wiser.

"He wanted to get rich, I suspect, because there was nothing he didn't crave. Like good liquor. Had it shipped in by the case from up north. And he'd give you good welcome with a glass of port or sherry, the best whiskey. A row of decanters gleams on his carved sideboard. For he furnished his house up grand for his new wife, even bought her a little rosewood piano for her to play. Every year he gave parties at Christmas and New Year's that threw certain townsfolk into a fit of expectation or disappointment, depending on whether they'd got one of his printed invitations. Generous to his friends, you could say that for him. Deadly to his enemies."

"Which were you?" I asked him, going along with him. I'd already done the chronology in my head and it didn't square.

He laughed. "Well, I wasn't a man to tackle somebody who'd put himself beyond the law—a force of nature. I was a spectator, you might say. Old enough to know a few things. So," he said, in a low voice, "I'm one of the guilty ones."

I must have looked puzzled as hell—where did that fit in? He wasn't even born till after the flood. He said. "Don't fret over it. It won't do you any good. Wait a while." Then he took up his tale again.

"Land was where the future was, and like I say, Jack wanted land. He started out with one good-sized parcel, put in a road and built a handsome house and bunkhouses for the hands. Started running cattle. About that time he married the daughter of a man with sizeable holdings both in California and up by Dalton. She brought him some money. She was a pretty thing, who liked to dance and loved to go to theatricals. All the ladies took her up and thought her charming.

"Jack was buying more land, all he could get his hands on. The kind of land he wanted, good land with water, was settled all around him, but he wasn't a man to be dismayed by obstacles. There was a ranch bordering his, settled by a family named Rivdell, and he made Rivdell an offer. But Rivdell wasn't about to sell. His father had come there not long after the Battle of Glorieta Pass and cleared the land, built up the place, and it was home. They had words. Cameron told Rivdell he'd better sell if he knew what was good for him.

"Just about that time two things happened that caught the town up short. His wife, like I said, was frolicsome, and she had taken to going to the plays a little group was putting on. A young man had come to town, with a passion for the theater. He'd come to give singing lessons to the young ladies, and pretty soon he was putting together musical evenings. A little merry fellow, dark-haired and fair complexioned, he was known as Little Van. He had the most delicate hands you ever saw, and a sweet high tenor voice. He was a popular fellow, though the men mostly laughed at him for his refined ways, thinking he wasn't but a sissy. But that didn't seem to bother him as he went here and there, invited to dinner by all the families who had their daughters trilling scales under his tutelage.

"It began to be noticed that Lila Cameron spent a good deal of time in the company of Little Van—you know how gossip gets around. Small town like this, you spit on the sidewalk and it's known all around the county. Anyway, they sang together in the church choir and afterwards he'd walk her home. For the Camerons had a house in town, and while Jack was taken up with the workings of the ranch, she entertained her friends. Little Van came to her house to sing duets and drink a cup of tea or a glass of sherry, and she went to his theatricals. She was half a head taller than he was, but it didn't seem to matter; he had a taste for culture, and maybe that was what she fancied. She was the sort of woman who loved men, loved to tease and be teased by them—maybe you've seen a girl or two like that. They'll touch you on the arm and smile at you in a way to win your heart. Most of the time they don't mean a thing by it, and if you think they're giving you the nod, if you know what I mean, you're dead wrong. They mostly want the pleasure of your attention. And they revel in it mightily. I think she was of that kind—"

He was warming to his story now, the whiskey floating him along. He poured himself another slug, while I tried to imagine that

32

pair on the streets of the town, still raw from all the cottonwoods being taken off in the flood.

"But Jack Cameron didn't take kindly to what was going on. And he must have had a deep, jealous streak, particularly when he imagined other men sniggering behind his back. Because one night he was waiting for Little Van after he'd done his piece in the theatrical, and the moment he appeared, before he could speak a word of greeting or protest, Jack shot him through the heart. An article came out in the paper the next day, not a big piece, mind you. And even though men still got killed in fights, and every man was armed against the Indians when he rode out, some were genuinely shocked that one of the leading citizens would shoot down a man that way, a man who never carried a gun and wouldn't have known how to use one. But Cameron declared the fellow had compromised his wife, had made indecent advances. And finally, whether folks were convinced by the argument or just afraid to tackle Cameron, who was beginning to have some clout in the region now, no charges were ever filed against him."

He thought a moment. "It used to be a man could do about anything if he thought somebody was fooling with his woman. And some still do—that instinct runs deep in the blood. There wasn't anybody around to take on Jack Cameron, certainly not in Little Van's defense. He must've stepped across a boundary then: he'd killed a man. Do that and you put yourself into a different territory."

He paused and let me take it in. It would take me a while.

"Only wasn't a region he disliked. He found he could kill and get away with it. He was getting that powerful.

"But something happened to the wife. It was like you opened a spigot and the juice just ran right out of her. She kept to herself after the murder—" He looked at me. "I'd call it that anyway. Didn't go out much—hardly even to church. When Cameron gave a party, she might be there to welcome the guests, but it was like she was an automaton, putting on her smile. Then she'd fade off like a ghost and nobody would see her the rest of the evening. When you did see her in church, it was amazing how thin she'd got, and there was a hectic flush across her cheeks, as though her flesh burned from having people's eyes on her. Some opined she'd contracted tb. and others thought she was grieving over Little Van. But whatever she felt about the man, I suspect, myself, it ate at her vitals to have been the reason for his death."

Angus let me consider that a moment. "You don't have to hold the gun yourself to be taken to a different place. When something like that touches your life, it can never be the same."

"Like the flood," I said. "Whether you've lived through it or not."

"I think you've got the hang of it."

"*Nothing's* happened to me yet," I said.

"Wait a bit. You haven't learned the corollary. You think it's got to be something big."

"Well, it has to be something I can at least hold onto," I said.

"Maybe somebody has to come along and tell you what you're living if you can't pick it out for yourself. People don't know it, maybe not for a long time. Even if they have the experience...." He sat silent for a long moment. I didn't dare interrupt him. Then he said: "The greatest tragedy," he said slowly, "is never to have experience." I had no idea then what he meant.

He went on. "Yes, the flood made a difference. The town looked different after that, and maybe it was different in itself. Not quite so certain everything was being done for its special benefit. Anyway, there's nothing so impresses the human memory as a good rousing catastrophe: earthquake, fire, flood. A hurricane hits and levels half a city, the inhabitants wandering around in a daze, everything lost and broken. As though it had been sent to wipe out the lot of us. Only some of us get left behind to witness the destruction, wonder what was at the back of it. Now we can do the job maybe better than the elements, blow ourselves to kingdom come, past the Last Judgment even, and boast the greatest catastrophe ever. All the winds, fires and floods together in one big clash." I expected him to lay in a description of something beyond The Deluge Leonardo once pictured. He'd had whiskey enough....

"Why, if we all went, there wouldn't be a witness to try to figure out who put on the display and who ought to get the credit. Nobody to put a rainbow in the sky for; nobody to build things back up again and put the old wheels in motion. No builder under the morning sun, the plants and birds returning, the earth all sweet with readiness."

He was going all right, the old imagination leaping right along. I didn't even have room to say, *Do you think it'll happen?*

"For the rest, maybe it's to remind us of caprice, keep us on our toes: *Watch out, here it comes, from an unsuspected quarter. Flood this time.*"

I've looked at all the pictures before and after, thinking to myself. Yes, something's been lost. It was a more civilized-looking place when Tom Weston's hotel was standing and the two rows of cottonwoods lined the streets. And I couldn't help thinking even after the streets got paved, for the alleys and side streets were dirt and mud for a good many decades after, that the town had never got back up to what it had been in that first rush of energy and enthusiasm.

"Certainly, Gil had been marked by that event in a way more personal than most. You can tell a lot by what has marked a man and sends him in a certain direction. And if the first was the killing of Little Van that set Jack Cameron onto his path, then the second was the death of Rivdell, the rancher—found with a bullet in his neck."

"Cameron's work?"

"That's what some folks thought. The sheriff investigated. They took the bullet from the wound, but it was from a common type of gun. Could have belonged to any number of men. Nobody knew of a motive for killing Dan Rivdell, except one—Cameron's telling him he'd better sell, or else. We've heard stories ever since, of how the hands that ran Cameron's ranch were hired guns threatening the settlers whose land he wanted. There were a couple of other murders, again unsolved. The threat was in the air, and enough murders to make it convincing, though Cameron denied he'd been guilty of any violence.

"But the common notion whispered back and forth, as his holdings grew and he settled his men as foremen on the various ranches he'd acquired, even giving them some land, that it was all threat and intimidation. He didn't have to kill any more folks, and pretty soon he built his holdings into the biggest ranch that ever was—a million acres, think of it. And 60,000 head of cattle."

Like some conqueror taking over. "The Weston ranch as well?"

"Not yet, not for a long time. Nina Weston must have been some woman all right. Like I say, Cameron came courting her. That started early, a year or so after she'd been widowed, and Gil was still a boy. And there's the story of how the boy hated him, hated having him come round and what Jack did to him...."

He wasn't good for any more story, not that day. And before I could get any more out of him, he'd taken all his stories with him, succumbing to a bout of pneumonia. But before I left him and he left me, he said, "I knew them; I knew them all. Like I said, you may be taking on more than you'll ever want. But I have a feeling you've a restless heart as well."

For a time, what Angus had told me buzzed arou nd in my head, coming and going at odd moments. Then voices began to speak to me and faces appear. Nina Weston; Gil, the boy; Jack, the land baron. Coming and going, they filled my mind with their conflicts, their debates, their anguish, as though they wanted to live again. Knocking at the door of my mind, teasing me till I couldn't leave off with what I knew. So this is how I see it, what I put together out of what I knew and didn't know.

For the past is always to be reinvented.

III. The Well

It might be fair to say he was marked out from boyhood. No flesh-and-blood father to guide his steps and interpose between that restive spirit and the boundless. Only the bodiless ideal, the ghost.

As I see it, he had to invent himself as he went along. Not just breathe in the ordinary as most of us do, as we struggle with our mortal clay.

He wasn't one to settle for that.

Elevated by circumstance that spoke to whatever lived in him, he was called beyond mere flesh and blood. Everybody suffers, but some are born to suffer in unique and remarkable ways. Or maybe that view lies in the eye looking back at him, projecting him into the heroic. Take a violent land and it takes heroes to meet the challenge, and villains rise up as well to figure in the great dramas of lust and risk and vengeance.

The imagination expands with the heights of mountains and into the reaches of distance.

But wait. It, too, has a terrible task in trying to reach him.

The boy must have had to look sharp, always keep an eye out, because he never knew what might be standing behind him waiting to put its claws in his neck when he made the wrong move. The play of laughter from somebody itching to get his kicks at his expense.

At school, the kids making faces behind his back, mimicking the way he walked and spoke, for there was a lingering of a British accent from his father and an Eastern cast of speech from his mother.

He rebuffed his schoolmates with indifference—they were beneath his notice. .He refused to join their games or to have friends among them. He could hardly conceal his contempt for his teachers, for their pitiful knowledge. He was hopelessly bored. For a time, they didn't know he could read, until they found him off reading books well beyond his years.

He lived in the worlds of Genghis Khan and Alexander the Great, Marco Polo and the Arabian nights. There, nobody could bother him.

At the ranch he took over his father's telescope to study the night sky and in his father's library he found books too hard for him, books on the constellations and planets that he took on anyway. An overwhelming world. The ordinary world of men was no more than a piece of dust.

He read a passage in a science book that fascinated him. If a man had an arm long enough to reach the sun and suddenly touched it, he'd turn immediately into an old man. Living under the sun gave you an expanse of time, he decided. And what was there to do with it?

At the ranch he at least had his forays out onto the land— explorations of caves, fishing in streams, clambering over the rocks.

His wildness made the men leery of him.

Nina Weston's hand was too gentle to bridle him, and he had her dancing in circles.He needed a father to whup him one—that's what the hands said among themselves. That would straighten him up.

Whatever drove him never seemed to wear him out, but exhausted any creature in his path, as he took himself to the outer edges of daring. So it was with the wild roan they captured when they rounded up the calves. Strawberry color. The boy heard the commotion out in the corral, the animal slamming itself against the fence, bucking and kicking all around the space.. As he watched the animal, he must have seen a nature like his own, one that put its freedom before its death and would batter itself against the corral until it got one or the other.

"He's one mean critter," Joe, one of the hands, said. "An outlaw, that's what."

"I want to ride him," the boy said.

"You crazy? You looking for a way to bust your bones and break your neck?"

A couple of the others muttered quietly that it might be an improvement.

"I'm going to ride him," the boy insisted. "And I can do it too."

"Your mama would have my hide," the foreman, Buddy Quicksend, said.

They had a battle royal over it, he and his mother, till Gil had her almost crazy: he wouldn't give in. He'd run away to California, he threatened her.

Finally, Buddy, who could handle nearly everything that moved, got her gentled down and proposed a solution. Gil was a strong boy and a good rider, he assured her, and they'd get the horse to where it would take a bridle and saddle, and maybe it would be reasonably tractable. He'd broken more than one such horse.

They set about starving the beast into submission, that wild roan, kept it tied up and weakened him till it could barely stand. Every day for that week young Gil came out to look at his horse, whose eye, no matter what its condition, was still as wild as ever.

On the fifth day, Gil watched as two of the men forced a bit into the creature's mouth and led it around the corral—docile enough. His horse. Nina Weston still wasn't convinced, when she came out and stood beside her son, both of them giving the horse a onceover.

"Gilbert, you don't know what you're getting into."

"I can ride him," Gil insisted. "I know I can." Now he couldn't wait for the opportunity.

"At least he'll get it out of his system," Buddy told her. "Maybe they'll tame each other—who knows?" They were well matched in temperament at least.

When the horse was used to the bridle, they tried the saddle, let Gil climb on its back and lead it around. The roan pawed the ground nervously, danced sideways a couple of times, but let itself be walked around the corral.

The next day Gil was on his own. Nina couldn't watch; she couldn't let go of a mother's fear, but the men, eager for the show, were quietly making bets. In their book, nobody could ride that horse.

"Well, I don't know," Joe said to one of his buddies. "That boy is meaner than any horse—a real match."

It was a tense moment as Ortiz, one of the trainers, saddled up the roan, then held the stirrips as Gil climbed on. He could feel the meanness of the horse pumping underneath him and it called up his own determination and a certain mad delight in pitting himself against the creature. He'd beat the outlaw at his own game, hang on till he brought him round. He'd even give him his spurs at some point. The hands stood by, ready to come to his rescue, if need be.

A towering big-boned, sturdy boy, but still a boy.

No more than twelve.

And crazy.

He'd been on horseback since he was a tot.

"Think he'll do it? " one of the newer cowboys ventured. He was almost convinced.

"Of course not," Buddy Quicksend said. "Haven't you worked up any sense yet?" Ortiz unloosed the rope. For a second the roan stood stock still, as though it couldn't believe it was unbound. Then his freedom hit him in the blood and bones, and he exploded with it in all directions, bucking, leaping, kicking.

Afterwards, the men swore that horse defied the laws of gravity, its mangy hide a streak of lightning, its reddish color flashing back the sun. The boy hung onto the maddened animal and gave his body to its leaps and doublings. It was a marvel he stayed on as long as he did.

But then the horse lowered its head, kicked its hind legs high as the sun and threw him. Not content, it headed for him there on the ground and would have trampled him to death if the men hadn't pulled him out in time. He'd scared them at the same time he'd won their admiration.

"A right smart ride," they told him after they'd shaken the dust off him, and he could stand up alone.

"Boy, you sure hung on, even when you slipped onto the side." He was fool enough to dare.

Crazy for danger, Buddy said to himself. *Or just plain crazy.* But he'd been brought down to size, after all, for all he set himself up so high.

Then came the little snicker that had been both nervous for his safety as well as glad he'd got what was coming to him.

Thus Gil was ever a trouble to his mother, and her heart was torn over him. At times she wondered if he was not quite human. She was afraid he'd grow into a real bully, trample those around him.. Headstrong and aloof, he acted as though he was being shaped in the direction of some large pattern of expectation. But where would he ever find his domain, his niche?

Not just for herself, she mourned his loss of a father, who might have curbed his excesses.

"Nina, that boy is going to give you nothing but grief," the minister's wife, Annabelle Griffith, said to her. "I think a military academy might straighten him out."

He needed someone to act as a father. That was Nina Weston's only thought. Nor could she imagine anyone taking her husband's place. Who else could take the boy on? It would have to be someone he could look up to.

When Jack Cameron stepped across the path of her vision, what did she imagine then? He came to church one Sunday after the walk was laid. He had, after all, contributed handsomely toward its construction. She'd provoked him into doing it, and now he was there, sitting right next to her, smiling as she helped him locate the hymn they were called upon to sing. His voice joined hers in song, a surprisingly good voice that took up the words and melody as naturally as if they'd been bred by piety. She felt a tremor, realizing she'd set in motion something she could not see the end of. He, too, was alone, without a wife, and some of her women friends gossiped that he was looking for a replacement.

His pretty little missus was gone, and though it wasn't clear what had happened to her, everybody knew she'd never be coming back.

"Poor thing," they said. "Poor thing." He'd sent her away to a sanitarium, they said, because she'd gone out of her head and there was only one word left hovering in the air.

Murderer! Murderer! Murderer!

Some went so far as to think he'd had her killed.

That was the way rumor whirled around him, though Cameron moved through it like the eye of a hurricane, seeming never to know or care what he was whipping up in the common mind.

It soon became clear that he was courting Nina Weston, maybe even out of a real liking for her. He had a buggy and a pair of high-stepping greys he prided himself on. Sunday afternoons he'd drive them out and take her for a ride. A friendly gesture.

Sometimes he took Gil along, thinking perhaps to impress the boy, try to win his friendship. But the boy looked at the stretch of cactus and yuccas and joshua trees with indifference.He hated it that his mother allowed this man in her company, but very likely he'd have hated any man who came calling, jealous of anyone who tried to stand between them.   But Jack was his adversary.

No need for him to worry. Nina Weston would never marry Jack Cameron—that was clear to everybody but the boy and Jack. She'd be married all her life to one man, to his memory.

And for all his attentions, his sweet ministerings, Nina knew in her bones it was her land that really attracted Jack to her.

For Cameron, as I see him, was a man fixed on one idea, long after it was useful to him. Grabbing up one homestead after another. It was clear he'd taken himself beyond the point where anyone could stop him. The law wouldn't oppose him; he'd stepped beyond the law. Towering and enormous, he cast his shadow over the town. He stood before Nina Weston, a presence.

Now that she'd unthinkingly beckoned him, it was best not to be on his bad side. She had an instinct that her survival depended on it. Not that he wasn't courtly, for he knew well enough how to please a woman. He knew manners, wherever he'd learned them, and had got himself some culture, maybe from his forebears. And he admired Nina Weston; I would say she magnetized him, drew him to her, exercised a certain power.

Here was a woman of strength, a woman capable of loyalty.Who wouldn't like to imagine himself the object of such a loyalty? What a victory to add to all the other conqests!

In the midst of all his calculations, Jack Cameron found himself dreaming like a young fool. It was dream in the more substantial company of ambition that brought him to the parlor of the Weston ranch on a mild afternoon in late May after the branding was over for the year. He'd been hard at it, riding round his various holdings, overseeing the operation, exhausted beyond fatigue. Now it was over.

Leisure had hatched the right moment.

All that winter and spring he'd been at Nina Weston's side, taking her to square dances and various social gatherings. Suddenly there were parties in a house he'd scarcely visited once his wife was gone. Now the lamps were lit for the friends he had among the merchants of the town, eager for his trade, those from whom he bought feed and supplies, as well as others who were creating the politics of the town and the region, who traveled back and forth to Santa Fe.

He could come courting Nina Weston with a certain confidence, seeing what he could offer her: money, comfort, status. Indeed, a place in society beyond any she could envision for herself. Considering her Eastern origins, where her family had some status, she could appreciate what he represented. Not to mention a future for her son. Besides, a lonely widow had no business trying to run a ranch by herself. He'd been generous with his advice about improving the quality of her cattle, helped her breed her stock with his bulls, offered to ship her cattle with his, as would happen in the future when they pooled their resources.

It occurred to him along the way that if he married, he was getting a son into the bargain and might have others. That gave a man a certain steadiness and pride, to know that what he'd turned to hand could safely pass to future generations.

When he heard about Gil's attempt to ride the wild roan, he was impressed—the boy had mettle. He brought him a beauty of a horse, a young black gelding, newly broken that could run like the wind. With spirit enough to capture the heart of any boy and keep him out of mischief.

"What do you think of this?" he said, when he offered his gift.

The animal took Gil's breath away.

Jack waved aside Nina's protests. "A boy like this deserves a horse to match."

Whenever Jack spoke to him during this time, he called him *son*, as though to get him used to the idea, and took an interest in his education. When the boy discovered a passion for chess, Jack became his teacher and partner on those Sunday afternoons they waited for the meal Martina was cooking.

At first the boy, skeptical but pleased, would play him game after game, trying to see how things worked.

And Jack would lie in wait for him. Just when it appeared Gil had the advantage, Jack, skillfully working the pieces, would lead him to checkmate.

"I'm teaching you some of the tricks of this world, son," Jack would say with an infuriating little smile, while Gil clenched his teeth. "They'll come in handy one of these days—you bet." He wanted a son he could take pride in, who could measure up to the woman who would do him credit. Now that Jack had worked his way, however devious, to the place he wanted to occupy, Nina Weston could soften the rough edges.

What was done was done—why not put some questionable deal in the past and make use of his talents? Build a future.

Nina herself, the subject of so much speculation around the town, where there was considerable disapproval of the match, had never told anyone her intentions.

But if she was determined not to marry him, she knew she had to walk a narrow line, allowing him to think he had her favor while not promising anything that could compromise her or be misinterpreted. A tricky business.

And finally came the moment she'd been dreading, for she knew she had no way of turning him aside without giving his pride a deadly blow.

She was hard pressed, and some nights she lay awake for hours trying to imagine the thread she could take hold of to lead her out of her predicament. No, she couldn't marry him, but how dangerous to refuse him. And if she'd let things go too far, it was because she knew that at any stage the rebuff would have meant the same. She could tell something was on his mind just from his manner as he sat on her brocaded love seat in her parlor that particular afternoon when he came to visit. She offered him a whiskey, which he set on a little table beside him. He regarded her thoughtfully, smiling now and then as he watched her move about or looked into her face, which still held a youthful charm. No doubt he was experiencing an equally delicate moment. In effect, he was competing with the former husband for the ornament of his life, the young thing that had let her eye wander in his direction. A bad bargain altogether. But for the present round, he was called upon for sentiment. He'd read in novels how it was done, and *The Gentleman's Book of Etiquette* stood on his shelf. He'd spent time trying to fit himself to its notion of decorum. It was like acting a part in a play, and he'd tried to rehearse in his mind the proper lines for the role, had spoken them aloud to his image in the mirror.

Just as Nina Weston had lain awake nights trying to prepare her refusal. You can see the two of them caught there, both in their awkward and contradictory poses: It all had to be done the right way, when there was no way for things to come out right.

He struck out first.

"You know, Nina, I've always admired you," he said in a low voice, after they had reached a pause, having wrung the last drop from such matters as this year's grass and rainfall, and the state of her cattle. "And maybe now I can offer you some of the comforts that will ease your life and give you company." Thus he wanted to remind her of his bounty without being crass.

"I know there are tales about me that have made the rounds, and maybe I've done some things I'm not proud of, but what's done is done." There was no point glossing them over. He had to ease her mind about his unsavory reputation. "I'm humbly ready to make amends." The humility was a momentary concession for the sake of the changed man he must now appear to be.

He'd put out good solid cash for the paving stones before the church, an act that showed his heart was in the right place. He'd stood with her there inside listening with utter boredom to a parson's tiresomeness.

Now let him reap the benefit from his sacrifices, claim what rightfully belonged to him.

He'd carved out a place for himself in the region. He had the power to take things where they needed to go, which is all any man wants in this world. But he could do with a woman's touch.

The celebrated woman's touch touted by the ladies' magazines, the notion that a woman could indeed change a man. A heady notion, perhaps somewhat nebulous when put to the test. Or as one wag put it, "Depends on what part a woman touches."

And not just any woman either, he hastened to assure her. "It's you I want, a real partner to share my life. We see eye to eye. Together, there'd be no stopping us. Together we'd rule the roost. Every eye would be turned in your direction."

It was a vision of the future that fired his brain, and she could see how he'd defined her role in it, willy-nilly. All she had to do was step into the place prepared for her.

He rose from his chair and went over to Nina and actually knelt down in front of her. It was all part of the performance and its expected drama.

No matter how the blood beat against the ribs in the varying combination of will and motive, with even a touch of sentiment, it had to flow into the required pose. "I'm asking you to be my wife."

Embarrassed, even a little flustered, she made him stand up. For a moment, she stood and looked at him, trying to summon her will, as he clasped her hands.

Then she released herself, went over to the window, and stood looking out before she spoke, at first not really seeing anything in the yard, but trying to shape her response in the words manners called for—such a silken refusal it made a balm for the wound it created.

Gil had just come in from wherever he'd been riding, hair flying in all directions, his horse in a lather.

She watched and did not watch as he dismounted, and hoped for an interruption. But she knew it would only postpone the inevitable.

Jack, pressing his advantage, came up beside her. He knew the ploy of women who say no and again no, intending to say yes, a fixed corollary of propriety.

"I'd be a good husband to you, Nina," he said with careful softness as he almost ground his teeth for the appearance of horse and rider, "and a father to your boy."

For a moment they both watched as Gil led the panting animal towards the stable and gave him over to one of the hands.

He was coming toward the house. "And that fine boy deserves a future," Jack said, cursing the possible interruption at the worst possible moment. "I know my duty."

She had two cards she could play, and one of them she drew upon now. If Jack knew his duty, she knew hers.

"I've always considered you a steadfast friend," Nina began. "And I hope I'll always have your friendship. You've given me help when I most needed it." Indeed the gratitude was real.

He took her hand. "I hope you consider me more than a friend, Nina."

What sort of man did a woman want simply as a friend? It irked him to have her think of him so. As I think it would irk any man with any thought for his manhood.

"You are a man of great power," she began tentatively, more than ready to acknowledge the gulf that divided them.

"It's yours for the asking, Nina." As, in a manner of speaking, it always belonged to women for the asking.

"A man of great power, called upon to do undreamed of things for the Territory. And I am deeply honored," she said. Now she had to give back the image of a woman who was unworthy of him.

"But you must understand me. I'm just a simple frail woman, broken by great loss. I have survived that loss, but like my poor husband, my heart was carried away in the flood. I made a vow I would never marry."

Though tears might have helped her cause, she did not resort to them, but gave him a full direct look. She wasn't trying for a picture of virtue worthy of melodrama—such sentimentality wasn't in her—yet she banked on something he might give homage to. Her hand was still in his, as though he wanted lay claim to it that very minute.

"I understand your grief," he said in a low voice. "The man lost in that flood I'd gladly claim as a brother," he went on with some intensity, for he had to find the matching words required to win this overwrought woman's heart. Being called upon for eloquence was taxing to his powers, but he gave it his best shot: such a mind and such a heart had preceded him, he acknowledged, in a man who could see great things for this piece of wilderness. A man of foresight, who could make the future come to pass. He had to give him his due. Only by that path could he make his own way. "How deeply I understand that you not only lost a husband, but that fine boy of yours lost a father that could have guided him to manhood in the best of ways."

Now that he had given the man his due, he had to nudge her toward a little common sense.

"He is all I have in the world that matters to me," Nina murmured, taking back her hand. She touched her handkerchief to her eyes as she readied her second card. "And I cannot think of myself until he has found the right place for himself in the world."

That might be helped along, he thought—no different from the rest—with a good thrashing.

He'd have liked to break him like a horse. Put the fear of God into him to docile him down.

"I know your deep concern. That would be my most pressing duty," he insisted, "to see that he finds a place worthy of him." His gorge was beginning to rise.

It was clear he needed a diplomat's finesse to snake his way past all her objections, the heaviness of motive requiring the most delicate finesse. He was not a patient man, but too much was at stake for him not to let her take her full sweet time.

They heard Gil come blustering in, as though he'd brought wind and weather for partners.

A door slammed. Jack gritted his teeth. Had no one ever taught him how to close a door?

It would be just like him to blunder into their midst and wreck the careful structure Jack had been trying to assemble. He knew the kid's signature not only first hand but from a variety of anecdotes.

He had to press his suit, here, now in what he considered the right moment. Otherwise he would lose all momentum. "A boy needs a father's firmness together with a woman's touch. Otherwise..." The right phrase that stopped short of threatening her did not come readily to mind. "Otherwise things get out of hand."

He could feel her stiffen and, despite his sense that he was treading on precarious ground, he felt the urge to beat down her resistance.

"Face the facts, Nina," he said, with more vehemence than he intended. "The boy's getting more rambunctious day by day, more than a woman can handle, and needs to be whipped into shape before it's too late." He wasn't used to being countered, and, in spite of himself, he'd run out of tactics. He longed for some fresh inspiration to let him know how far you needed to go before a woman's no turns sweetly to yes.

"I know you have my best interests in mind," Nina said, "but it would be unfair to you, Jack, with your position and your lofty ambitions, to burden you with my son." She'd taken him in and spit him out in a single breath.

"Let me at least try to make up to you for your great loss." The words rushed out of him, but they had a hollow sound. "Let me put everything before you to take your pleasure from. Let me give the boy..."

The two of them had met at the same corner, face to face.

"You're more than generous," she said, seized with panic. "All you have done I do appreciate." Her voice subsided into a whisper.

"Right now, I can I see you're overwrought," he granted her. A hunter could finally wear out his quarry, but a woman had the unfair advantage of being able to take refuge in her weaknesses.

"I can't t take this as a final answer," he said. "Give me a chance,

Nina," he said, with enough emotion in his voice to cover his chagrin, as he tried to convince himself he could mean something to her.

He took one final tack, inspired by the ladies'magazines. It was a woman's duty to improve a man's moral character. "It would make a difference to my life—all the difference. Nina, I need something to live up to. And you're an angel."

"Jack, you know you have my admiration. And I'm here for you to..."

"Think about it," he importuned her.

He had to lift her mind to another level, enlarge her vision before she slipped away altogether. "Turn your eyes to the future. This may be a raw and savage place, not something the centuries have built. But think of us—how we can build it. Look that far ahead."

She'd been a force behind the schools and hospital; let him lure her with the notion of how much the public good might benefit.

"I can't think anymore," she said, her hand in front of her face as though to push him away. "Please leave me now," she begged him. "You must excuse me."

He took her wrist, gently touched her palm with his fingers, looked intently into her eyes and let her go with this final impression of his sincerity. He had to be content with that.

"I'll see the boy a moment before I go," he said, his voice scraping the edge of still pent up exasperation.

He wanted her land, but he wanted her with it. Now with her nod of acquiescence, he had to retreat. He could still work on the boy, hoping thereby to curry favor with the mother.It was his one remaining hope, though it would cost him some effort to speak a friendly word. The way the rascal had ridden the horse was a scandal. He hated to see a fine animal mistreated in that fashion. He wanted to take the young pup to task, but he couldn't risk irritating the mother by alienating the son. A ticklish business, all of it.

As he approached the dining room, he saw the boy at the table, with a chess game set up. A book of instruction for mastering the game lay open beside him.

He was deeply absorbed, studying the book and moving the

pieces, meanwhile chanting something in a monotonous singsong: "Cameron Jack, Cameron Jack," he heard.

So he lived in the boy's mind after all. He still had a chance. He stepped closer.

"—your heart is black. Look for the bullet hole in the back."

The little bastard—how dare he!

"What are you saying?" he thundered. "Who do your think you are?"

The boy looked up, dumbstruck. He'd been so intent on his game, he'd gotten lost in the rhythm of the chant, until the words had gone blank of all meaning and he'd simply been repeating them without knowing what he said. He sat there blinking.

And then the figure that loomed in the doorway was on him, pulling him up by the hair.He was seized, his arm twisted behind his back, the breath snatched out of him.

He didn't utter a sound, but struggled savagely for a moment. Jack, by far the stronger, kept twisting his arm, till he went limp from pain.

Then Jack's face was in his own, a wavering red blotch "Now tell me what you were saying."

Defiance shot through him—he repeated the words: "Cameron Jack, your heart is black."

He felt himself shaken furiously. "You say that again and..."

Somehow he'd pushed the fear away from himself; his breath found him again, and with it, his voice. "What will you do? I don't care."

"You think I can't make you care? Let's just see what I can do," Jack said, shaking him again. "Rotten spoiled and thinks he can get away with murder. You just wait."

Jack let him go with a shove, let him stand there in the full force of his threat.

"It's because you're a bully," the boy blurted out. "And a murderer. And I hate you." He rushed forward, head down, his fists balled.

"You want to have it out, do you, you little savage? I'll be glad to do my part."

Suddenly Gil was being pulled through the dining room and

kitchen, out through the back door. Martina gave out a yell as the boy shrieked in fury: "Let go of me. I hate you."

By now the house was in an uproar.

A couple of hands down by the stables came belting up as Nina and Martina came running from the kitchen. When they emerged into the yard, they were in time to see Jack bending over the side of the well, the boy's legs in his grip as Jack held him head down in the well.

"Look down there, boy—maybe you'll see a few stars." Jack could barely keep hold of the flailing legs.

"Take it back, or I'll drop you."

"Are you mad?" Nina cried.

"Get away," Jack yelled, as the men rushed up. "Lay your hands on me and you'll regret it."

Nina waved them off, as Martina stood praying aloud. "Do you want to kill me? Is that what you want?" Nina panted.

Jack pulled the boy out.

"He needs..." and left it at that. Gil stood on the ground, getting back his legs.

He moved to his mother's side, where he stood—tearless but with burning eyes.

Jack was clearly shaken, caught as he was, put in the wrong—a spot he'd never had to occupy, whatever people said.

"Get out,' Nina told him. "Get out and don't come back. Ever."

Fortunately, his Stetson had fallen to the ground, and Jack could take his time to bend over, retrieve it, and dust it off. Then without a look at anyone, he strode across the courtyard and around to where his horse was tethered, mounted and was gone.

IV. Hippolyta

An extraordinary incident finally convinced Nina Weston to send her son back East to a military academy. Without a father's authority, it would take more than her flailing efforts at discipline to put the boy on the right path. She had to let go of him, let others take up the challenge She was not the sort of doting mother who, blind to any fault, unwittingly encourages her son to become a monster.

She had tried, at first gently, to take him in hand, and in an agony of remorse over his excesses, he would promise her better things of himself. But his own nature was against him. She was at a loss; and though she might blame circumstance or even herself for his behavior, as mothers ar apt to do, she sometimes gently questioned the darkness before sleep, "Oh, where did he get his rash blood? What am I supposed to do with him?" If she was beset by any lingering fear because she'd lost the favor of Jack Cameron, a man who'd gladly savor a certain triumph over the woman who'd refused him, she never revealed it. Though she had only to look at what was going on around her to give her pause. He was still grabbing up everything in reach, squeezing out the small homesteaders on the way, his long shadow ever moving toward the far horizon. A man to be reckoned with. A prominent figure beyond the town, a man in the public eye, whose influence reached all the way to the Governor's Palace. He'd thrown himself into the fight for statehood. Whatever fear or hatred he'd engendered, public sentiment was on his side. He had a talent for mending the fences he crashed through, perhaps because so much occurred under the cloak of secrecy.

If he hadn't come any further in Nina Weston's direction, it was not because he couldn't. And what prevented him from coming after her? I have entertained various speculations. Perhaps he had more pressing concerns to occupy his mind. Very likely he enjoyed the unspoken threat he presented—toying with her fears at a distance, letting her feel that it was only his mercy that stood between his desire and its execution. Or perhaps he was merely biding his time, letting the distance grow between the offense and his revenge. The moment was to be savored in the imagination when, with a snap of his fingers, he'd simply gobble her up. But nothing happened for ten years—till it appeared he simply didn't care and then the turn things took came in a way nobody expected, himself least of all, I would say.

All this time her son continued on his rocky course.   H o w they managed to keep the boy in school till he got his diploma is a task for the imagination.   Though there were periods of exemplary behavior and excellent scholarship, you couldn't count on their continuity. He didn't take kindly to discipline, and the punishments he was given for thumbing his nose at the rules did nothing to soften his recalcitrance. Only the stern warnings of the Headmaster, who saw him as a bad influence on certain susceptible minds, kept him more or less in tow. What's more, the boy didn't want to shame his mother by being kicked out of school.

Certain of his masters, especially Mr. Long, who taught history, and Mr. Waggoner, who taught physics and chemistry, were convinced of his brilliance and made allowances for him. Even so, they must have experienced considerable relief when he graduated. He would make his mark, they quipped, or be branded with one.

He was enrolled at Harvard at his mother's insistence but did not last there. Something deep within rebelled at that manner of becoming cultivated. Neither the ministry nor education, nor the law appealed to him. Reports of him were not encouraging.

Nina's older brother, a ship's chandler in Boston, tried to take him under his wing, show him how a young man of good family should conduct himself, but the two did not get on. Her son, he told Nina Weston, was a disgrace. Instead of attending classes and looking to his future, he took up with a couple of scamps and spent most of his time gambling and drinking. What else occupied his time her brother refused to disclose.

A stern lecture from his uncle during his second year, when he was indeed on the verge of flunking out, brought things to a head. On his own, Gil dropped out of college and for a few months worked as a messenger for Western Union. He'd earn his own way, he wrote his mother—she needn't trouble herself over him any longer. He traveled some along the coast, took from the East whatever it offered, spit out the rest and made his way to California. There he worked on sailing ships going north to Washington and Alaska, spent time in the dockyards. His was an unsettled, wandering life. An occasional postcard with a brief note assured his mother he was still among the living. He refused to let her send him money.

Meanwhile she refrained from any effort to influence his future. At times she wondered if she would see him again. It was ten years and more from the time he left until he came back home—with callused hands and darkened skin. Perhaps he'd had enough of whatever sort of education his way of living had offered.

To Nina Weston's surprise, things prospered during the decade of his absence and she found herself growing rich. She bought some land herself. Then an inheritance from her father came, and with it the thought of rebuilding the house. A cramped, irregular house, much patched and repaired, that had served them over the years. Not the sort of dwelling to which Gil could bring a wife. In spite of herself, she could not help looking ahead now to the next generation, to her grandchildren, to the noise and laughter of their play and a sense of life continuing. A new era.

She'd done her part, carried on with the ranch, helped launch the first public school, petitioned for the establishment of a high school, served as one of the patrons of the hospital. Proudly the citizens claimed the town now resembled an Eastern town, and strangers who braved the journey there were surprised by its amenities, instead of the rough and lawless outpost they had expected. A real pearl in the wilderness, they wrote to their friends and relations back East. Her generation had paved the way, if not the streets. Now Gil could make his peace with the past and find a niche for himself. Now and then she made some tentative reference to that future in the hope she might stir something in his blood, appeal to some as yet unknown ambition.

But before she could think of turning the reins over to him, there came a spell of bad luck that set back all her plans. First an early heavy snowfall. About every seven years or so it happens; for the most part winters in the region are seldom marked by deep enough snow to threaten the cattle . You can find it in the higher peaks like Mogollon Baldy. In the lower regions it lasts a few days, then melts into the ground.

Only a few times can I remember the town shutting down, the kids let out of school, happy to be outdoors with their sleds, and hardly anyone else on the streets except those handling emergencies.

This time the cattle couldn't get to the grass, and the ranchers had to use their hay to get them by until the snow melted. But just when it appeared they'd got past the worst, a blizzard hit them full force. Jack Cameron, who had more hay than anybody else stored throughout his holdings, was equipped for the emergency. And he offered to anyone who cared to bargain out of desperation, a trade of so many head of cattle in exchange for feed to take care of the rest. Cursing him, some took his terms, figuring to salvage whatever they could.

Nina Weston debated with herself what to do, after having used up all her feed and finding none among her neighbors. She dared not approach Jack Cameron. But one morning when she went to town to see if the freighters had been able to haul in any hay from the Mesilla Valley, she came upon the man himself in the hardware store, and he graciously tipped his hat and asked her how she was faring.

"Like everybody else," she said.

"It's been a hard winter all right," he acknowledged. "Folks have been coming to me for feed to tide them over. It was good haying this year, and by a lucky stroke I laid in a supply."

"I don't suppose you'd be sparing any," she said, taking her chances.

He gave her a little ironic smile. "I can spare some for you. Not a lot at this point. But it may be enough to take you through the worst. For a price," he added.

That was to be expected. She weighed the consequences of

letting the cattle starve, and though she was well enough off to survive a disaster that would also make the next year harder, she didn't want Gil to begin under a cloud. She debated whether to take the consequences of the weather or put herself at the mercy of a man ready to gobble her up.

"Tell me what it is," she said, expecting a price beyond what she could pay. "So I'll know if I can afford it."

This time he laughed, as though at a private joke. "What I want is a visit from your son. I hear he's coming back," he said. "I owe it to him to make up for my inexcusable behavior."

She looked at him in astonishment. She could not take him in. A man who could achieve his ends, it was pretty clear, through murder and intimidation, whose effrontery had taken him into the strongholds of power all over the state and heaven knew where else. Wonder of wonders, this little episode was still on his mind and had perhaps given him some thorny moments. He was a puzzle to her. She found herself growing wary. She had the feeling that this too rode upon some motive.

"I can't answer for my son," she said, "though I thank you for your offer." Giving him a little smile, she turned to go about her business.

"You don't have to," he said, stepping round in front of her. "I'll ask him myself when the time comes."

He tipped his hat again and left the store. But the next day, his wagons were at her door, delivering their load of baled hay.

And then it snowed again, and even Jack Cameron couldn't prevent the losses that occurred, though he survived in far better shape than most.

It was spring before Gil finally returned, whether lured by his mother's promises and thoughts of home, or grown weary of his rootless, wandering life. For when the time was ripe, the ranch was to be his. To Nina, it was worth the gamble, and Nina played her trump card. He'd work with Buddy Quicksend at his side until he learned the ropes and then take charge. Although the two men were of vastly different temperaments, they at least had a respect for the work of the ranch.

The responsibility for it, having a stake in its prospects, would settle him down, so Nina had convinced herself as she watched Gil's progress, and he could then fulfill his role of landowner and citizen, husband and father—the pursuits that allow a man to live up to the best measure of what's in him.

She hardly recognized him when she met him at the train station, though she had been to see him during various visits East before he dropped out of college. The sturdy boy, as tall as she was, had become the man who towered before her. A man whose dark hair had bleached with the sun, his face deeply tanned from long periods out-of-doors. A handsome fellow, her son. His young man's features held a certain maturity now, and she thought she detected in them a kind of assurance, something solid to build on. Though she caught from his eyes flashes of the old fire. They threw their arms around one another.

For the first few months Gil was home and they were rediscovering one another, Nina Weston experienced a joy that had been denied her for many a year. Indeed her son seemed a changed man, willing to be guided by Buddy in all that had to do with the operation of the ranch. At sun-up he was ready to saddle his horse, the fine animal Jack had given him some years before, and ride out with the men to inspect the stock, look over the water supply, help keep the cattle off the loco weed. He learned to wean a calf with a small board on its nose to keep it from nursing from an emaciated mother, and to lay traps for pumas and wolves. He listened as Buddy spoke about the difficulties of guarding the herd during winter, of exhausted men and horses working in the freezing cold, trying to find the places where the snow was shallow and the grass under it thick.

He learned what could happen during a blizzard or a lightning storm when the cattle got spooked, and the men had to work their hardest to keep the cattle from drifting or stampeding. He asked intelligent questions, took Buddy's advice, learned how things were always done and worked alongside the men repairing fence and shoeing horses. He was ready for the roughest work. He was part of the spring roundup, lying out on the ground with the others during the nights under the stars, and he helped with the branding when the calves had been corralled. The exhaustion he reached seemed to fill him with a newfound satisfaction. Buddy had to be favorably impressed.

During the summer that followed he perhaps rediscovered a certain freedom in that life, as he rode off to hunt or roam the land as he'd done as a boy. And if he was still moody, self–absorbed, at least he didn't inflict himself on those around him.

That fall, after the cattle had been rounded up and sold, followed by a night of celebration, Nina Weston and Gil, on the occasion of his twenty-fifth birthday, held a little ceremony of their own in the office of her attorney: she signed the ranch over to him. It was his now. She could let go. He stood there, towering over her, a man come fully to his manhood, full of vigor, with a face much like his father's, a pride in his expression and a suggestion of the same kind of ambition, ready to take on anything.

Despite Gil's various accommodations, Buddy Quicksend, for one, was not eager to see him put in charge. He harbored certain strong misgivings. He couldn't help it; he'd always managed things with a free hand, practical but flexible. What bothered him was a sense that Gil wouldn't be satisfied with anything the world could boast, least of all himself. He watched as the young man took on the work of the ranch with a vengeance, reading long hours into the night what books he could find on the raising of cattle and the use of the land. His head was full of projects.

He wanted to raise horses, wanted to try new ways of breeding cattle. He had visions of a great ranch, a hacienda and outbuildings where not only those who worked the cattle lived, but others who'd make their tools and build their carts and fit out the horses, and plant their supply of hay, an enterprise as noble as Jefferson's Monticello, with visitors from the ranks of science and agriculture.

Nina could only wonder at him when he came to her brimming over with plans that had taken hold of his imagination. No doubt he'd been influenced by his father's large aspirations of bringing civilization to the raw wilderness. And who among us has not had at least once the dream of breaking the mold of the familiar and creating something beyond imagination? What would we do without the power to dream?

But it seemed like Gil couldn't find his way. Maybe his dream was too grand, so that what he tried was shot through with caprice. One week he had the men setting up another windmill for some project he had in mind; then suddenly his enthusiasm would flag, the effort outstripped by his idea, and he'd skulk around in a black mood. Then overtaken by another fit of enthusiasm, he'd forget all about the windmill while the men laid in the base for a smithy. Whatever grand scheme he carried in his head seemed always cheated in the efforts to make it real. For he could tolerate nothing less than the beckoning ideal.

"A dreamer," Buddy said, "of the worst kind," and spat with disgust. There was no living with him. He had a hard enough time as it was just getting the basic work done.

Then for a time Gil left the ranch alone and turned his attention to the house. He called in an architect all the way from Santa Fe to design the dwelling that he wanted—in the Spanish style, such as he'd seen in photos of the old cities of Mexico and Central America. Enter a great central patio planted with trees and cacti and flowering shrubs and see around you a three–sided two- story dwelling, with a grand ballroom, music room, library and a great dining room on the first floor, kitchen, kitchen garden, and storerooms at the side. Upstairs, various bedrooms and a special study for himself. Nina gasped at the scale of his fantasy, the expense it would entail.

The architect drew up the plans accordingly, the contractors were brought in, but then came ceaseless arguments over materials and arrangements, till they were ready to tear their own hair, but not before tearing Gil limb from limb. Nothing suited him, and were it not for Nina Weston's cajoling one, persuading another, soothing tempers and frayed nerves, remonstrating with Gil that his stubbornness would leave them without a roof over their heads, the house, too, would have been abandoned.

Finally it was finished, the basic structure stripped down and rebuilt, rooms added at the side and back. Not nearly so grand as he would have liked. It would have to do. In the future perhaps.... Already there were still images in his head to be realized. Then he entirely lost interest.

Fortunately, he set his mother to the task of furnishing the new rooms, sending her to Santa Fe to find old pieces in the Spanish style and order others made, while he turned his attention elsewhere.

The men began to rebel. Though they couldn't say he worked them any harder than he worked himself, they chafed under his tyranny and complained openly. They'd be better off working for Cameron, that sonuvabitch—so they muttered. Buddy Quicksend was ready to throttle Gil himself. He'd been running the ranch for nearly twenty years, had taken it through hard times, held on through the worst of winters, urged it toward prosperity—given Nina his best. His life's blood had gone into the place. Now the boy he'd watched grow up had reached the full height of his arrogance. He'd simply shoved him aside now that the ranch was his, and turned things upside down with his hare-brained schemes. The fact gnawed at him. Not that all the notions were wrong-headed: breeding bulls to improve the herd, looking for new strains. But Gil was quixotic and perverse; there was no way to plan from one day to the next. He was of a mind to leave. And he knew exactly where to go. Cameron had been after him for years, though he'd never said a word to Nina Weston. He could go as foreman of one of Jack's holdings—for bigger pay.

True, he could see what Cameron was about, though he had a pretty clear notion of that already.

He knew he'd be leaving Nina Weston in the lurch; the ranch would collapse around her. That was Jack's game—to pull out the props. Buddy Quicksend had kept his loyalty to her. He cherished her. Only now it was a different kettle of fish. Gil had driven him to the wall with nary a thought for all he'd done, certainly without a shred of gratitude. What of those months they'd worked side by side, when he'd undertaken to teach the young man everything he knew about land and cattle and weather? So much chaff in the wind.

One moment he was raw with anger; the next, sick at heart.

Nina Weston was no less torn. Whenever she raised some objection, Gil said mildly, "Mother, you're the one who put me in charge. I know what I'm doing. Things can't just go on the same old way."

"Things were working well enough," she ventured. "Buddy's done so much with this ranch, especially when times were tough. I couldn't have managed without him."

He gave an impatient shrug. "Like being dead," he said. "That works well enough too—living in the same rut for years and centuries. The world is changing."

No more than she should have expected. The rash blood she'd always known. *Does the leopard change his spots, the Ethiope his skin?* She'd deluded herself from the very beginning—hoped the East might tame him, give him reverence for all she remembered from her girlhood. He could have shone with such brilliance. Then she'd hoped the sweat of physical labor, the unsettled life he'd led would sober him. But these experiences had touched him no more deeply than the wind: he would give things his own stamp even if it meant his undoing. As always she was faced with excess—everything pushed too far. A torment to himself and those around him.

More than ever, she deplored the loss of a father who'd have put some sense into him, forced him to continue what custom demanded. She'd tricked herself into thinking he had changed, from the way he'd yielded to Buddy's experience and ordering of things. He'd never tried to take charge then. Now he seemed goaded by the need to prove himself, to create something beyond anything the town could conceive. Her own son reminded her of Jack Cameron: the same display of arrogance—too much intelligence and pride compressed into a single human frame—as though the earth existed for a single grand scheme. Madness. Her husband reaching for his piano, his notion of culture brought to the wild...

And Gil, what was he reaching for? The very thought

overwhelmed her. Whatever goaded him on allowed him to become ruthless, besotted with ambition. She prayed, Oh, don't let Buddy leave.

"What do you think, Buddy? What is there to do?" she implored him, fully aware of the state of things with the men.

"Well, ma'am, he can't go on bossing the men like they're just a bunch of cattle. They won't stand for it." Then came the outburst: "He's got me thinking I'd be better off on the worst starve–out spread than here."

"I've made a terrible mistake," she admitted, shaking her head. "I'm afraid we're all going to suffer for it." She touched Buddy on the arm. "Forgive me," she said. "Leave if you must, but..."

Quickly she turned away. And once again the man was caught by his feeling for her, something more than loyalty.

Other reasonable hopes Gil dashed as well. The respectable families, whose doors had been opened to him, with some thought about the prospects of their marriageable daughters, began to see what they had let into their midst. Nina hated to admit she was ashamed of him, a young man who threw out whatever notion came into his head, laughed openly at ideas he didn't countenance, and made decent people look like fools. She'd hoped he might marry Dr. Healy's older daughter, Mary, who'd had the benefit of a tutor and a music teacher and who could not only sing like a canary but also embroidered with delicate skill tea towels and pillow cases and crocheted doilies and coverlets to grace a house with polished surfaces to put them on, and who shone in the silks she wore, bearing such an amiable smile and countenance people were drawn to her. Nina Weston pronounced her a lovely, accomplished girl. She hoped she might exert a softening influence on her son. It was the women, she reminded herself, who'd brought their taming force to the West, to this remote and isolated town. Now that the last bits of recalcitrance had been subdued in the interests of the new order, Geronimo and his band of Apaches, having been defeated a decade ago, the frontier was at peace, and the way was open for a settled life. It had taken five thousand soldiers to put down a hundred Apaches.

What would it take for a son who was a law unto himself? It was worth hoping Mary Healy might be equal to the task.

At first, Gil seemed to find pleasure in the company of this pretty, likable young woman, though he failed to notice that the force of his personality made her agree to opinions she later had to wonder at. Now and then she'd make a little moue and draw a quick breath.

"And what do you think about when you're sitting there indoors all day?" he asked her as they walked out one evening.

"I don't have time to think," Mary said. "There's always so much to do, Besides, there are the visits to the poor and sick. The church choir and the china painting lessons. I'm always busy."

Gil considered. "Would you like to go out on the range on horseback?" He looked at her hopefully. "It's coming into grass this time of year, and the calves are being born. Would you like to see a calf born?"

She looked at him with a charming smile. "I've been a town girl all my life," she said. "Hardly a pioneer. Nothing of the rough and ready. All I've seen are kittens being born."

"You can do something different," he insisted. "It's not a sin. I've spent nearly my whole life outdoors. My mother has a gentle mare you can ride, and I know she'll be glad to lend you a pair of riding breeches. You're about the same size." He paused "Or I can give you a pair of my breeches, so you can really ride," he said, perhaps to see her reaction.

"Wear your trousers," she said with such disdain the young man laughed.

"You could even ride side-saddle, like they do back East."

She did not seize on the opportunity. "It sounds like a rough life on a ranch."

"There are always dangers," he granted. "Just a couple of weeks ago, Buddy Quicksend, that's our foreman, nearly got himself killed when a mule shied at a rattlesnake and bolted, and he got tangled in his horse's reins."

"I abhor snakes," she said. "And scorpions and wild animals. They frighten me. I like being in town because it's safe. I can still remember the story about how the judge went out with his family and got ambushed by the Indians. It makes me shiver all over—like it happened yesterday."

"I saw the Apache Kid once when I was young," Gil said. "He'd stolen off the reservation with his woman. He took water from our well for his horses. I saw him. We stood and looked at one another for a moment. I'll never forget it."

She shuddered. "I'm glad it's peaceful here—and civilized."

"Not so civilized as Kingston," he said. "They got twenty-two saloons there and eighty brands of liquor. We got only sixteen saloons where the miners and the cowhands can get drunk and brawl."

"What are you saying?" she demanded.

"I'm just saying," he drawled, "that they've got more places for the men to get into fights and stab each other. Even the Indians, if they're of a mind. Think of all the benefits."

She looked at him, her blood rising. She knew well enough that he was making fun of her. "You think you can change all that?" she said with scorn.

"No indeed," he said. "I think we'll only improve on it—invite the celebrated Madam Varnish to come and deal out faro. We're a little behind on the gambling end. There are still some fools not separated from their money."

He made her feel dull and wretched, as he plunged on, praising that fine citizen Jack Cameron and the sheriff and all the local politicians awake nights thinking of the public good. And how beneficial it had been for the town to have all the Apaches sent off to Florida to die like flies, even the Indian scouts who'd helped General Crook track them down in the wild mountain country of Mexico...."

"It's all past and done with," she blurted out, angry now. She wanted a beau she could walk out with to admire the evening and look up at the stars, one who looked for her smile and the light in her eyes and spoke his adoration.

"I see you're interested in justice," he said.

Her eyes were points of fire and her cheeks were flushed. He almost liked her then, she had some spark to her.

"Keep your justice," she flung at him. And before he could further appreciate her fine burst of temper—they were near her house—she fled inside and left him standing.

"Keep your civilization," he yelled after her.

Nothing spoke to his blood. These decorous daughters were like weak tea, with their tepid femininity and their Victorian manners. And he roared around the town in his hunger.

Better to drink in the saloons, where the crude jokes and rough manners allowed him something of himself. Or else he joined the poker players at the back or upstairs. He liked risk, and from his raw beginnings in college he had learned from cowpunchers, and from sailors, from betting men on trains, to gamble. He was open to any game of chance or skill, and no matter what he lost, he was not too daunted to play again. Indeed he had a mania for gambling. When the cards went against him, some impulse goaded him into recklessness, and even if he had a winning streak, he often couldn't quit until he'd ridden it into loss. Thus he was creating his own legend as he went along, the townsfolk holding their breath.

"His poor mother," they commiserated, meanwhile, I suspect, holding onto a secret relish. Hedged in by our fears, we most of us can't help being titillated by a little scandal. Can't keep our eyes and ears away from it. And should I claim my own disinterest, declare myself a mere recorder for the imagination? Holding only the spectator's role? Spectator or voyeur—where does one cross the line? Don't I have any life of my own, or is this the way I go looking for my life as I try to imagine the story?

As yet I don't know. Only that here we have the maverick throwing aside convention—or at least pushing past what was tolerable into excess. For he did openly what a good many did in secret and pretended to the opposite—courting ruin in more ways than one.

That's how they saw it. But they said so with a certain relish. It wasn't just amusing, it was downright absorbing. Whatever else he'd contributed to gossip and rumor, he'd now openly taken up with Hippolyta. In the eyes of the town, he couldn't sink any lower.

Set off a little by itself, but still a regular house, it was accepted by the town: a respectable man deserved a place where he might go for a little diversion. The madam kept a good house, with a parlor furnished in sofas and chairs and lamps with fringed shades and mirrors and a piano. And after the liquid refreshments, a punch the madam made herself, that drew away any awkwardness or reserve and brought on a light, bubbling hilarity, the entertainment would begin. One of the girls would open her sheet music and play the tunes she knew, while one by one the girls went off with the men, till at last, it was her turn too. For she had her special friend waiting.

But Hippolyta lived up on Chihuahua Hill, and certain men came to her alone. Who these were Gil had no inkling, but he concluded that her customers were not only the Mexicans she lived among and possibly a few cowboys and miners who found the refinements of the local house too inhibiting, but others who found her charms alluring: owners of the mines and ranches and local businesses as well. She was not only beautiful; she was, he'd heard some people say, a bruja, a witch. For she grew herbs and practiced her own kind of magic. In her garden were herbs with which to assail the great mysteries governing but small lives, and she knew their potencies for good or ill. Both men and women came to her for charms to bring good fortune or to keep off the evil eye and the vengeful wrath of dead ancestors; for love potions guaranteed to arouse the affections of even the most disdainful.

The priest would not allow her inside the church, she had so fallen beyond redemption. If she worked her baleful charms on Gil, she herself was likely the worse for it, so people said; he was already so far gone. Like had met like—she'd met her match. Curiosity had led him to her, for he was born curious. He found out where her adobe house sat on the Hill, and when he found it, he was overtaken by surprise. It stood out from among her neighbors', an adobe simple enough, but well-built, extensive. She had set out not only a garden but a small orchard, in which apple, peach and cherry trees grew and, along the walls, nasturtiums and black-eyed Susans and beds of herbs and chilies. She drew her water from a well in back, and farther back were pens with goats and a little enclosure with a flock of chickens. Also at the rear, she had a small stable with a horse and a cow. Beyond these, an open field allowed them to graze. Among the houses around her with their patches of weed and prickly pear, she had created a little island of cultivation.

Near the house he saw an old woman stooped over a tub washing clothes and hanging them to dry. As he was surveying Hippolyta's domain, a woman appeared from inside the house, gave some instruction to the old woman and glanced in his direction. She was formidable: taller than the Mexican or Indian women he had seen, with honey-colored skin and dark hair. He stood for a moment admiring the curve of her neck and breast, the tangle of black hair that leapt back from her face as though charged with electricity. For her presence, intense as the colors of her flowers, drew the eye and held it. She turned and stared at him, then asked him in Spanish what he wanted. For the moment he wanted only to look at her, to let his eye ride the curve of shoulder and breast, to satisfy himself that enough harm flashed in her eyes to make it worth his while, enough promise of delight in the flesh. It was all there, he could see at a glance, a passion that could take him in, perhaps do him in. A difficult love for any man, if she chose any man to love. But well worth the gamble—he'd so despaired of finding anyone who could sound his heart. Flesh wasn't enough—although he took his appetites to where they might have temporary satisfaction, until the excesses nauseated him; nor had the spirit made its soundings. He told her in passable Spanish he needed a love charm for a woman who had no eyes for him.

"No eyes for you?" she said, looking him up and down. "For a big man like you with strength in his body, who blocks the path, and the eye as well? Maybe you have the wrong woman."

She gave him a long, bold assessment. He could feel the sharpness of her gaze as though it could not only take the measure of every muscle and sinew, handle liver and lights and reach to his very vitals, but weigh his heart and decide what truth was in him and what was false.

He struggled with his discomfort. "But you have charms," he said. "Or so they tell me—that can turn pride into yielding softness."

He spoke softly, as though to suggest the desired result.

"But you wouldn't want her after you got it," she said. "If such a woman woman threw herself in front of you, you would give her a kick and turn aside." She could indeed see into him, and he stood dazzled and exposed.

"Then I come for you," he said.

"You think you can have me just like that?" she said, snapping her fingers. "You think I give myself to every man who walks by?"

"I thought," he ventured, "you gave yourself to those willing to pay a price." He'd been deceived, he saw at once. She was not there for any man to claim. And those whom she allowed to come to her knew her worth and had left their bounty.

"Not you," she said, turning away. "For you there is no price."

She had driven a dagger through him, this bitch of a woman, and he wanted to seize her and throttle her. But even as she annihilated him, he was held in thrall.

"Yes, there are those who come to take me as though I were a piece of trash. Especially those who think they can touch the sky. They want to light their candles and call the fire an evil thing."

He had no idea what she was talking about or what she wanted or didn't want. "They won't let me in the church," she said. "They think I'm so much beneath them. Not even human. As though God belongs only to them."

She trembled with anger. "They think I've turned God into the devil. As though light and dark were the only powers."

"Build a church of your own," he said, "if they wont let you in. Theirs isn't the only one, the fools."

There was a shift of the ions in the air. She looked at him as though she'd been struck by lightning. And he wasn't clear himself about what he'd said. But he went on. "You say there are other powers. I don't know what they are, but sometimes things enter me, take hold of me...."

Not the Sunday sermons and or hymns that left him without the least enthusiasm, but had given him the fidgets all through boyhood. Who was the god that sent the flood and let his father die? He couldn't find any god to claim or look to for comfort. But there had been plenty of gods and goddesses to worship—now just pictures in an outworn book. Old names that poets stuck in poems. That lived in the books in which he'd once lost himself. Who'd once inspired a great belief, held names of power.

Perhaps there was a goddess somewhere not yet given her due. Hippolyta knew what it was to live a life of the flesh—but perhaps more. Like Mary Magdalene. He thought of both virginity and experience, how both had lived in the same woman, though people acted as if you couldn't have innocence back once it had skipped out. If there was a time in the newness of the world, if the time could be remembered.... She wasn't such a fool, this woman.

"My own church?" she said. "What an idea," she said, dismissing it. "Blasphemy. Lightning would strike it down."

But now he could not let go. "Who knows?" he said. "Who are they to say you don't belong there? Suppose you built a church. You say there are powers... God or the devil? Only those?" He didn't know. "If you were the priestess, what would you say?"

"You're mocking me."

"No," he said. "I wouldn't think of it." Just now he'd have been glad to fall at her feet and worship whatever power lived in her. For something had been sparked, and it spoke to a deep emptiness in him—with all the struggle to reach beyond torment, the mind all mired in hidden speculations, trying to describe what has no name. Real enough for all that. You can struggle in that agony for years and centuries if you're not born to take the known path and take comfort in the old pieties. But once sealed off from the common dream, by what avenue can you find your way back? Or forward? And to what?

That conversation made her even more widely known in the town. For, yes, she built her own chapel—it's been written in the annals of the town—because she'd been ruled out. And Gil was drawn to her, because of what they both were. A curiosity, a wonder at a creature who'd strayed beyond the others. Her own church. Whatever she was, she looked beyond herself. And he wanted to look into her, follow the changing aspects of her image in time.

"I mean what I said," he told her. "If you want a church, we'll make you one."

And he stepped over her fence, into her garden where her herbs grew in little beds. He took her hand, which sent his own tingling.

She looked at him, looked deeply. Then she took him inside. She took him inside cool white walls hung with *retablos* of saints and martyrs all in red and gold. And brightly painted gourds and a tree made of clay filled with ceramic birds, orange and green, blue and yellow. She led him to the carved bed of dark wood, slipping away the bodice from her honey-colored breasts with their dark nipples. Her skirt and petticoats slipped to the floor, revealing her sleek thighs. She took him to where he came to know her for the first time, in a rush of blood and action that left him breathless, all used up, the whole of him. And for the first time lying in her bed with his arms around her, he felt a loosening away of the tight knots that held him in and which he continually strained against, like the wild horse he'd once tried to ride.

V. The Hunt

He had both a dog and a horse, his most prized possessions. The dog was a hunter, the best dog in the county—that was his boast. It was a beast born of surmise, for he'd found the animal half-starved, lying in a ditch when he was out riding. A hound of mixed breed, but with a good head and heavy paws, still in its first soft puppy fur, tawny dark. He'd gotten down to have a look, his first thought being that it was a wounded puma or coyote. But no, a dog that whined and thumped its tail at his approach. Gil stroked its head and invited it to eat the sandwich he'd brought with him. The dog wolfed it down, looked for more, and finding none but still grateful, gathered up its energies to throw itself against his leg in an offering of friendship. He lifted the pup onto his horse and held it carefully as he rode home. He took charge of the pup himself. She slept at the foot of his bed until she found her strength again and wrestled with and tore up everything in sight. Then he built a house and pen for her and trained her as a hunter. She had courage and speed for flushing up wild turkeys and tracking deer and antelope. Once she treed a bear and clamored for him till he came. He named her Battle.

The horse had been Cameron's gift to his boyhood, a horse now in its prime. He rode it now not as if he were astride a whirlwind, though he still liked to gallop across the mesas. Now the horse was part of him and flowed beneath him, joined in an intricate exchange of signals and movements. With the two animals he felt as close as he had ever come to kinship. And there, perhaps, with horse and dog as he went off to hunt, some part of him could come into play that lay outside all that grated upon him and allowed his rage to subside. He could lose himself in the day, in the land, in the sense that something might be discovered—leave off his contest with the world and whatever seized him that wouldn't let go.

That's why you'd have come West with all the nameless others, to break through the fences and take off, celebrating the chance. Gold and land a lure to the blood, but maybe you don't even need that incentive. Just beckoning possibility. The call of freedom with all its risks. That's the way I see it.

So you can see riding out into the land, where the cattle ranged half wild and mingled with the game. High grass to feed on and other bounty. He could take his pleasure in the good shot that brought the taste of the wild into the kitchen. He could carve up a deer with as much skill as an Indian did. And he knew the satisfaction of the kill.

But one day he was caught up short by a movement that disturbed the grass, made a sudden turmoil in his vision. Strangeness took him captive —he could not believe his eyes. First he caught sight of a cow he startled into a frightened run—a cow whose brand he couldn't make out, not theirs. Often when they rounded up the herd, they found a few strays and wild cattle mixed in. Those without brands they branded, added them to the herd and let them go again. Sometimes he and the men went out by moonlight to rope wild cattle where the ranch bordered the bush, or to set a v-shaped trap with poles, baited with salt, whose ends they could close. Every now and then, there was a *ladino* they couldn't capture, but which eluded them time and again. Even if they captured it, the wily beast, somehow it managed to escape.

This cow he galloped after and saw that she ran in the company of another creature he couldn't at first identify. Dark-skinned and hairy, covered with some sort of hide, or so he thought. He gave chase until both eluded him in the brush. But in the moment before they disappeared, it struck him with a sudden burst of recognition that the animal he pursued was a man. He got down off his horse and kneeling beside the tracks, he found a human footprint.

He was dumbfounded. What sort of man? All the way back he turned over the question in his mind. A man who lived as an animal, and, so it appeared, ran with a cow. And how did he live? On prickly pear apples and pine nuts, mesquite beans. Perhaps he caught birds in a trap, snared rabbits, or even rats. For the Apaches they were

73

a delicacy. Maybe he was an Indian. A man alone without other men—or women. The freedom, the sheer stark loneliness of such a condition made his head spin. He envied it, even as he guessed something of its vulnerability.

He asked Buddy if he knew anything about a man living out in the bush. Buddy remembered that there was a Yaqui Indian who used to come around selling wood. He hadn't seen the fellow for a long time, thought he'd maybe gone back to Mexico. But could be he'd gone wild and snuck off to live on the land, the way some of the fellows do—the Indians, that is. And there was another, who'd been tossed into the pokey down in El Paso, and come up this way to try his luck—Mexican or Indian, who'd got in trouble whenever he turned around. Big man, though most Mexicans are small. Must be Indian then, since these were the only two breeds of people he knew—though he hadn't seen any tall Indians himself. Heard about them though. And then old Jake, as he was known. Mauled by a bear. Wouldn't come back to live among civilized folks. But he was old, must be seventy, eighty. He'd seen him once, back when was it? In short, after half an hour of rambling conjectures, at the end of which Gil was ready to throttle him for his tiresomeness, Buddy Quicksend was no help at all.

The discovery unsettled Gil, like a shadow fallen across his mind. From the midst of all that land in which so many creatures moved, a strange eye was taking him in, and he could not turn his head away from it. It looked at him from a different attitude, and what did it see? Did it recognize itself in him; yet if it did, it could only run. Fascination drew and maddened him. The creature crossed his dreams at night. He had strange dreams that made him grind his teeth. He dreamt that he had taken hold of a great ax to chop down a giant tree, but that he couldn't budge it. No matter how hard he tried to lift it, it remained immovable. Then he dreamt that a meteor had fallen from the sky and landed on his foot, so that he couldn't move. In this, too, he was helpless. No matter how he tried to lift it off and continue on his path, it was beyond his power.

He rose from sleep, dream-tossed and irritable. For reasons he couldn't explain, he couldn't bear himself and daylight, and human speech lacerated his nerves. His mother, who anguished over him still, begged him to tell her what was wrong. And he told her his dreams. "There's going to be a change in your life," she said.

"Are you just saying that? How do you know?"

" Just a feeling," she said.

At times he thought her merely superstitious she put such stock now in omens and premonitions. Even before his father was carried away by the flood, she had sensed a warning, though she hadn't put any stock in it. She'd told him that things came to her sometimes, and though at first she hadn't given them any heed, now she paid attention. Dreams were like hints, she said, from the other side of things. What that meant he didn't know, but somehow he couldn't put it aside.

He rode out again and searched for the wild man's tracks, and lost and found them. He looked for clues at the edges of what he guessed to be the creature's life, the evidence of a kill, the remains of fires, but found no charred wood beside the creek. Did the creature eat only raw food, live without any consoling warmth? He roved through the hills and into the canyons. He began exploring caves, thinking one of these might be the wild man's lair. How did he survive in winter? And finally when he 'd begun to despair and was making his way back to the ranch, he chanced upon the game he sought kneeling by a water hole, bending over to drink. He stopped his horse and held his breath, watching.

The cow stood a little way back. They were companions, man and cow. The cow lifted up her head, caught his scent and snorted, then leapt away. The wild man looked up from his drinking, hair sopping, water flowing down his chin, and fled. Before Gil could reach him, both had disappeared. And though he wove through the bush for hours, he could find no trace.

He sent the men out. "There's a wild man on the land," he told them. "He's been thieving cattle, and I want him captured." Thereby he translated strangeness into the daylight world. How else could he get them to act? They went out by moonlight to see if they could trap the outlaw. And after several nights of fruitless search, they came upon him, lying against the cow's side under the shelter of a cottonwood along a quick-moving creek. The noise of the water covered their approach as he slept innocent of danger. And before he knew what was happening, they seized him, got a rope around him, and roped the cow as she stood up. But somehow she got free and charged them, bellowing as they tried to jump the man. She buffeted them from all sides, making a great turmoil in the moonlight. One of them shot at her, and the wild man yelled out in fury. Then he broke away, dodged aside, clambered up the tree to prevent himself from being trampled, while the cow, her head lowered, charged this way and that, with a bellowing that mounted to the moon. She was a whole herd of cows. The horses were spooked, and started running. And while the cow distracted men and horses, maddened to fury by the threat to her man, ready to protect him to the death, the man escaped as well. Frustration and relief. A stampede they could understand, but this was a whole new experience. So they returned to Gil and reported the night's adventure.

"I never seen such a thing, never spent such a night," Buddy Quicksend said. "And I swear I'll never spend another like it." It wouldn't fit into the words they knew. A man and a cow, by God. And it must be her milk he drank, for her udders were full and she had no calf. Perhaps she'd lost one and adopted the wild man instead. But where had he come from and how long had he survived in this uncertain life? Down in the bunkhouse, they worried the subject this way and that; then they let it go. They had the herd to think about, other chores to do. Such nights would ruin them for a good day's work. Gil sent them out again—he kept the matter to himself to trouble over.

Gil told the strange tale to Hippolyta , and she grew thoughtful. Then she said, "Let me go out to the water hole where you saw him drinking. "

"Why, what would you do?"

"There are herbs to put into the water," she said. "There are charms that subdue wildness. And then, well, perhaps we'll see."

He rose up on his elbow to look at her as he lay beside her. She had come to know men. There had always been a man around her, so people said. He might be thirty or sixty, it didn't seem to matter to her. And he busied himself keeping up her yard or working to buy her food. Then she only sold charms and herbs. They came and went, the men. And in between, men visited her, taking from her a momentary pleasure. But either way, they left behind more than they knew, a residue of something more than themselves. They left a woman who had known many men. Gil wanted this kind of knowledge for himself, an ability to see beyond whatever a man brought in himself. Or a woman—that was of a different order perhaps.

Something winked at him and drew him on. He and his men could only try to capture this strange creature, take him by surprise and tie him up, confront his wildness as captors. But Hippolyta would not take him by force; she would take him by her wiles. By what she knew. He had to wonder. It was a strange thing to be doing; he felt a curious disquiet, and yet he could not leave it alone.

Hippolyta rode out with him. She carried in one of her saddle bags packets of herbs and scents and charms; in the other, beans and meat and tortillas, and a chicken she had killed and roasted. "Do not come for me," she said.

"How will you get back?"

"The horse will find its way. I have a blanket, and I have food."

"It gets cold at night," Gil said.

"I'll be safe."

"If you're not back in three days, I'll come to get you."

"Trust me," she said.

And he left her not far from the watering hole. During the time she was gone, he felt such restlessness and misgivings surge within him, he could hardly bear it. It was as though he had a rival, one he'd himself created. Alone in bed he wrestled with the dark and rose raw- eyed in the daylight. He couldn't concentrate, and if anyone came to him with a question or report, he dismissed him hastily, though things weren't going well. Several days after those nights of turmoil, Buddy came to his mother and gave his notice. That he'd

77

avoided him stung Gil to the quick, and though he'd gone to the older man and told him how great his loss would be and offered to double his pay, Quicksend had simply looked at him with a little smile and said, "I think the time has come for us to go our separate ways. You got your way of doing things—I got mine."

Then he learned that Jack Cameron had hired Buddy away. That put him in a fury, and though at first he tried to convince himself that Jack must have threatened him with lying dead in a ditch if he didn't accept, he knew better and acknowledged he could blame no one but himself. The man he'd known from boyhood would be gone. In that moment, he knew he'd counted on his continuing presence as one of the props holding up his life. In that state of mind, he alternately thought of and forgot about Hippolyta.

He went off to town to pick up supplies or busied himself with unnecessary tasks. He ate erratically or didn't bother to eat. To lose himself, he spent his evenings in the Pioneer Bar and sat alone with a bottle of whiskey. He sent down one shot after another until he roared and started looking to pick a fight and the bartender threw him out. Other times he drank in deadly quiet until he fell asleep at one of the tables, and they had to roust him up and carry him across the street and into the hotel. Or if the gambling urge took him over, he stayed sober and played poker in the back.

The fifth night he rode into town he came upon Jack Cameron dealing pinochle in the back room. Gil recognized him immediately, though it had been more than ten years since he'd seen him last. In his fifties now, Jack Cameron carried a certain distinction, his dark hair streaked along the temples, his mustache entirely gray, the hawk nose more prominent than ever. He'd glanced up at the young man without recognition, and would have ignored him for his cards, but his sidekick jogged his memory. "It's Gil Weston."

"Well, long time no see," Jack said, rising up and greeting him as though he'd been expecting him all along. "Sit down and join us."

"Not tonight," Gil said. It rankled him to have Cameron sitting there shuffling the cards with a kind of insolent ease, knowing that he'd gotten the better of him. At the height of his power. He controlled all the range this side of Duck Creek to above Mule Springs, and every meadow and water hole in a day's ride, now a million acres, with sixty thousand head of cattle. He'd started his own breeding ranch and swore he'd have a better cow than the longhorns and wild cattle that had roamed the land, scrawny and tough. He'd put his beef on the tables of the East, and taken the toughness out of it. And now he had Buddy Quicksend to help him do it. Over the years he'd built a series of bigger and finer houses to keep up with each new stage of success, and now his pride was a hunting lodge where sometimes he entertained as many as thirty or forty guests. He'd had fancy chandeliers brought in to grace the dining room, and faucets plated with gold. Goblets of Waterford crystal held his wine; Wedgwood china from England and sterling silver and Belgian laces made his table a glittering display. At Christmastime a huge tree was transported by many hands into the living room, to be decked with candy canes and gingerbread men, and lit with candles, and all the children from the town, the cowhands' kids, the children of Mexican miners, one and all, were invited to join the celebration and take home bags of candy.

"I've been hoping to have you come out and see my spread," Jack told him, "now that you're in charge of your own affairs. I owe you a little debt."

"What might that be?" Gil said, immediately suspicious. One by one the other men, as though at a signal, got up and moseyed off to the bar, and Gil noticed that only one of them still remained, a fellow named Pard, Jack's right-hand man, who, as rumor had it, did his dirty work. He remembered the man.

"I'd take it in a kindly way if you'd sit down for a little friendly game," Jack said. "I heard you've got a bit of skill at it."

How would he know that? Such obvious flattery. He wouldn't be taken in, though he rather prided himself on his gambling skill. He was ready to insult the man, pick a fight, let him have his henchman waylay him in the dark.

"Don't think I'd be much of a challenge for a man of your skill," Gil said, putting him off.

"Who knows? " Jack said, riffling the deck in a slow fashion, head cocked, looking at him narrowly. "And it might prove worth your while."

"I doubt it," Gil said. "I don't go in for your methods."

Jack ignored him. "I've got a little piece of land, sweet little section with a fine meadow. It's yours if you win."

"I've got enough land of my own," Gil said. "But I can't play for stakes like that anyway." He turned to leave.

"You're suggesting I'd have the whole advantage," Jack said, "since I wouldn't miss the loss. But I'm willing to take a handicap. Just for the sake of amusement—it's been a dull evening. You can put up your dog against my land. I hear she's a pretty fair animal."

"I wouldn't take any amount of money for her," Gil said.

"You don't have much confidence in your card-playing ability," Jack said casually. "Or maybe you're just scared."

Jack was trying to get his goat—he could see right through him. "I won my spending money all through college," Gil declared. "Without cheating."

"So—a fair way to support scholarship and get a little practice to boot. Admirable. But then who knows—maybe I'd just let you win. "

"What I win, I win on my own," Gil said.

"Spoken like a man," Jack said. "I like your style. I like a man with guts."

And though Gil knew he should simply walk into the saloon and order a whiskey, he sat down and told him to deal the cards. "My land for your dog. Name your game," Jack said. "Poker, pinochle, black jack, dice."

They started off with pinochle, set the points they'd play to. Gil won the deal. Having the advantage of a hundred aces, he bet the hand strongly and won. His blood was up; he wanted to beat this man. And luck was on his side. But though he started soberly enough, perhaps because he was convinced he couldn't lose, he got caught up, became giddy with the need to risk, betting for what was in the widow, putting his trust in a luck that he determined should be his. Jack was a shrewd man in a game of cards, and he could see what was happening. The only thing required was for him to take the fullest advantage of his own cards, remember what had been played, while the young fool played the high cards first and neglected to calculate what he should hold for melds or else, having made a mistake of that sort, held cards too long that should have been played early. As the hands played out, Gil could see himself going wrong. The moment he made a bid he knew he shouldn't have done it, knew after he'd thrown down a card, he should have held it. It was as though some demon bent on his destruction had caught him up, running with all speed toward his undoing while he stood by, helpless. Jack sat imperturbable, his long shadow seeming to pull him in, defeating his will.

The men, drawn from the bar to their table, gathered around to watch them play. The air grew charged and smoky, filled with the shadowy play of their own emotions: what they held in under the surface of jokes and banter. Resentments and envy that flowed towards what they lusted after; what they feared in some dim way for themselves; what they had failed to risk and never claimed. As the smoke filled the room, it seemed to move and take the shape of all the tensions, to float like a miasma. Though they had no love for Jack Cameron, something made them glad to watch Gil's luck turn against him. For he'd never had to deserve all he'd been given. Aloof, he could stand above them, delivering a contempt that shrank them into the ordinary and dismissed them. Yet a certain shame mingled with their grudge against him, for Nina Weston had ministered to the town, and they knew her generosity, her desire to serve the public good, which was themselves.

And the shame reminded them that underneath any notion of themselves as decent and law-abiding men lurked something that rose up against their pretensions, bristling with antagonisms sharp as knives and just as deadly. So they waited and saw Gil throw away his chances and lose his dog.

"I see I have the advantage," Jack said. "I tell you what, let's switch to something that depends more on luck than ability—and you can have your chance to win back your bitch." Cameron didn't want to be accused of robbing a simpleton, but he knew his mark. Child's play. Secretly he could laugh, and the triumph had allowed him the condescension that would drive his victim to greater fury and loss—inevitably.

Gil himself could see it coming: he caught a smell out of the past, a moist rankness that made him want to choke: his head down inside the well, enveloped by a mossy darkness. He saw that now again he'd been trapped, had allowed himself to be, no one to rescue him, and that if he went on, he'd lose everything. A voice in his ear said *, Don't do it, Gil,* and he looked around to see who had admonished him, softly as a woman might. Some voice that seemed to be in the room even as it filled his head. He wanted to obey the voice, even if it meant his losing face. He could hear rumor filling the air, *Yes, lost his dog that was so precious to him. Now he won't have anything to boast about. Puffed himself up about his gambling too. That'll teach him. Naw, ain't nothing'll teach him. He's got a heart like a bear trap, and even a bear can't bear it—haw haw.*

It was the glitter of Cameron's eye, the soft smile that played modestly under his mustache that snared his prey, drew him against his will.

"Name your game," Cameron said.

"Dice," Gil said.

Dawson, who ran the place and always kept his neutrality for the sake of general good will, brought the dice.

"And the bet?" Gil said.

"Well, how about your dog and that sweet little piece of land—" Jack said, "against your horse. Was always sorry I let go of that horse. Best animal that's ever come my way."

He couldn't lose this time, Gil convinced himself, because only he could ride that animal, ride with the intimacy of their deep instinctual bond. If he lost it, he'd be losing half himself. He shook the dice. No snake eyes, but no seven either. But though he shook and shook again for the five he'd first thrown, it wouldn't come. Once again the voice admonished him to let go his losses and retreat. But his head whirled with a vision of his horse, his dog. And when they moved beyond him, he knew he couldn't bear his life. "If you want to go on playing," Jack said, in a low voice, "You'll have to put up your ranch.."

A hush fell in the room, and now it was hard to read the sentiment that played about. Hard for the men to know their own minds. For if they'd wanted to see Gil lose, they didn't particularly ache to see Jack win; and now the stakes had grown beyond all reason. They didn't want to see Gil lose everything. It brought them to the edge of that dark fear that Cameron would swallow them up too, swallow up everything and tyrannize them all. The Weston ranch still held its own character, a small island that had so far, for whatever reason, been spared. A numbness settled over Gil, as if he were a fly stung with poison, stricken until the spider came to eat it. He sat immobile. He no longer cared about the ranch or his own fate. So that as he watched the dice form the configuration that took everything away and put it into Cameron's hands, he was a spectator watching the unfolding of a drama that had no connection with him. And when they watched Jack throw the winning eleven, the room felt a low hum move through it that was, if not moan or protest, a letting go. Gil still sat unmoving.

"Well now, neighbors. Don't think I'm not a fair man," Jack said, "or that I want to rob a young fellow of his chances in life. I won't allow any man or woman to starve—" He looked to see how he was faring in the sentiments of those whose eyes were on him. He could see the play of irony: no man or woman to starve if he manages against the odds to stay alive. And he allowed them to consider that he could have got this piece of land, too, if he'd wanted to go after it. But they couldn't object: he'd won it fair and square. And now they could experience his largesse.

"Gilbert here," he said, reducing him to the name of his boyhood, "can stay and work the ranch as he's been doing. And he won't starve, and his mother will have her home, everything just the way it's been. Excepting that it's my land now, and I expect him to work it the way he'd work his own and make it prosper. Not neglect the fences or the cattle. Now is that what you'd call fair, or not?" he appealed to the rest. But there was no demur.

He turned to Gil directly, as though to cement things with his smile. But Gill understood his real message. *Because now you can't leave it—you've got a debt owing. You've made your mother a hostage to your fortunes.* Gil stood up from the table, grabbed his jacket and strode through the bar and into the street.

But Jack Cameron was right behind him. He caught Gil by the shoulder and made him turn around. . "Let's have a little man-to-man," he said, as Gil pushed his hand away, "just to show you I'm not one to bear a grudge. Let me say this: I've always had a soft spot for your mother, and if she were willing..."

"Leave her out of this. She's not a whore." And he strode away without looking back. That was how Gil lost what so far his mother had managed so determinedly to hold onto. Well might he grind his teeth at night. His head reeled with loss. And round and down more deeply the thought ground into him that he'd had things he loved and had been rich with their possession. Had had them. Like the air he breathed. They'd made him what he was. And without them he didn't exist, was sickened by the very thought of his existence. He was nothing; he'd struck bottom.

VI. Flower Woman

Hippolyta tethered her horse a little distance from the water hole, beyond a thicket near a little hill where her mare could graze and where she might spend the night. The sun was high, and under the cottony clouds the land glowed with midday heat. She heard the trill of a meadowlark as it flew up and small rushes in the grass: birds and lizards, horned toads or rabbits, all the small, busy, hidden life. The barrel cactus, the choya and the prickly pear had finished blooming and were now forming their fruit, but the yuccas were still in blossom, their white bulbs incandescent with the sunlight. She liked being on the land out under the open sky. It gave space to the landscape around her.

Freedom. Everything called to her: cloud and bird and glint of rock, the red of Indian paintbrush. She breathed all of it in. Except for the birds, it was very quiet. She would have made her way through the brush to the water hole and stood for a long moment studying her reflection in its pool, but she thought better of it. She did not want to forewarn the wild man with her scent.

She moved off a little way behind a trailing growth of scrub cedar to wait for whatever might find its way there to drink. The afternoon heat hit its peak—then a shower fell, as it usually did mid-afternoon that time of year. Her hunger grew as the shadows lengthened, but she did not eat. Hunger sharpened her senses to exquisite keenness. She watched a deer approach, sniff the air, and drink. She had tried to put herself where the breeze couldn't catch her scent. The deer seemed untroubled. She saw a coyote creep up, continually looking over its shoulder. It lapped the water and moved back into the tall grass.

Then a new noise disturbed the brush, and she saw the unlikely pair emerge. She held her breath at the apparition, for she, too, was visited by a sense of strangeness, as first she watched the man drink while the cow stood watching over him, and then as the cow came forward and lapped up the water with her broad tongue.

They could have been lovers, so deep an unspoken intimacy entwined them. Hippolyta could recognize such things. She'd seen the play of all kinds of emotions, and something more, between lovers; she'd known all these in her own flesh and heard them spoken of when lovers came to buy her charms. It was what she knew best, her lifelong study, not simply the isolated expression. She had come to know the force that pushed forward into attraction and repulsion, into love and disdain, into power and submission— the force that swept everything before it. She knew how it must be in that unspoken language underlying all speech: the cow's thoughts were those of the wild man and his were hers, fused into one, uncomplicated by any spoken word. They moved together in a single instinct. And she wondered how it would be to dwell in just that, if a man' s thoughts could run with hers and her own with those of a man in whom she could lose herself. In certain moments it had happened. But she had no time to dwell on that interesting question.

Having turned over several schemes in her mind, she now let out a little soft moan as if she were in pain. She saw the man look up, turn his eyes in her direction without seeing her. Then she made her moan again, louder this time and more insistent. He stood up and came toward the clump of cedar, still keeping a distance. She moaned again, softly pleading. And slowly he approached to where she was and looked down at her, this creature on the ground, curious but fearful too. Now she grabbed her leg and groaned and rolled on the ground to show him she was hurt. And he bent down beside her, drawn toward her in sympathy but confused as to how to act. The cow held back, as though afraid, for she lowed softly, as if to call him away.

Hippolyta put out her most pitiful groan, for the two of them were rivals now, and both were calling to him. She reached out and touched his leg. The man leapt back. She was afraid she'd startled

86

him away, but he didn't run; instead he continued to regard her, his attention riveted on her face. She groaned again and waited for his tentative approach.

He didn't want to come, but neither could he simply go and leave her. A heart was there, she decided, something to appeal to, even if not yet wholly formed. Once again she held out her hand, and he came slowly forward. She touched his leg, slowly let her hand run along the calf with its long, soft hair. He must have liked the sensation, for he drew back the leg she had stroked and held the other one toward her. Finally she reached for his hand and drew him down beside her. Then she played her hand along his arm, nuzzled him and stroked his neck.

The cow stood there stupidly, made a mutter that took up a rhythm of short insistent sounds then turned into a bellow. Angry now, she was importuning him. She trotted off a little way and pawed the ground, as if to tell him she was leaving and he'd better come along. Then when she saw he wasn't coming, she gave voice to the first notes of an anguish beginning to dawn on her.

Hippolyta took one of the wild man's hands in both of hers and began to stroke and caress one then the other. The nails were long and sharp, thick and yellow, and the hands were calloused like a hide. She could scarcely see his face, the hair was so thick and shaggy, in places matted beyond the comb, filled with burs. She tried to read the eyes, large and brown and deep, somewhat like the water hole. She saw a mixture of puzzlement and fear, but with these a fascination that pulled him toward her. She began to sing, and he looked at her as if struck dumb, as if he'd never heard such sounds, but which struck his ears as more than sound, suggesting, if not a meaning, something that was awakening in his blood. She was trying to weave around him a net of sensations. to put new touches on his body, new sounds into his ear.

Under her hands he grew less wary, seemed to grow soft as the mud at the edge of the water hole. He felt himself become his sensations, as a certain heat grew in his flesh, went racing along his veins, all the hills and valleys of what he was, to locate itself between his legs. Such sensations had come before, but had no connection to the creature lying on the ground. And what he did with them depended on where he was and what was handy. A sudden sharp noise aroused him, and he saw that the cow was going to charge in their direction, very likely trample the creature in the grass.

He yelled out, stood up, and chased her. She must have thought they were finally running off from the interloper, and Hippolyta thought so, too, as the pair ran off a little way. But then the man came back, and she began again to soothe and caress him.

The cow had not given up the contest, but this time the wild man took up a stick and when she charged in their direction, he rose against her, beating her flank and yelling out in anger. The beast did not leave but trotted off a little way and stood bellowing, the long tones reaching as though toward the growing anguish that must have been new to her. This time when he returned, Hippolyta put her lips against his neck, and a long sigh came out of him like a reluctant moan; she put her lips to his mouth, a mouth that did not know cooked food. She had to overcome her disgust. Then she drew his hand under her blouse and put it on her breast. She could see the sweat break out on his face, which shone against the light that filled his eyes, even as a glancing fear struck the surface. She crooned soft words as though to a child to reassure him, coaxed him to lie back in the grass, where what had grown under her caresses was ready to receive her.

She came down on him and took him expertly in the ways she knew. He ejaculated with a cry, then lay there in the grass, spent with new emotions and a strange delight. He didn't know what had happened to him. He tried to remember, to strike upon some impression that lay back somewhere in a mind that was but the press of hunger and thirst, the motion of running in the grass and the comforting flank of the cow, little that would link to this; his mind grew confused with the effort. Anything he did before, what he knew of the cow and her way of satisfying him was function, and the creature in front of him was more than that and different. And he himself now seemed more full, more vivid to himself.

He found his mind moving back to some dim time when other creatures like this one had been part of what he knew, to when he suckled at a breast and someone other than a cow had tended him. But these were like stuttered syllables that rose and were sucked back again into the currents of his sensations. And he was suddenly caught up sharp as his mind seemed to move away from the warm pool in which he had been floating, to a colder air outside. He had a sensation of floundering, sinking, of forgetting what he'd known—of helplessness.

He pulled away, got up quickly and ran to where the cow still stood. But she merely looked at him, snorted as if she were about to attack him and moved away. This time she went off and did not come back. She'd shunned him and was gone for good; he knew this but didn't fully comprehend. And he gave a great cry. Tears poured out of his eyes and great racking sobs seized him, and he wept until his voice grew hoarse.

Hippolyta left him to his grief until he had wearied himself, then came and took his hand and led him to her knoll. There she kissed his eyes and, sprinkled a soothing herb into the food she gave him: tortillas and beans and pieces of the chicken she had brought. He ate the new food tentatively at first, discovered its flavors and eagerly took it down. Afterwards they bedded down for the night. She kept her arms around him until he fell asleep, so that her warmth would keep from him the reminders of his loss. And when the sun rose she gave him the rest of the food.

He followed her docilely, for he had lost his way to what he'd been and had no sense of where he was being taken. He began to listen to the sounds she made, that called up echoes of something like those he once had heard. But these were different sounds. Then she took him to her horse, showed him how to climb up into the saddle, and together they rode across the ranch land and took the road to town. It would not do to take him to Gil; she had to keep him for a while both for his sake and her own: He was a plant uprooted. He was helpless as a baby—without speech or resources. She owed him both care and sustenance. But also she had a certain curiosity: what could emerge from this lump of rawness?

Astonished, he hardly knew where to look as they followed the road into town. Creatures walking back and forth, coming in and out, their bodies hidden under colors that seemed part of them. Once he'd gone in the direction of lights that played through a copse of trees until he came to a place that thrilled him. He saw horses like the one he now rode, heard the barking of dogs that sent fear chilling down his back. He'd raced away but sometimes came back to where, at a safe distance, he could watch while hiding in the grass. And sometimes the horses had invaded his own precincts as two-legged creatures came to drive the cattle. He had to look sharp then so as not to get caught. Once when the smells of food invaded his nostrils and twisted his gut, he'd sneaked up to where he saw a fire glowing, not far from where the cattle were penned in and moved with a thousand backs and bellowed and raised the dust. He recognized the creatures there that were not like the other animals, but always he'd turned away in fear.

Now he looked around in wonder at things he didn't recognize, holding on as the horse moved beneath him. People looked at them with similar wonder. Some greeted Hippolyta as she rode along, but she gave only a little smile. She took him along through the space where only horses and moving things attached to them passed by, where no plants grew and no rocks stood. He hung on as the horse strained uphill.

There were places like the one he used to sneak up to see. . . They went round to the back of one, next to a covered place, where she got off and so did he, and she set the horse free in a space of grass with sticks up all around closing in the space. He felt hollow, stramge to himself, as though all his life had leaked away. He felt her take his hand, but all the same his knees weakened under him; he'd left the place he knew, far from the cow and the other creatures he had run with, and whose thoughts had been his thoughts. He sank to the ground and put his hands over his eyes. Above him, her voice caressed him, encouraged him.

"Don't be afraid," her voice crooned. "Come now. Come inside, and I will cook good food for you." The sounds moved from one to the other and eased his mind like song. He felt her take his hand again, with a pressure to rise up from where he'd sunk down.

He stood up and followed where she led him. Plants grew here, he could see, and trees, but it was different from all he knew. There were colors like those he'd seen on cactus plants and mixed in with the grass. She showed him these, showed him the fruit forming on her trees, her cherries, peaches, and apples. She told him, as though he could understand, "Not ripe yet. Not yet good to eat." She made a face to show him. She picked a little yellow rose and held it to his nose. "Flower," she said, and touched his lips as if to draw the sound from him. But he could not say it.

Then she took him inside her house. He looked around in wonder at this new space, full with things he did not recognize. She took a large hollow thing and guided him to climb inside it. Then she poured water she had heated over him. She soaped him down, rinsed him off, wrapped him in a towel, sat him down and cut his hair. She held a mirror in front of him and he trembled before it, at the strange creature who stared out him. "Muy guapo," she said, smiling at him as she took it away. She'd bathed him, then fed him and took him into her bed.

Days passed and weeks, the time that was to him no time until he found it was held by certain bounds, when they rose and ate and went to bed. She led him around the objects in her house. Table and bed. Plate and cup. Tortillas and beans. He discovered that the sounds she made belonged to these things. She urged the first awkward syllables from his tongue and lips, got him to hold them in his mind until he could speak them. As his lips and tongue got used to speech and the words left their echoes, he began to remember back to when he'd known words like these. Pictures came to his mind of men sitting around a fire and women cooking food in pots. He remembered a time when he lived near houses but was alone. He rembembered snaring birds and rabbits in traps of twigs. He remembered these, but when they were and how he came to where he'd been were lost to him. Now his naked skin was covered with cloth, and his feet were encased in leather. They chafed at him at first, held him in, and he liked it better when he could take them off and lie in bed with Hippolyta's soft body next to his.

She was changing him. She filled his mind with things he'd never known. How strange the speaking was. Sounds that came back to the same things, but were his own. He began to remember things he'd seen and tried to describe them in the words that lived in his head. The words danced in his mind, filling its corners. And he knew himself to be himself. *Hombre*, she called him now, and it seemed to mean himself, not only when he was in her bed. But it meant other men as well. He was one of them but also himself. This confused him, but he didn't know how to ask about it.

He called her *Flower Woman,* for she grew flowers in her garden, and corn and peppers, chilies and onions and tomatoes. Together they picked them and put them in baskets. The chilies she hung on the outside wall to dry; the rest she took inside, where she cooked fragrant food to feed his hunger. She did all this and made a place for him. It was a magic she wove and everything she did filled him with wonder—the way her hands took the plants and fruits and made them savory; the way her hands kneaded the dough and made it into tortillas or bread. Hunger had always gnawed him, and the meat he'd eaten, taken sometimes from the remains of a kill by a mountain lion or a coyote's kill, had never been good to eat like the food she gave him. Once or twice he lingered over the raw chicken or piece of beef she laid out to be cooked. He remembered the taste of rawness as what had shaped his life. It made its own smell in his nostrils and he felt his gorge constrict.

But the great miracle was bread. She had to keep him from stuffing his mouth with it, for he could never eat enough of bread. It seemed he was reaching back to satisfy a hunger at its source that made him ravenous. Somewhere in his memory was bread.

Little by little, the hunger left him. In its place were the tortillas she gave him, filled with beans and chili sauce, and sometimes meat, the cherries he could eat until their redness filled him, the ripening tomatoes: all these made a different thing of hunger. His body, too, was changed by his sense of things. It belonged to a different creature, and the image he saw in her mirror, he knew now, was different from the animals he ran with. His body was no longer the carcass he flung down on the ground after the exhaustion of the day, finding warmth in a cow's flank.

Flower Woman's bed was softer than any spot he'd ever slept in, and her flesh and his own kept company there, with a warmth that filled them and overflowed. He learned to kiss her lips, what parts of her to touch, to kiss. And she opened to him like a flower. *"Tuo eres mucho hombre,"* she told him, with her rich, deep laugh. And something in him rejoiced when she said that.

At first he spent most of his time making the acquaintance of dogs and cats or talking to the horse and cow at the back of the lot. She taught him to feed the horse in his stall and bring hay for the cow, but she was the one who did the milking. Once when he was alone, he nuzzled the cow, but he made her nervous. He tried to remember what it was like when he ran in the wild, but his old life had been slipping away. At first he sat there with the cow. A strange feeling crept into him as though he'd done something wrong, but he was puzzled to know what it was. Hippolyta found him there. "You're here! Don't you like it in my house?" He was trembling, and she put her arms around him. "You are a man now," she said. "With great power. You are Hombre."

He was able to think now how different it was with Hippolyta. Cow had been warmth and food, for she'd given him her milk and he had slept by her side. They had run together in one thought. And so time had flowed through them, one day like another. But now Flower Woman gave him warmth not only when he was in her bed. Not only did she give him food and drink, but there was her smile, the light in her eyes, her expression, her words, everything that made up her presence. When they came together, he was aware of the part of himself she had awakened and that it belonged to him—that it drew from him a feeling the cow had never inspired. He had no word for this, but he knew it was important.

He began to recognize people from among those who came to Hippolyta for herbs and vegetables, and others he saw in the streets and shops she took him to. They asked him questions, and at first he couldn't answer and stood silent. She taught him things to say. "Hello, how are you?" and "Buenos dias. Como está usted?" He didn't know how he was, but she told him to say, "Very well, thank you. Muy bien, gracias." He noticed the way children played and women stopped to talk to one another in the street and men dressed in suits and Levis and shirts. He liked their hats. She bought one for him, and he liked the way he looked in her mirror.

He learned that some things stood longer than others in what Flower Woman called *tiempo*, that was like water flowing or clouds passing, yet it wasn't these. It was something that put lines in a man's face or a woman's and took away his strength and her smooth skin and bent their backs. It let the baby learn to walk and talk and children get their growth and become like himself. He was afraid time would come for him and strike blows to his face and back, and he wanted to hide under the covers. But Flower Woman laughed and said time was always there. Time was a puzzle to him.

She kept reminding him he was a man and showed him the ways he needed to live like a man. She explained how men married women and kept a house together and raised their children and sent them to a school. Inside of her were eggs like chickens laid, but different too, and together a man and a woman could make a child. She told him about money and how it bought things and how it had to be earned. She showed him all the ways people worked for it and explained how gold and silver came out of the ground. She took him by the church and told him not everything was here on the earth, but some things belonged to another world beyond this one, and that people went to worship the Creator of both worlds. This, too, puzzled him. Time was of this world, but what lay in another world that knew no time was quite beyond him.

So time passed, he didn't know how long, while Hippolyta taught him where words led and how things worked. He helped her in the garden and learned the use of herbs and how to speak to those who came for them. She sent him to the store to buy things she used and handle money. He spoke to people now, and sometimes went to visit their homes and walk the streets. He learned to manage on his own.

One day, when he was alone downtown, a cowboy named Zeke took him into the Pioneer Saloon and bought him a whiskey. "You never had that before? Why, fellow, you haven t lived." At first the whiskey burned his throat as it went down, and he coughed and sputtered. The men laughed at the face he made. "Come on, be a man," Zeke said. Hombre watched him take up his own shot and toss it down. "It takes a little getting used to. But then, boy, oh boy." Hombre did the same with his shot. Once again the whiskey burned his throat and made a fire in his belly. The cowboy winked to the bartender, who poured another for them both. Then the others bought drinks.

The liquor fired his brain, and before he knew it, he was yelling and pounding the top of the bar until the bartender told him to shut up or get out. "Take it easy, amigo," the cowboy said. "A man's got to hold his liquor."

But Hombre felt wild again and full of a sensation that lifted him more forcefully than delight. A fire was running through him. A fight started next to him, and the next thing he knew, the men were striking out with blows, and the stools fell, and there was a shattering of glass. Hombre stood as if bewitched. A burly fellow drinking next to him said, "You in this fight?" Hombre, holding onto the bar, the bottles along the wall blurring before his vision, shook his head no

A fist landed on his jaw. "Well, you're in it now."

Then his own fist shot out and he grabbed up a bottle and threw it, heard it smash. A wave of triumph broke over him. He felt like smashing things, throwing the chairs. He was hit again and struck back blindly. Then someone fired a gun, and he saw a man fall to the floor, the blood flowing from his chest. He wanted to run, but the sight of blood made a shrilling in his ears, and his feet refused to move. He stood paralyzed amid the crash of bottles and the tumult of bodies, as a scream filled his head. Then a blow he hadn't seen coming struck him and everything went dark.

He didn't know where he was when he felt his eyelids pull open.

He lifted his head from the ground where he lay, felt the sharp pebbles he'd been lying on. Dark shapes spun around and he lay back dizzily. It was dark as midnight. A wall rose next to him. He was outside, and it was quiet now. He struggled up and leaned against the wall. When he did, his stomach heaved and turned his insides out. Emptied, he felt strange and divided, as though he'd found something in his nature that belonged to him but that he didn't want to claim. He staggered to the street.

Hippolyta was awake when he finally found his way back to her. She'd been frightened when he didn't return. She washed the cut on his forehead and warned him that whiskey made men violent, drove them to fights and killing.

"The man lying on the floor could be dead now," she said. "It could have been you."

The idea of killing troubled him. Death happened to men as well as creatures. He'd watched the vultures come for the carcasses of dead cattle and deer. He'd eaten fresh kill. He knew the stench of rotting flesh. Once he'd watched a vulture sit on a deer a mountain lion had killed and dip its beak into the dead eye. He'd shuddered and turned away. And he'd been gripped by a fear of something old he'd stumbled on that now would never leave him. But despite her warning he went back and drank again, for the liquor brought to him a quickening he didn't want to forget. It chased away thoughts that troubled him and put him beyond them.

For the sensation of what he'd known before pulled at him, tormented him. It came to him in sudden flashes, when he dug around the plants in Hippolyta's garden and felt his hands in the soil or watched the clouds floating their white masses overhead. He felt it when his blood rose and he lost himself in Hippolyta. And sometimes he wanted desperately to go back and run on the land.

But Hippolyta kept telling him that now he was a man, Hombre; he was civilized and when he came to know all his new life offered, he wouldn't want to go back anymore to what he had been. And she told him that a day would come when he could go to work on the ranch of the man whose land he'd been living on. He would have a different life there taking charge of the cattle and horses instead of living like one of them. This, too, troubled him. Something else would be happening in time, and he would no longer be there with her, eating the food she cooked for him and lying next to her soft body, finding his way inside her and galloping with her toward the wonder he'd discovered. He wanted only to cleave to her, to hold onto what she had given him, and hold her in his arms. Why was it he would have to leave her?

She would say only that time would hold the answer. I can't help wondering if she meant that for herself as well. Considering all that she had invested in him from her having wooed him away from the only life he knew, could she simply let go of him without a backward glance? She had known many men. They had come to her and then moved on, most of them very likely at her bidding. Perhaps that was for the sake of her freedom, which she refused to sacrifice. But Hombre was different—with him she'd had to go deeper and stay longer, and she must have been awakened to new parts of herself as she went along. But perhaps she saw something beyond herself—that Hombe needed to move in the direction of further possibility in order to fulfill all he was capable of, that further adventure awaited him. Perhaps she knew that she had given all she could and needed to gather herself together for the sake of other discoveries for herself. She might feel loss, feel it keenly, but see its necessity—I'll give her that.

Outwardly at least, his new life had taken hold of Hombre. He became fascinated with all the new things he saw and how they worked: the wheels of wagons, the way a buggy rolled along the street; with parasols, how they opened and closed, and what the operation of a sewing machine accomplished. It was hard to believe it turned out the clothes he wore, with their buttons fastening and opening. Or his shoes, how they were made. He spent whole hours in the telegraph office or down by the train station. How was it that messages could travel over wires? He could not believe that these things could exist. They were magic. Hippolyta had her magic, but these were other magics. You entered them through a doorway into a different world.

But other times when he walked the street, he felt like a bull caged up in a pen. He wanted the women he saw, one after another. Wanted them all. But they were not to be touched—these were wives and daughters who belonged to other men. He grew timid under their gaze, trying to display his half-formed manners while his vitals simply clamored for them. Men wanted women in the way he had come to know, and the women needed to be protected, Hippolyta told him. Otherwise men couldn't live together, but would constantly fight and kill each other. That's why men came to her bed, Hippolyta said, because there was something left over that couldn't fit inside the rules. And there would come a time when he would leave her and find a woman of his own. He was left in painful confusion.

"If a woman is in danger, you must protect her."

More than a year had passed since Hippolyta had gone out on the land and brought the wild man back with her. Hombre. Gil she hadn't seen in public since he'd lost all his possessions. No one could come near him, and even Nina Weston feared for his sanity. The blood had drained from her face when she heard the news, and for a time she could not speak. But her son was full of noise.

First he raged against his own folly, then he railed against the universe. One night, unable to sleep, he'd put himself on horseback and went off to a hill not far distant from the ranch. He dismounted and for a time stood looking at the stars. Then he yelled out, "Who made this crazy world? Come out and show your face." In the answering silence, he yelled again. "You took my father." Another silence. "And what was the sense of that? Did it do anybody good? No, you love harm. You love to destroy things. That s what you love. Harm and evil. You let people die in fires and floods. Revel in the earthquake. Wars delight you. Does the cripple make you happy? All the deformed, diseased and ugly things? So much evil to keep you busy. How you must rejoice! And you've let a murderer despoil me and take everything I have. And leave me the dregs while you fatten the hide of the guilty. That's your universe. You want my love? I spit in your face. If this is your work I'll never believe in you. Better the devil—he's more honest."

While his mother mourned, he kept to himself, morose, ready to fly into a rage at the slightest word. Most of the time he refused to speak, but worked indifferently, kept his distance like one exiled. He seldom came to town, and when he did, he stood for a long time in the saloon drinking alone, deep in his own solitary thought. No one came up to him or spoke to him. They didn't dare. There was that air about him that suggested it would be a poor idea. He was beginning to fade from the town's attention, become a nobody. For he had nothing now except a foreman's job on another man's ranch. What was there to take notice of? And where had all his raging got him?

So that on this particular evening when he'd taken down several whiskeys and gone outside to take a breath of air, no one gave him any heed. The saloon was filled with men. He was but one more cowhand come to town. The place was booming, full of noise: miners in town after a week's work, cowboys in the streets who'd come in from the range. They had money burning in their pockets and they were looking for a good time. The downside of the year had begun; the cattle had been rounded up, driven down to where they could be herded onto railroad cars and shipped off to Kansas. Now was the time to get drunk and find a woman or gamble away the loose change.

The noise of the saloon had sent Gil out into the street, the din of raucous laughter in his ears. It called up the blackness inside him. He would have been glad for a fight. He was debating whether to go back and drink himself into a stupor or get on his horse and ride back to the ranch, when he saw Mary Healy. She was getting married. So the news had filtered through to him long enough ago that he'd forgotten. Betrothed to the new druggist, who was bound to give her a good house and an exemplary life. Gil could feature her looking demurely from a daguerreotype, her children clustered at her skirts and her young man, grown portly, beaming over the bounty he'd provided, seed and substance. He had taken his place beside her now, that young man, his round spectacles glinting benignly, his slightly receding hairline loosening his pact with youth, as he strolled out, ready to take on the duties of married life.

When they passed him, deep in conversation, without giving him so much as a glance, Gil, hardly knowing what he was doing, grabbed Mary s arm, and she, taken by surprise, cried out.

"You're not going to do this," he growled, "without a little taste of wild honey." Then he pulled her off down street, stumbling after, dragged along as if she had no weight or power to resist. Her young man ran behind, yelling. "Let her go. Are you a lunatic? Stop him!"

Gil stopped abruptly, turned and swatted the spectacles from his face. As the betrothed groped blindly for his antagonist, Gil struck him down.

Mary Healy tried to jerk away, drawn to her lover's distress and wanting to rescue him, but Gil yanked her away toward the saloon, determined to drag her upstairs. "I'll be the first," he cried. "You can have me as a wedding present."

Mary Healy, grown frantic, couldn't believe what was happening to her. A man she'd all but forgotten, had been most relieved to forget, was threatening her very being. Ready to force her and ruin her. A black hole yawned before her. She tried to yell, but, breathless, the words were lost. With her free hand she dug her nails into his back, kicked at his legs, but he was like a force of nature.

Truly he'd lost his wits now that he'd lost everything else. Dragging her along. To ruin and shame her, to leave her shunned by all. "Help me," she burst out, stumbling blindly. "Save me. From a madman."

Now men came running towards them, trying to waylay and seize him. But somehow Gil rammed his way through them, knocked the breath out of one, slammed another aside. The black cloud that rose inside him filled him with a more than human strength. Making an abrupt turn, he drew his gun. Someone ran to get the sheriff, as a crowd began to gather, yelling for him to release the girl.

At that moment, the wild man, who was coming down the street, saw the struggle, saw the girl being dragged along against her will by the towering figure who had captured her. A woman who cried for help. One to protect. Without another thought, he let out a whoop,

100

knocked the gun from Gil's hand, and gave him a punch in the jaw that sent him reeling.

"Run now, run," Hombre yelled to the girl, who shoved Gil away and took to her heels. Gil staggered a step, shaking away his astonishment. But in the next moment he was ready to take on the one who'd assailed him. And Hombre was ready for him. Here was a battle. Perhaps it had been waiting for him, or he for it. A sweet strength surged up inside him. He ran against Gil with all the force of his wildness. And so they locked in battle, striking and grappling one another back and forth, so evenly matched it was hard to know who would gain the upper hand. Even as he struggled with his antagonist, Gil marveled at the strength that rose up to challenge him. They sweated and groaned until the girl was forgotten altogether and only their bodies and wills mattered. So as they struggled in the street no one, not even the sheriff, interfered. Let them have it out, let them kill each other, for all he cared—it would be an entire benefit to the community. But that apparently was not in the cards, they were so evenly matched. The gun had fallen somewhere at the outset and been kicked aside. Even from the beginning Gil had no interest in using it, except to scare people off. It was his strength he prided himself on.

But the wild man was the more instinctive fighter, and finally he got his opponent down on the ground, where they rolled and fought. Then the wild man had his arms pinned and Gil had him for just a moment. In the next, the wild man knew, he would throw Gil off and they would go at it again. But in that moment they caught each other's eyes, and each saw something that held him and sealed a bond. They both burst into laughter. Gil rolled over and lay on the ground heaving with laughter, and Hombre rose up on his knees, bent over him and roared as well. Then Hombre helped him up, and they stood, their arms around each other, shaking with paroxysms of laughter, while the people gathered on the street muttered their disgust and incredulity. Finally having had enough of the craziness they were witnessing, they dispersed.

The girl and her lover had been reunited, shaken, but with their affections renewed by their experience. They spent the rest of the evening over a glass of sherry, recalling their fears, their relief over their rescue, their hopes for the future. Indeed it was something they would never forget. Spent by their exertions, Gil and the wild man paused, clapped each other on the back and went into the saloon and had a drink. They drank their way into friendship. Past that, into a need that made them inseparable. And that night Gil took Hombre to his ranch.

VII. Dark Eduardo

Dark Eduardo was a knock-about. His origins, his wanderings were both uncertain, for by his own account he never stayed long enough to take the imprint of any place he set his foot on. Perhaps that was why he left behind his legend everywhere. His whirlwind visits took up all settled objects, tossed them in the air like chaff, juggled them like plates and chairs, let them fall where they would into the shadow of his departure. In his flight through space and time, he'd momentarily lighted on the here-and-now. Where he'd been and what he'd done—that was to chew on, pick apart during the evenings in the bunkhouse or else the saloon. A little entertainment. Sometimes he told one tale, sometimes another, caring no more than a buffalo chip for gaps of time, clashes of fact, and other mysteries. If anybody tried to call his bluff on what he swore was truth, he stroked his mustache and said, "Well, if my memory has led me astray..."

He'd squinch up the side of his mouth, knit the brow that traveled from above one eye across his nose to the other in an unbroken line, make his face into a caricature, and come up with such an elaborate explanation the scoffer was struck dumb trying to piece together the new logic of things. Meanwhile his face grew mild and innocent. He could do anything with that face; he could be anybody. Then after his spiraling invention had violated all previous logic, he'd give a laugh, as though nothing was more surprising than the truth, and dive headlong into another unaccountable tale.

I have mightily the impression he'd gone about picking up bits of incident and anecdote, pieces of everybody else's stories, and let them mingle with his own till he himself couldn't distinguish what he'd lived from what he invented. One life was too undersized to fit his sprawling nature. He lived inside the world of chance, the outside chance. The only thing certain was that when he was through swearing in Spanish or English, he went on with equal gusto in Indian or Irish, and once in a while threw in a little German for good measure. Somehow he convinced the men he must indeed be all the things he claimed: had been a scout chasing the Apaches in one of General Crook's forays, had made and lost three fortunes mining and prospecting and gambling, had worked on ranches and was an experienced cattle driver. And though he came simply with the name Eduardo, because everything else about him was obscure, and even his mother could have been a Spanish beauty of noble family, a Mayan princess, or a Russian countess, and no telling about his father, he was known almost immediately as Dark Eduardo. He found the epithet flattering to his own shifting image of himself and very amusing. From then on, he would go by nothing else.

He'd turned up at the ranch one day wanting work. He was willing to do anything, to take up any piece of life, it seemed, and try it on for size. He was an experienced cowpuncher, so he claimed. He was a dead hit with a lasso, a dead shot with a revolver. They asked for proof—any man could brag that way. The demonstrations of his skill took their breath away. He could put a bullet into a silver dollar he tossed into the air. He'd done branding and could mend a fence. He could even cook; biscuits and chicken-gravy was his specialty. He wanted a place to hole up for the winter. He'd help out with the spring round-up and the branding.

Gil had no need of extra hands. Hombre could do the work of two men, and during the winter, unless they had bad weather, there was not all that much work to do, though it was true they'd be hard pressed come spring. But Dark Eduardo looked Gil in the eye and said, "I hear you've had bad luck. Lost things no man can bear to lose." He nodded sagely. "I know about getting caught with all your paws in the trap, not to mention your tail." He rubbed the side of his nose, added a wink of complicity. "I know also the moment that's ripe for plucking the jewel out of Fortune's crown and forty ways to do it. I know the old bitch like my mother."

That did it. Something spoke from eye or voice that went beyond what anyone can see or hear: it happens. A shudder went through Gil as though fate had twitched him on the shoulder. He hired Eduardo on the spot. To be let into the secrets of the man's knowledge, to have revealed the right moment for action and the way out of his predicament—who could resist? A farfetched undertaking. Let him take the chance. He had nothing more to lose, or so it seemed. Dark Eduardo s eye was everywhere, even when he didn't appear to be looking. But which eye? One was green, the other brown. Did one see what the other missed? And which offered the clearer vision? Whatever work was to be done he did cheerfully, without complaint, and won the men to him, though his manner suggested he was superior to any piece of common labor that fell to his hand. The men liked his jokes and bantering. What he'd been doing before he came, what had brought him to these parts, he didn't say. He was polite, even unassuming. But he was a man who filled a doorway and took possession of a room full of eyes, from the sheer force of his presence: a wave of black hair combed back from a face made bold by its cheekbones and jaw, accented by a black moustache. He was himself.

His pride had no sharp edges; at ease, he could look into men and situations. Sometimes the green eye gleamed sharp as a spike, and sometimes it was a green pool. But the dark eye was unfathomable, giving him at times a sinister look, a look both dangerous and compelling. Whatever he took in, he mulled over like a lizard sitting in the sun with half-lidded eyes. He was never in a hurry. Nights he pulled out his pack of cards, the dice he carried, and said to the men, "How about a little game of chance? Just to keep me in practice." And then a gleam came into his green eye, as he won hand after hand, roll upon roll. But when a man began to look glum and grumble about his luck, suddenly everything shifted. The stash in front of Dark Eduardo would begin to dwindle, and by the evening's end, he was back where he started from, still full of exuberance. "Ah, gentlemen, I should always quit after the first half. That s where all my luck lies." And he'd give a deep, full-throated laugh. "You see how it is—luck can turn on you like a woman." He'd laugh again: the joke was on him.

But Gil kept the impression most of his tricks still lay in the bag—that he could have kept on winning had that been his desire. "I'm a man for a game," he said to Gil. "A man should be on top of all his chances, so he can get his best shot."

And Gil started watching him, looked over his shoulder at his hands, studied his expressions. Watched the way he danced with his luck, letting himself be led at times, drawing his inspiration from a run of cards, but growing cautious when the cards didn't go his way. Much of the time they did, and he made the most of his chances, taking risks, even to the point of daring, pulling it off. All with marvelous aplomb. Nothing rattled him. He knew the odds. He had a kind of high-hearted confidence, but he wasn't reckless, wasn't carried away by arrogance or desperation. Gil put aside all thought of himself, became his apprentice by putting himself inside him. Tried to imitate his state of mind. For that s what it was, he decided. And if you put yourself there and gave it your concentration, then perhaps the outward configurations might take their shape from that. Was it true? He was intrigued, ready to make the experiment. Little by little, he began to climb out of his funk, not let his losses plague him. He left off replaying the scene in his mind when he'd thrown everything away in the desperation of the gamble. He tried not to think of Cameron Jack, as people spoke of him now, though not in his hearing.

As they played one game and another, Dark Eduardo paused now and then and said, "Let me show you something," and watched Gil closely and gave him a little nod, the corner of a smile, as if he'd somehow learned the necessary trick, the stroke of judgment, and was finally getting it right. Gil began to see, clearly enough, how Cameron Jack had hooked him away from his concentration, played on his emotions, when he should have watched himself like a spectator, fixed single-mindedly on the game and where his luck was taking him—the outer edge of his chances. He'd been led by the nose, like a donkey. A simpleton—that's what he'd been. He groaned to think of it. But he knew he couldn't afford the replaying of his rage or the desire for revenge. Only calm and calculation. He had to make a little island of himself in the midst of any disturbance around him.

Meanwhile Dark Eduardo spun his tales. He'd gambled on riverboats and tried his luck in San Francisco, in all the gambling salons where he could smell out a game of chance or skill. He played pinochle and black jack and poker and dice, liked euchre for a change and had played whist with socialites and politicians.

"Why I remember this one time, a lady entered the room, all in silks and finery and made her way to the gaming tables. And they all made way for her. she was the Madam there, and she had money, believe me. She rolled those dice like she'd done it all her life. She took a fancy to me right off."

"Yeah, we believe it," the men said. "You've had more women than Solomon had wives."

His favorite game was billiards, for it took the sharpest eye, the steadiest hand, the utmost calculation: the greatest challenge to a man. Now there were moments as Gil lay awake at night when he felt something changing inside him, as though he was being brought up from his defeat. And Hombre, too, was taking him in another direction he could not yet define. Dark Eduardo played about him like a volatile element, not to be pinned down. But Hombre was of the earth, firmly planted there. Hombre spoke to his blood, brought into his mind new images or old images made new that opened him toward seeing the world with fresh eyes. These influences pulsed within him.

He and Hombre were everywhere together. They went out hunting on the land. He taught Hombre how to shoot and drop the wild turkeys. They brought back a deer and had Martina cook the venison. She dried some of the meat for jerky. They explored the hills, galloped their horses in the open country. Now the same thoughts seemed to run in their heads, as their intimacy grew deeper. Friends they were, but more—brothers. The idea of friendship was new to him, a discovery. Before sleep, Gil lay awake thinking what it meant, where it took him. It made of him something he'd never been before, brought him to new emotions.

Those he'd caroused with had never been his friends. He'd kept close to himself, for he seemed to walk outside some boundary of custom and correct behavior that gave the town its notion of virtue— even though it could take in roughnecks, who could shoot a man in an instant of violence, and Cameron Jack, who'd made his murderous tyranny respectable. But Hombre took him beyond all that. And though he could never imagine living as Hombre had, still his blood warmed with unspoken knowledge. Their experience belonged to no one else. If Dark Eduardo was his fate, Hombre was his good fortune.

His luck would change; he knew it in his bones. Dark Eduardo spoke of the right moment, and now he was waiting for it to arrive. If only he could recognize it when it appeared, not let it pass him by. He was learning patience, the patience that had always been beyond his reach, and a trust now in his instincts. There were things he did not attempt to understand.

All that winter, Dark Eduardo appeared to be carrying on another life he never spoke of and did not explain. At times he was gone for a few days, even as long as a week, on certain matters of business, but he would be back, he told Gil. And he always turned up when he said he would. On one of these occasions when Dark Eduardo returned, he'd shaved off his mustache, and clean-shaven, looked to be a far younger man. With him, he had a friend whose arm was in a sling. Fell off his horse when the animal spooked, and broke his arm, Dark Eduardo told him. When he healed up, he rode off again. Gil never asked any questions, and if his surmises ever made a connection between a poster that appeared in the Post Office offering a reward for the apprehension of the outlaws that had robbed several trains in the northern part of the state, he never said so. Just before his departure for Mexico, when Dark Eduardo revealed his identity, Gil told him he'd known for a long time. But by then all that followed had been set in motion.

There was a day that could be called the beginning: Dark Eduardo said to Gil,

"Your dog would come back if she were off her chain. If she

could just get a smell of you... You saved her life. She'll remember that always, if she's given a chance."

"How would I bring it off? Sneak up at night and cut her collar! The other dogs would tear me to pieces."

"Throw them meat to keep them quiet. Take Hombre with you. He can see in the dark and find his way like an Indian. And let the horses loose if there's time. Sometime start up the rumor there are Apaches roaming around—sneaked off the reservation. They can take the blame. You might find your own, get him back".

It was getting on towards the full moon, and during those nights when a soft blaze left the imprint of the mountains against the sky, the two of them, Gil and Hombre, rode their horses out and made their way through the woods that led to Cameron's lodge. They tethered them by the river, came partway up a trail that led up close to the lodge, but not so close as to set the dogs into an uproar. Then they returned and camped by the river among the salt cedars and cottonwoods that grew along the banks. One was a huge tree, bigger than any tree Hombre had ever seen. He couldn't see around the trunk and its main branches, thick as the trunks of smaller trees, were like a ladder into the sky, awash with moonlight. He lay in his blanket, looking up into the branches, letting his eye wander upward to where the smaller branches and twigs filled out a great framework, a net that snared the moon. But not for long, for the moon was a wanderer, and though she visited the tree on her journey across the sky, she moved higher, freed herself to hide among the clouds and appear again. He fell asleep under the silvered branches. In the middle of the night his own cry awoke him.

"What? What's the matter?" Gil demanded, startled awake. For a moment Hombre could say nothing, fear so clutched at him. When had he been so much afraid? He'd been attacked, but though he searched the darkness that surrounded him, he could not find what threatened.

"What is it?" Gil said, also searching the night.

"The cow ran at me, to trample me to death," Hombre said. "Her eyes were full of fire and her horns were like tree branches."

"You were dreaming," Gil said.

He had dreamt before. Dreams ran through his head on their way to somewhere else. He had always had the sense of things moving through his sleep. But this dream wrung his heart. The cow had come running at him, and he rose up, seized her and tore her apart. Never had he felt such madness in his blood, not even when the whiskey had seized him up and sent him hurtling. And then from his rage, triumph. He'd whirled her great haunch, then thrown it to the top of the tree with a mighty shout. *This is what I think of you, filthy animal.* And still he trembled with fear, though he could no longer say why.

"It's all right," Gil assured him. "Everybody has dreams, sometimes nightmares. Don't be afraid—they can't follow you."

All around was a stillness. Hombre did not know what to do with the terror he felt. It gnawed at him for days afterward and wouldn't be dispelled. And though he could find his way through the woods with ease, he couldn't push away the sense that something boded ill. Three nights they spent tracking in the woods until they knew their way perfectly, had decided where to tether the horses and left marks they would recognize to ease their escape. They'd staked out a little trail that led through a canyon, probably used by the Indians, one not likely to be discovered. They would wait for the dark of the moon to make their theft, then hide until the following night.

It took all of Gil s persuasion to get Hombre to go through with the raid, but when the time came, Hombre seemed to have gotten back his nerve. Though the night was black, Hombre could see in the dark as well as any night animal, make his way through silent woods along the river without a sound. Gil followed behind him, somewhat disoriented now that the moon was no longer there to show him the way. When they approached the lodge, Hombre went first, stood still as the dogs bounded out, barking, but as they came running to surround him, he threw them meat. He drew back listening, as one of Cameron's men came out, studied the night for a moment, then yelled at the dogs. Sometimes the appearance of a skunk or a coyote set them to barking. The dogs quieted down, and

Hombre led them around the wall and into the woods, throwing the meat, leading them away. Meanwhile Gil made his way in the dark, heard a muffled barking near the stables, and found his way to the pen where his dog was chained. Quickly he was over the fence, recognized, jumped on eagerly. She licked and nuzzled him as he cut the collar, opened the gate and led her out. Then he went on to the stables, moved inside until he found his own horse, and throwing loose ropes around their necks, managed to lead out three of the others, mounted his own and took off into the woods.

A shout went up and torches were lit. Men came running; shots rang out. But Gil had already slipped into the woods, his dog running after him in the direction of the spot where his and Hombre's own horses were tethered. Cameron's men were shooting and shouting in the dark, trying to scare off whoever had raided them. "Apaches," someone yelled, for at times they left the reservation to raid the settlers. Some of the dogs came racing back home, and there was a brief confusion of horses and dogs. But there was no point in chasing the marauders by night. For a time, Gil and Hombre dodged about among the trees as they made their way back to their horses near the river. But when they reached the spot, the dog had somehow disappeared. She'd been right behind him most of the way, and though Gil whistled for her, she didn't come. "What could have happened to her? he kept asking. She had been right there. "But she's free now," Hombre said. "She has your scent and she'll find you. Don't worry." Gil paused uncertainly.

"We'd better get out of here," Hombre said. "Come the dawn and they'll look for our tracks." Gil was reluctant to leave without his dog, to be only half successful. It seemed a bad sign. But he had to give her over, and the two of them took a long circle to where the trail cut off to their hiding place. Gil had stolen back his horse and freed his dog, and except for Hombre and Dark Eduardo, no one knew about it. He didn't want anybody to know. There was a cave at the end of a canyon, and he took the horse there, left Hombre to take care of him and went back to the ranch. He rode out later that day with food and supplies, an ax for chopping wood.

A few days later, Dark Eduardo said, "Maybe you're ready now."

"To do what?" The little raid had bolstered him, had allowed him to walk around with a small triumph: He'd hit Jack at a vulnerable spot. And did Jack guess that he had come for his horse and dog? He'd have been better pleased if he'd gotten back with the dog, ready then to move on to the main thing. After all, Cameron still had the ranch. Now was the time to win it back. Indeed he was ready. He was itching to take up the challenge of a game, but a man like Cameron would be a fool to take him on when he had nothing to gain by it. How would he manage to lure him into taking up the challenge? Cameron knew better. Gil shook his head.

"Come on," Dark Eduardo goaded him. "Don't think along the bend of a dog's hind leg. Nobody holds all the luck all the time. You've put a little crimp in Cameron's luck, made a bad omen for him. Only a little cloud maybe, but now there is a dark spot in his thoughts. Now's the time to let that darkness spread. It's all in the game."

"Suppose he doesn't go for it?"

"Not man enough? How would that make him look? And maybe, just maybe, he's still sweet on your mother. You could..."

"Make her a pawn! You think I'd do that?"

"Wait a minute," Dark Eduardo said. "We're looking for stratagems, *es verdad*? We're dangling the bait. A man like that can hear the *maybe*." To win back the ranch was in Gil's power, or so Dark Eduardo assured him. The right moment, and maybe his last chance, had arrived. And it was true, the whole configuration of things was different. He was different. Now that he was out of the hole he'd been in, he felt toughened for the fight. Gambling was in his blood, and theft by night.

He rode into town one evening to see if he could goad Cameron Jack into a bet, but that night and the next, Jack wasn't there. The third night he appeared. Gil was standing at the bar, and Jack, seeing him, ambled over. "You've been keeping yourself pretty scarce these days." To the bartender he said, "Bring this man a drink." Gil waved it away. It was one more than he could afford. Only one to give him nerve. "Nose to the grindstone," Gil said. "But things are letting up a bit. All in good order."

"I suppose you've heard about the trouble at my place," Jack said. "I reckon it would be the Indians out scavenging. They came up the way Indians know about. Made off with horses, like you might expect. I've put the warning out just in case. And I've had my men up and down scouting the territory."

"Never can tell about those Indians," Gil said. "They're not happy on the reservations. I imagine they've got to Mexico by now."

"Wouldn't surprise me," Jack said grimly. "But your horse and dog, they got stolen with the rest." Maybe he was glad to tell him so. "They were two fine animals. I haven't found their equals—not by a long ways. Not to mention the ranch. You're a sorry lot all right," Jack said, clapping him on the shoulder. Maybe he needed to rub it in. "Had everything just lying in your lap and let it go to the bottom."

Though his scalp prickled, Gil took it in. That much he'd learned—to let some part of himself stand aside and not get riled.

"Well, then," Gil said, "seems like a man ought to have a chance to win some of what he lost."

Jack laughed. "Well, I've got it now, and I'm not about to let it go. You can't bank all that much on your gambling skill after what happened. You'd just land in a bigger fix—if that's possible. "

"I bank on it anyway."

"But you got nothing worth losing." He laughed again. "Only everything to gain. A man would be a fool..."

"But who knows but that there's something more,'" Gil insinuated. "There are those whose friendship —"

Jack scoffed. "I don't t need any of that foolishness. There's nothing I need any more. And if I did, I've got ways to get it."

"I thought you were big enough to take the risk," Gil said.

"Trying to goad me, are you? I see what you re about and you'll see you can't do it. I got what I wanted and I've got you exactly where I want you." With that he downed his drink and turned away towards the back room to play his round of poker.

"Your luck's turned inside out," Gil said. "You're afraid to play me this round because you'll lose. One way or another."

Jack turned to look at him. "Is that a threat?"

"Sometimes it's the real thing."

Jack rubbed his finger over his mustache. He said. "You've got to get your nose rubbed in it, wouldn't you know. I'm on to your kind. You've got to go down on your knees, wallow in your own shit. Okay, I'll let you do it. This time it'll be your skin. A thrashing or a pistol whipping. You want to gamble on that? You'll have something to lose all right—your hide. "

"I'll take you on," Gil said.

Jack looked at him with contempt. "What's your game? Poker? Your funeral." There was already a game going on in the back room. Nat Phillips was there, who owned the hotel—a poker hound who played nearly every night. And mostly won. And Clyde Nichols, who kept the stables, as well as Bearsoup Wiggins and Frank Worth, a couple of the ranchers from close by. The two sat down and joined the game. For a time the stakes were small, the hands middling, and the winnings no one man's. Then Jack took a big hand with a straight he'd drawn to, an inside straight at that.

"Looks like I m set up for the evening," Jack said, raking in the chips.

"Sometimes luck lasts only the first half," Gil said.

"And sometimes it lasts all night. I've been pretty lucky in my life."

"The next time the Indians might kill you," Gil said. "Think of that." He sat calmly. He'd given up recklessness and wouldn't be pushed into desperation either. Jack won the next hand as well.

"Maybe my luck's going to run to the second half after all." The next two hands went to Phillips, then Nichols. Gil had to fold. Then Gil was dealt two pairs, aces and eights, the Dead Man s hand. "I'll take one," he said. Two of the others folded. Jack took none. Phillips took one and threw in a blue chip. Jack threw in two. Gil, three. Jack raised him, and Gil raised and called. "Everything s on it," Gil said. "I'm going to take it all back."

"You've got a lot of confidence with a couple of pairs," Jack insisted, laying out a full house, kings and tens. But Gil's hand was three aces and a pair of eights. "You see,' Gil said, "you haven't cornered all the luck."

"It was a cheat," Jack said, leaping up, sweeping the cards from the table.

"Check the cards, search me," Gil said. "I've won fair." He took off his shirt, turned his pockets inside out. And to his surprise, the men did not turn against him. "Looks like he did it," Clyde Nichols said.

Jack stood there, perhaps in that quick second wondering if he should draw his gun, but thinking better of it. "It was a goddam lucky draw," he said, with grudging admiration.

"I'll be around to pick up the deed," Gil said, "unless you re a man who goes back on his word."

The two men stood caught in each other's glare. But then Jack let it go and said, "You won, you got back what was yours. But you haven't got the last word yet. You never know about a dead man's hand."

Gil rode to the ranch at a gallop. When he strode into the bunkhouse, the men, too, had their own game going. "You won," said Dark Eduardo looking up at him. "I can see it in your walk, in your face."

"The ranch is mine now," Gil said quietly. "But then, something told me how it would come out." He stood there, giddy, suddenly weak in the knees, as the men congratulated him. "That must have been some game."

After their game broke up and they'd drunk some beers, Dark Eduardo asked him for a word alone. "Well, you've done it," Dark Eduardo said as they walked towards the corral. He lit up a small cigar, took a slow puff and let out the smoke as if a smoke was what he most relished at that moment. Then he said to Gil in a soft voice, as though delivering a compliment to a lady, "Now you must go and kill him." Gil stared at him. "Don't you see, amigo," Dark Eduardo persisted, "You've reached into the darkest gamble. He's not going to hand over that deed unless there's a gun pointing in his face. You must understand he won't let you get away with that. He can't let himself be beaten by the likes of you. If you don't kill him, he'll have you killed instead. And Gil knew why his knees had gone suddenly weak after it was all over: he was a dead man unless he was the one to kill.

VIII.   The Gamble

Now that he'd won and could see clearly what the stakes had been, he recognized that part of himself that had fallen to the depths. He saw how low he had sunk in his own regard, how he'd even pushed aside his shame, dragging himself along the ground of his existence, face in the dirt. Yet all the while shame had stunk in his nostrils. He wondered why he hadn't killed himself. He'd avoided his mother these past months, retreating from even the sound of her voice in the hallway or the kitchen. He hid himself, ate alone, scarcely spoke. The thought of looking into her face unmanned him, the worse for him that she never turned upon him in accusation. Even now it took all his courage to face her. Exhausted from the hazards of the night before, he'd thrown himself into sleep as though to the bottom of the well Jack had once threatened him with, and lay like one drugged till well past noon. He rose slowly, blinking himself back into the reality of his changed condition. But he did not go to her until that part of the afternoon she gave herself quietly to sitting alone and reading. It was a small room she closeted herself within, where the windows looked out over the land, from which she could watch the sunset if she chose.

Nina Weston had been deeply marked by all that had passed. Not just the loss of the ranch and all she'd hoped for, but she'd been stricken by what had happened to her son. A light had gone out. Sometimes she didn't see him for days while he kept himself and his torment from her. To spend her time reading, tending her flowers, giving instructions for the day to Martina in the kitchen was all that was left to her. She knew little about the newcomers who had arrived, though she had seen her son in their company. If she came upon Dark Eduardo, he tipped his hat and addressed her as if she were the governor's wife. Hombre, on the other hand, grew shy in her presence. If there were new influences operating on her son, she did not try to gauge them. She was glad for his diversions, to take his mind off the state of things. Hombre impressed her with a kind of innocence; Dark Eduardo struck her as a man who knew too much.

When Gil appeared the afternoon following his adventure, she was struck by a new expression in his face, not exactly triumph, though there was a strain of it. Rather, a profound relief, as though a great weight had been lifted from him. "There's been a change," he said, after he'd given her a hug and felt her anguish over him. "You can't change what's been done—I know that now. This ranch..."

"Don't speak of it," she said. "What's done is done."

"This ranch I lost through sheer recklessness. And became a worse man than the man who won it."

"Please no more." She held up her hand in front of her. It was his pain as much as her own that she couldn't bear.

"Only now I've won it back."

She gave a little startled cry—it was almost beyond belief. She listened to him tell what had happened, how a lucky draw had put things back into his hands. For a long moment, she looked at him, suddenly seized with dread. "I fear for you," she said, rising up. "He will not take this lightly. He knows no bounds—you know that, don't you? He'll lie in wait for you, try to catch you unawares. There will always be a price on your head."

"It was worse before," he said. "A craven life. I couldn't live that way".

She embraced him. "I always saw something in you—a great spirit," she began.

"Don't speak of it," he said, afraid to give a name to the impulse that lived in him, good or evil, he could not say, the forces warring in his nature. But she was not a woman for shallow sentiment. She knew her son. "You've been marked," she said, "by all that's happened to you. Whether curse or blessing I know no better than you. But now..." She paused, for she could see all too clearly the difficulties that faced him, as circumstance met his temperament in a world where to survive is warfare. And to find a place was all but impossible for difficult natures. "Leave him alone," she counseled, at the same time knowing she was asking the impossible. "Even if he doesn't give up the deed, the ranch is yours. We can stay here," she said, desperately now, contradicting everything she'd said before, what she most deeply knew, "and live our lives."

"You're deluding yourself. You know that as well as I. Everybody knows what happened—do you count that a refuge? Shout it to the world. You think Jack gives a damn. A little temporary setback, that's all. He'll wait till things quiet down a bit, then some night a bunch of men will ride up, set this place on fire and shoot us down."

She could see it happening. "We could go away from here," she said, even as she knew he'd never consent. He did not respond. "What will you do?"

"I don't know yet," he temporized. He'd have to force Jack's hand. Try to get him to yield up the deed to the ranch, at least to get a fact nailed down. Then if he wouldn't deliver... He'd cross that bridge when he came to it. When he left his mother, he walked outside into the waning day, the sun illuminating a high bank of cumulus cloud before it sent down a fan of closing rays. The mountains were hung with blue shadow, except where the light fell, and the land was settling into the quiet that comes before darkness gathers everything into itself. The darkness of snakes and owls and coyotes, as well as the darkness of men who need to cover theirs tracks.

But the sun would rise again, revealing what had been concealed: the twisted desires of men, their blood lust and demented dreams. In spite of himself, Gil believed in the light, something existing beyond the heaviness of earth, the dawning of an order all things reached towards however imperfectly. He wanted to call this justice, this exercise of sunlight. And he would be its instrument. He was canny enough now, on his guard, open to the right moment for action.

But suppose Cameron Jack thought him witless enough to make a grudging peace: turned over the deed, momentarily taking the wind from his sails then lying in wait to do him in. The smarter choice. Or maybe he'd line up his gunmen and come after him. The question was left hanging, for after the game, Jack left town. Gave it out that he had business that took him to the East. He was gone for weeks.

Meanwhile Gil chafed at the bit. Jack had him where he wanted him; he could amble along, without hurry. Tease him as much as he liked. Gil sent him a message that he was expecting him to make good what he'd lost; now he claimed the deed even as he'd given it up before. Such were the terms he put it in. If Jack was waiting for a threat so that he could justify some kind of retaliation, Gil knew better than to give him cause. "Getting impatient, are you?" Jack wrote. "All in good time. I haven't left the territory." Then he sent word he'd meet Gil in the lawyer's office one afternoon later that week. But Jack didn't show."

"He sent me a message this morning," Ames, the lawyer, told him. "Said he was sick as a dog."

"I don't believe a word of it," Gil said. "Now we"ll go and kill him," Gil said to Hombre that night. "He's not going to deliver," he said, inwardly rejoicing. "Now it's our turn. We're going to get Cameron," he told him. "It's what we've been waiting for."

"I've never killed a man," Hombre said, remembering death, how it stank in his nostrils.

"I think it must be an evil thing." Evil he wasn't sure of, nor good either. He knew only what he embraced as life. But death had left the odor of rotting carcass that reached a sense beyond his nose.

"I've got to fight him, Gil said. "Otherwise the evil feeds on itself. That has always been true. We're men, we're human beings. God won't do what's to be done—He's above all that. He allows the wrong. Only men are left are to fight it. Even against God Himself, he thought as he refused to believe in Him. Whatever god is. Maybe it was what men were needed for—to fill in for god's absence. Jack would trample every one until someone rose up and put him down. That was for a man like him to do. The task he'd hungered for all his life. For a man like himself, it might be the last opportunity to come his way. He could see a new world coming into being that would sweep away a place for men like him, where everything would be taken out of their hands.

It must have flowed through his mind before, the desire for some memorable action to mark his time here. A chance to live past forgetfulness among all the forgotten.

To recall even one man's circumstances is challenge enough to tax the imagination, as I have come to know, as I set about the doing of it, trying to call certain ones back from among the lost, so that I can remember something of myself. Some things sink into forgetfullness—like ancient animals, their bones turning to fossils, and all their experience buried with their dust. Till someone digs them up in the excitement of discovery. So I have gone swimming along the surface of the tide flowing to the present, diving under, losing myself in what lies below, coming back up, puffing and blowing. All that tangle of what I bring back from among the bones and muck. Trying to reclaim exactly what? As if there were words for all that lies pulsing below the surface, creating what we live, words to fit our longings.

And so I return to that moment when Gil put on the yoke of what would become the burden of his life. While there was still a place for a man to accomplish something signal and all his own, or so he thought. He wanted to claim the action that would define his fate. He was the one to take it on, enter the doorway at which he stood, face what beckoned from beyond—the only way to be human, he insisted, as Hombre's face held out his denial.

"Look what's going on," Gil countered. "Life poisoned at the source. He chokes it out all for himself. And we're supposed to stand by, just let it happen?" The idea had hardened into dogma. The same words kept going round and round.

Hombre stared at him for a long moment, trying to work his mouth into an answer. It was beyond him. Then slowly his expression became suffused with warmth. "We're friends," he said. "Anything you want to do, I do with you, whatever happens."

Gratitude and amazement struck Gil with sudden weakness, as though a light dazzled his eyes . Something almost too lonely for him became a connection between the two of them. They clasped hands and were joined as deep as life. And he thought how it would be when they'd gone past this adventure, the way it would seal their lives together, their experience, the magnitude of what they'd accomplished together.

Before they set about their strategy, they had a visit from the sheriff with a writ of arrest. Dark Eduardo was wanted for train robberies in three states. He'd been identified beyond a doubt by Pinkerton's detectives, who'd seen to it that a poster with his picture was plastered on the walls of city halls, banks, and post offices throughout the territory. So much Gil had already surmised. "Sorry I can't help you out, Sheriff," Gil said. Much to his relief, the man himself was gone. Even at the time, Gil's instincts told him he would never see Dark Eduardo again. "Any man can help his luck along," he'd told Gil as he prepared to depart, the day after the poker game. "But you have to approach with a little disguise. Jack thought you were one kind of man, now he sees you are another. You are in the open. You must take him by surprise." Dark Eduardo turned to leave, then turned back.

"You've always treated me fair and square," he said. "Do you know who I am?"

"I knew after the last train robbery," Gil said.

"I figured," he said, as though glad of the discovery. Then he said, "They're going to be on my tail now. But I want to see you win out. If they corner you, if you need some men, leave a message for me with Jose Benevidez. Lives over by Magdalena. You see," he said, "I still want to be your luck." Then he mounted his pinto and rode off. Whenever Gil bent his thought to what lay ahead, Dark Eduardo stood at his shoulder, as though he hadn't left at all.

Instead of pursuing the renegade with a few questions, the sheriff shifted ground. "I hear," he said, "that you and Cameron have had a little difference of opinion. If I were you, I wouldn't push matters any farther. He's a man with a nasty temper."

It occurred to Gil that Dark Eduardo was simply a pretext for his coming. "A legal debt," Gil said, "a matter of who owns this ranch."

"If I were you," the sheriff offered, "it might be better if you tried your fortunes elsewhere." He had lowered his gaze so that it didn't meet Gil's directly, for he'd always done Jack's bidding, and was suspected of, if not doing his own share of the killing, at least covering up those who did. Always something feeble in his expression. Sam Colby. He got mean drunk sometimes and had been seen on more than one occasion staggering along the street. Folks kept out of his way. No reason to add to their troubles.

"He send you here, Sam? Afraid to come on his own?"

"I'd advise you not to get on your high horse," Colby said testily. "You don't know who you re dealing with. Or else you're a fool. He runs this town. Anybody sensible knows that. No one's crossed him yet but didn't end up in a bad way. He's giving you a chance to clear out before he's decided you've lived too long. He doesn't have to take anything off you. He could have the whole territory up in arms if he gave the word. Only he doesn't have to."

Gil didn't smart off. He caught himself before he gave himself away. "I'm glad for your advice, Sheriff," he said, as though he meant it. He was indeed glad to have put in front of him what he knew he was up against. He and Hombre couldn't repeat what they'd done before, bearding the lion in his den. Jack would have his men around him, armed to the teeth. And if Gil became a nuisance, they'd come after him. Disguise, he remembered. "I'll tell you straight, Sheriff," he said. "I'm downright disgusted with things, so help me. There's no profit in the ranch anymore. And the truth is, I want to get out of here and try my luck where there's real opportunity."

"I knew you had some brains," the sheriff said. "You've been to the East." He seemed relieved. "1 wish you luck, son. I can tell you, I envy you. Going off, making a fresh start. I'm too far along myself, but I tell you, you've got the goods to do something yet." Gil watched him go. *Go back and spread the word, my friend.*

The following day he bought a railroad ticket for his mother to go back East to visit her brother and his family. He was trying to buy time. He gave it out that he was going north right after the roundup. And that spring after the cattle and the calves had been rounded up, they sold them off without a hitch. He'd already sent

Jose Benevidez a message that he needed help. Before that, he'd gone round on the sly to a few men he knew who hated Cameron, from families that he'd harmed. Among the men who worked for him, he chose three he could count on when the time came. He wanted to keep the number small. As it was, the task had spread beyond him, and become complicated. Not what he wanted. He'd have liked to settle things on his own, just with Hombre at his side. Dark Eduardo would come to him with half a dozen men, maybe more. They arranged to meet at the place where the unknown trail wound through the mountains. This time they'd go after Jack just at dawn. Meanwhile all that spring they lived in the tension of whether Jack would send his men to converge on the ranch or send a picked man to lie in ambush and shoot Gil down without an argument. Jack had the advantage certainly. Now that the sheriff had done his official duty, Jack could sit back chortling as he kept them guessing. Maybe he'd come after Gil, maybe he wouldn't right then. Now that the cattle had been sold off. the question was whether Gil would leave. Jack was too smart to think Gil was a coward. And though he might keep himself aloof, Jack had his spies out to let him know what was going on. Gil suspected that even if he were actually doing what he was trying to create the semblance of—his leaving—Jack wouldn't necessarily be content. Two days before they would gather and take Jack on, the sheriff came to Gil once again. He stood in the doorway and hemmed and hawed before he mentioned what he'd come for. Gil took him into the kitchen and offered him a cup of coffee.

"I've put out my nose," the sheriff said, "And it's come to me there's something in the wind."

"You got it wrong, Sheriff. I'm fixing to leave these parts and not give a look behind." He'd been outfoxed, he decided, but he'd have to face it out anyway. Jack would be lying in wait, and the question now was who'd strike first. The sheriff tried to light a cigar, searched his pockets for matches, finally gave it up. Gil did not offer him any help.

'I know you've got no reason to trust me," he said, taking a different tack. "I know you think Jack's bought me for good and all." He drew himself up to look at Gil directly. "But there are some people who've gotten pretty restless. Jack don't necessarily keep his promises. He thinks he's got everybody in his pocket." He paused. "I'll be on your side." It came out as though it were a labor for him to say it. "Me and the boys."

Gil looked at him narrowly. "You're right—I don't have any reason to trust you," he said. "To me, you've done nothing but crawl around on your belly with the rest. But if it's true what you're saying, just you keep out of it, not taking sides. You and the rest. Can I count on you for that much?" Or was that revealing his hand in a way to go against him? "And you can let me know how many men he's got around him."

The sheriff wanted to shake hands on it. If things worked out, Gil figured, it was a victory of sorts: the town would be behind him. At least Jack couldn't count on having everything under his control. The night before the raid, he and Hombre and the three men from the ranch—the others had since been let go to ride north to meet the gang Dark Eduardo said he'd bring, seven men—all save Dark Eduardo himself. He'd been set upon one night when he'd been holed up with Jose Benevidez and had barely escaped. He'd fled to Mexico.

A dozen men in all. And that many or more around Jack's spread.

"I've come to take what's mine by rights," Gil told his men, "and the rest belongs to you and those he stole from."

They camped that night a few miles above Jack's ranch and planned how they would converge. Ride up on the ranch from three different sides, let five of them mount the attack at dawn, the rest serving as cover, waiting to cut down Jack's men. Gil and Hombre would take care of the rest. That night as they lay under the stars. Gil slept fitfully. A thousand shadows plagued his mind. It was as though he'd opened the passage to all the shadows of dreams that can haunt a man, winding round the brain like sirens, refusing to depart. Already it seemed as though the ghost of vengeance stood over him, Jack's ghost as well, to make him mad, to make a terror of his life. And he woke, struggling to lift himself out of the fit. This

125

time Hombre woke in response. "What's wrong?" For a moment Gil couldn't speak. When he did speak, his voice quavered like an old man's. "I didn't expect to feel this fear," he said.

"It'll be all right," Hombre said, as if he were comforting a child. "Tomorrow when you wake, it'll all be gone. As soon as the light comes.... There are dark shapes that take away your strength. Fear belongs to shadows. But in the light it all comes back—what you need to do."

For now he saw how it was, why certain things were to be called evil, because they choked out life. He could see that a man like Jack wanted to swallow up the world and leave nothing for the rest. He had tried to push away the knowledge; he'd have been glad to go back to Hippolyta's bed, to her garden, to live in her luxury and put thought out of mind. Thinking created a burden in the moment, made you stand outside alone. Somehow Hippolyta, and then Gil, had brought his mind beyond all he'd known before.

Gil gave a sigh and lay back down, blinking in the dark. He felt cleaved by doubt, as though he were two people. "I thought my way was clear," he said. "Now suddenly, I don't know anymore."

"The town is behind you now," Hombre said. "You're not risking anything. They're scared, but they're waiting for you to set them free."

"There are always those who wait and straddle the fence," Gil said bitterly.

For a time the two men lay quiet. Then Hombre said, "But you have to do it. Otherwise you couldn't live."

"It's true," Gil said, remembering. Still he tossed about restlessly, unable to sleep.

They rose before dawn, ate hastily the biscuits they had brought, made their way through the woods, and divided up. Three groups from three directions, two of them concentrating on the bunkhouse, The others would cover Hombre and himself as they entered the lodge. On the far side was a steep canyon.

They descended on the ranch, yelling like a hundred men. The element of surprise was on their side. Perhaps it hadn't occurred to

Jack that Gil might look to outside help, he was so used to having things his way. The sheriff had done his bidding since he'd been a sheriff, and he wasn't looking to his defection. He'd allowed himself to get cut off from some of those he most depended on. And though he wasn't looking to Gil simply to clear out, still Gil had been warned: he had a mother to think about, and if he tried anything, the sheriff and his boys would make him think better of it. Jack kept a light guard over his place, a couple of men who made the rounds and found out what the dogs were barking at. One of these men had been shot directly as Gil's men burst into the yard. The rest, roused from sleep, hastening to their guns, defended the bunkhouse. One of Dark Eduardo's men was hit in the shoulder but managed to shoot his assailant. A couple of the others, now on foot, took refuge behind the trees and kept up a steady barrage, for several of Jack's men had made it out the back door of the bunkhouse, a couple through the windows.

Meanwhile Gi and Hombre made their way to the lodge under the cover of the men behind them and at their flanks, who shot down a couple of Jack's hands as they came running toward the house. Hombre hurled a great rock at a window and hurled himself in, Gil just behind. They ducked behind the black leather couch in the living room as shots rang out in their direction. "We're coming to get you, Jack," Gil yelled as a bullet flew over his head.

"Just try it," Jack yelled.

After that, it was as if a dance went on between them as they fired at one another back and forth. Gil crept along the wall, while Hombre kept Jack engaged.. From the living room they backed him down the hall, and Hombre came around to cut him off at the other end. Then suddenly the shooting stopped. Jack had disappeared. Silence. They threw one door open, then another. The third was locked. "You're in there, Jack. We've got you. Come on out." Silence. "You don't come out, we'll be in there to get you."

"Come on in," Jack yelled.

Gil kicked in the door, as Hombre covered him, but no bullets rang out. They found Jack sitting quietly at his desk, his gun in front of him. Gil and Hombre strode into the room, their guns leveled. Seeing him there sitting as though he was waiting for them to stop by for a little chat almost disarmed Gil. What was this man? Did he think he was above being killed? He who'd killed so many or had them killed, acting like he was bullet proof.

"I'm going to kill you, Jack," Gil said. Perhaps he needed to be given the news.

Jack laughed. "I figured you were going to try it." He waved them off as if he could make them disappear. "You really think you can pull it off?"

"You know how bullets work. You've killed enough men to know ... In the back, if I remember rightly."

Jack laughed again. "Yes, that's the legend. And that's what'll happen to *you*. Maybe someone's sneaking up on you this very instant."

"The old trick. I want your guns. Not just the one in front of you that's empty. But whatever's on you, whatever's in the drawer. I know you're trying to play me for the fool," Gil said, motioning with his gun.

"If you kill me, you'll never get the deed," Jack said. "And suppose I've destroyed it. All your inheritance will end up in the courts. The lawyers will feed off your carcass like vultures. You'll end up with nothing."

"You think that'll bluff me out? I don't care about the ranch. All I want now is to kill you," Gil said. The man was stalling him. "The rest will take care of itself."

"Come to your senses, boy. You have nothing to gain."

"Stand up against the wall." It would be done right, this act of justice. Jack stood up and moved back as Hombre pulled out the drawers and overturned them one by one. Gil moved closer, and took aim. Whether a sudden craven moment hit him, or whether he was simply stalling for time, Jack went down on his knees. "Look, don't do it. Listen, you're everything I've always wanted in a son. Together we can..."

"Go to hell."

"No, wait—listen, I haven't told you my secret. I haven t told anybody yet. I found the Lost Diggings. There s a carload of nuggets in there big as bullets. It's yours. They found it years ago, but Cochise chased them out. And it's yours. Everything of mine—it can all be yours. You can make the town whatever you like. I'll have the power."

And for a single instant, Gil tasted the sweetness of the thought. All that power to create something splendid out of the chaos. Tempted, it may be that he waited a moment too long, enjoying his advantage, the triumph of all those whom Jack had done in. But then he saw how he was being led on.

"It's too late," he said, and shot. But in that same instant another shot rang out and Gil whirled around, and Hombre too, and shot wildly at whoever had sneaked up.

"Buddy," he cried out, as his old foreman slumped to the floor. Then another shot came. Jack, dying, had managed to get into his hand a small derringer in a side holster. And Hombre yelled, clutched his chest and staggered against the wall. Gil shot again, emptied his gun, but Jack was past any bullet. "Oh, my God," Gil cried, when he saw the blood coming from Hombre's chest. He knelt and staunched the flow as best he could, hoisted him up on back and shoulder, and carried him outside. Then, keeping an eye out for any of Jack's men who'd come back through the woods, he laid Hombre near a pyrocanthus bush. The battle was over now. The men were dispersing. "Hombre's hurt," he told them. "I'll take him back." Gil reached their horses and led them to where Hombre fought for breath. He lifted Hombre into the saddle, slumping forward over his horse's neck, and mounted his own. Slowly they made their way through the woods and into town, to the hospital, from where a doctor took charge.

"Just missed the heart," the doctor said, when he finally emerged from his efforts to remove the bullet. "Damaged the lung as well "We'll have to be patient," he told Gil and would not say more. Hombre lay unconscious, Gil sitting beside him. He had no thought or room to rejoice that Jack was dead. His only concern was Hombre. A long night lay ahead of him.

IX. The Wound

For three days Hombre lay in a fever, pouring sweat—out of his head. And Gil sat with him. Hippolyta had come, and the two of them took turns sitting by his bed, sponging his forehead, trying to speak words of comfort while he raged and tossed. For the wound, the disorder to his mind, took him back into spaces of forgetfulness he had long since abandoned. And old memories returned like a brush fire in the wind. His arms flailed, and he would strain to push away what he saw. *Enrique. No, no, Enique.*

For there was a man on top of his mother, pushing into her, riding her to a place where she cried out, while he stood by, helpless. He hated the man who took her there. And to his cries of protest came whacks and blows. Her man—who was this man? For his face kept changing, melting from one into another, looming over him like a great shadow. And his mother was pushing him away, the man melting into the great shadows on the wall. Hombre sank back exhausted, his forehead beaded with sweat. The coolness touched his brow momentarily, a hand pressed his. Then he heard footsteps coming after him, and he was torn away again. Running and running. He felt his running as he tossed away from the words that were spoken to calm him. But he could not stop running. He dared not turn to see what pursued him. Running, running. He ran into the loneliest place he'd ever been, a space that was himself.

He could not escape. He ran from one hiding place into another and waited panting, but there was someone who lived in him, who pushed him on until the fear choked him. Then he had to look out sharp with an animal eye, until he could escape. He ran until he forgot what he ran from, for no one came after him. He ran until his body wouldn't let him move. He ran into hunger and thirst, into an aching that was all of him.

Warm in his mouth, liquid from a spoon he was being fed with. He swallowed and moved beyond whoever was feeding him. The liquid burned his throat, and he had to push it away. Let him only run. Not to the refuse bins he rummaged through, that he found along alleys, until he was chased away. Not into the throng of older boys who teased and tormented him. Where now? Where? Ah—to the tree that stood in the weedy vacant lot. A tree with fruit ripening into little yellowy suns, soft, sweet, fleshy suns. He shinnied up the tree and glutted himself on the half-ripe fruit until he was griped by cramps and had to flee from his own stomach. He vomited like a dog, and reeled toward a shed to lay himself in the straw, a sick dog, panting as he did now. Only let him find coolness. He was in a heat from running, waves of heat rolling from his flesh.

Let him only... Let him... The cool green of a garden with the water flowing. He kept looking for it, up and down the dusty streets. It hung in front of him like a mirage, a gleam of green in the dust as the dogs barked and ran at him. Where was it? Where? The garden where the fruit hung like jewels, red and green, purple and lush gold. Fruit that would satisfy all hunger—sweet and juicy. And the branches a shelter. Away from the gnawing that was his belly. Now he saw it: red and green and yellow and orange. A play of colors made for his appetite—all the shapes. He wanted to hold them in hands, stroke them with his fingers, run his tongue along their color. And taste. Bite in with his teeth, tear away the soft flesh and let the juices run down his chin.

For the farmers brought in from the valley their melons and apples, their corn and squash and onions and tomatoes.

They brought their burros laden. The women brought their clay pots and shawls and woven blankets. And they sold tamales from their covered galvanized buckets, the smell of meat and chili twisting his nose. Around the square everything was made bright with the color of things to eat and wear, all spread out, piled up. He lay in wait, sharp with cunning, watching for the vendor to turn her back. Then slowly, like the cats that stalked the alleys, he crept up and snatched a tomato. It was warm in his hands, red and soft in his mouth. He laughed for gladness.

He couldn't lie still, not for a moment. The fever kept after him. A smell was teasing him, pulling at him, tearing at his stomach, and he had to go back to find it. In the morning early, it hooked his nose. He drank it in to where it confronted his hunger, snatched him up and pulled him forward. He had to follow along the street, then to the alley where the smell lived. And there he discovered the source. As he drank it in, a face appeared in the window. He stood watching, and then the door opened. From inside, the heat of the ovens. And she beckoned him, put the warm bread in his hand. He tore into it, wolfed it down until it filled in his stomach, and for a moment he knew contentment, a stillness of motion. Every morning he followed the smell. But sometimes she wasn't there, and the others ran him off.

He was a wolf. He became a pair of eyes, a pair of hands, a set of feet. Spying, snatching up what he could find, running, always running. Sometimes he snatched up a child's toy on a porch, a piece of clothing from a clothesline, whatever he could trade for food. And then, his stomach full, he could find a place to hide away and sleep. The nights were cold enough at times to turn him into a shivering, aching sack of bones, and only that. He'd go to where the horses lived and sleep in the hay. He'd find a shed where chickens closed their chicken eyes against the dark. Sneak into the midst of their urgent clucking and ruffling of feathers and roost there himself. So as not to get caught, he stole away before sun-up.

He found himself going to places he'd never been, bars with drunken men. They let him hang around. Gave him the dregs of beer, laughed at his antics. He learned to make them laugh, and they would throw him coins. And once an older boy gave him money to do things that were strange to him. He yelled out as the image overtook his mind. All these things he had forgotten as he grew into the silence that left things mute. Words slipping away. He no longer needed them. They stood between himself and the warmth of the sun, the shade where he sought relief from the heat. Where he could sit for hours and look at the grass, the lizards on the rocks.

He chewed on stalks of grass and let go of everything.

When the cow came to him and became his mother, his companion, he could no longer remember. Time had taken him, turned him round and round, moved him forward from one forgetfulness into another. How he'd walked and must have walked for many days, wandering the land far away from where he was—this was like a bridge he'd crossed over and left behind—to warmth, flowing with generosity. He'd walked until his feet were raw. Far enough to walk everything into forgetfulness, the streets where he had wandered, the language he spoke, all human ties. Into the land he walked, with his nakedness, only himself, throwing behind him alien things. And the land did not destroy him, but took him in—the animals and birds that lived there, the wind and rain. He suffered it and took whatever offered of bounty. The comfort of warm milk and what was left over from a kill; the shelter of trees and caves. Long days of lounging in the sun. Another language: the language of sight, hearing and touch. He came to know what flowed deeper than any words, all that joined him to his cow.

For a long time Hombre lay on the border between this world and the one to which he'd wandered back. He raved against remembering, even as he fought not to forget. What was given to him in one space was taken away in another, only to return with a new thing to tremble over.

Then one day, his head cleared and he woke as from a long dream. Gil was there—he recognized Hippolyta. And felt something being stripped away of the burden of remembering and forgetting, as though a light were blinding him.

He tried to sit up, but he was too weak. He tried to call back where he'd been, but what he'd been taken from and where he'd gone began to dim and lose itself. He heard their rejoicing as he sank away from himself like a stone. He'd have to rest, they told him. They'd been able to feed him only a little water, a few mouthfuls of soup. The doctor had taken out the bullet, but the wound still festered. He looked at strange walls, at a ceiling with a large blot that grew before his eyes and terrorized him. He closed his eyes against its fierceness.

"Take me away from here," he pleaded. " Let me die in peace."

"It's all right," Gil said.

"I've come around?"

"You'll feel better when you've had some food."

"This is an evil place you've brought me to," Hombre insisted. He looked around as though at monsters emerging from the walls. He tried to rise up from his bed and tore his wound until it bled. They didn't want to move him yet, but he could not be calmed. There was poison in the air, evil things. They had to give way to his panic; to keep him there would only do him harm. They summoned a carriage from the livery stable, had it brought round and with the help of the driver and Gil and one of the nurses, they carried him out. They would take him to Hippoly's house. He refused to be taken inside. Only outdoors could he be content. Let him lie near the shed where Hippolyta kept the feed for her chickens, the hay for her horse. In the end, they did as he wished. They piled up straw and brought out blankets and made a couch for him. Then Hippolyta summoned her neighbors, who put up a shelter for him, made with poles and covered with brances of sweet-smelling cedar. He seemed satisfied then as he lay there gazing, it seemed, at objects far away.

There he could lie and watch Hippolyta in her garden or the workers she had hired to mix bricks for the chapel she was building behind her house. For a long time she'd turned the idea over in her mind. It seemed strange to her, and yet not so strange. She wondered how it was to give a shape to reverence. She wasn't sure she knew what she was about, yet the idea compelled her. Perhaps she'd give her chapel to the priest, if he would take it.

Hombre watched the men mix the adobe and straw and form the bricks and leave them drying in the sun. He watched the sparrows come to take the breadcrumbs he threw to them, watched the clouds move across the sky and the shadows lengthen.

"I wish I'd never come here," he said to Hyppolyta as she bathed him and dressed his wound. I was happy running on the land."

"But think of all you'd have missed," she said, smoothing his arm with her hand.. "All that you have come to know. You were born a man and now you've had a man's experience. An animal doesn't know itself."

"But there were no troubles to burden my mind." Yet he remembered how he had to struggle against the cold and sometimes the lack of food, the threat of bear and puma.

"You lived from one day to the next," she said. "You got past cold and hunger and managed to survive. Would that have been enough for you? Tell me the truth now. What could you do with that proud body? Only think what you've learned to do with that. The horses you've ridden, the cattle you've herded. The women you've been with, who put their arms around your neck and laughed and teased you, who put their lips on yours. They'd be here now if I let them. What about them? Didn't they give you pleasure? And all the tricks I taught you. And the way you took them in and become a lover."

She sighed. " I didn't want you to leave me for that ranch, even though we couldn't roll around and play forever. Temptation though it was. . But when you have your strength, I wouldn't mind a few more of those nights and days," she said, giving him a melting look. So she tried to woo him toward recovery.

The knowing in his flesh that came after a sweet lust satisfied drew him. But sometimes when the lust raged in his blood, he hadn't known what would satisfy it. When his blood rose, it brought him strength—this he knew. He'd felt a momentum, a desire to throw himself into action, into the stream that flowed around him. Then a woman was only a distraction, but one he'd come to with pleasure. And where was all that now? Taken away, never to return, he felt. He was an empty sack.

Every day Hippolyta dressed his wound, fed him with nourishing soups made with herbs and good vegetables and meat to bring back his strength. But he ate with little appetite.. She could not understand where his hunger had gone.

"Why did you come after me?" he challenged her after a restless night. I wasn't doing harm to anyone."

He was beyond her. She could only try once again to remind him of all he'd seen and put his hand to, all he'd learned and accomplished.

He shrugged. All these were fascinating once. He was a child in front of them, overtaken by wonder.

"At night I could lie under the stars and they visited me with their light-arrows. The animals and birds were not afraid of me. They had their own language, and I understood." Tears came to his eyes. "Only now no longer."

She worried over him, disturbed by the way his thoughts all canted in the same direction, resisting her. She'd never met with such resistance. She taxed herself to win him back.

It is far stronger than I, she thought. A dark power— as though Jack had sent it with the bullet. "Did you have a friend like Gil?" she reminded him.

And he thought of friendship. A friend, a brother. He remembered how they wrestled and came to know each other before they knew one another's names. He'd pushed against a wall of strength, strained his muscles against it as he'd never done before. And the other had pressed to his utmost limit as well. A strength that had the living fire behind it, that lived in everything he knew. And they both pushed it to their utmost limit. It was as though they hadn't known themselves until that moment when they both dissolved in laughter that reached into an underlying delight. He had never laughed like that, it had come from so deep a place. He was consumed with longing.

When Gil came to see him, and sat beside him, he saw in his eyes the depths to which their friendship reached. He saw how they met in one another, and what was missing in each that they gave to one another, and where Gil went beyond him. He wanted to live again in that discovery. But though he tried to summon his strength to fight against it, a dark thing sat on his chest.

He could only rail against him: "You see what you've brought me to," he raged. "I'm going to die because of this bullet. Why did you have to fight against such a snake?" He watched his friend's face fall into anguish.

"Don't die, he pleaded. "I couldn't bear it, nor to think it was because of me. You know what there is between us, what we've lived through together. You know I can't do without you."

Hombre lay quietly. It was true. He yearned to be cured by such words.

"The two of us together—we could take on anything. That's what I thought," Gil went on. "And I always wanted to do something great enough that I wouldn't be just a piece of straw in the wind."

Hombre knew that was true as well. The excitement he'd felt along with the terror. What else could have brought him to that place? And if he listened to the wind, might not something come again that would stir his blood?

"He was like a great cloud blocking the sun," Gil said. He'd said this so many times, the words came automatically. "Ever since I was a boy—a shadow over my life ever since I was a boy. Jack Cameron." He himself was weary of his words, even as he sought justification in the after-clap of the event. Even if nothing ever decreed it, surely something would rise up and declare a limit to what any man might have or do. Yet Jack had had his way, far beyond decency and law. It was all he had to take refuge in. "Tyranny," he said. "And murder to make it possible. People can't live that way. It was..."

Hombre agreed. "Even animals don't have tyrants. Only men."

"It's true. Anyway, you're a man," Gil said. "At least together we rid this town of its sickness."

"But then," Hombre said, "that leaves room for how many more just like him. All the little ones to spring up, grabbing and taking."

What had given Hombre such a dark picture in his mind, as though he now knew the world for what it was? "Only that?" he said with a sinking feeling. "Is that all you can see?"

Hombre would give him no assurances. He was exhausted of arguments. The dance of shadows troubled his sight, darkness broken into pieces. Gil could see them even as he wanted to deny them. If he had known the outcome, would he have gone after Jack?

Hombre lay still. True, he'd had his moment; he'd have to be content with that.

But Gil persisted: "You're a hero to the folks here. There've been articles in the newspaper, and every time I walk the streets people stop me to talk about you. There was a crowd gathered round the hospital your first days there clamoring for news. We had to send them away. And they would have come here too, except we've asked them not to. They'll always remember us in this town, you and me, especially those who saw their men killed and their land taken."

"You think so? Hombre said, with what seemed a momentary brightness.

"Of course. There are the newspapers. I can read you what they say."

Gil brought Hombre the clippings. But only some few of them. For there were those in the town who thought the pair ought to be tried for murder: they'd gone outside the law to take their vengeance, and that was no longer the way things ought to be done. How could you have a civilized town if men took it upon themselves to kill? Those with vested interests in the future of the town viewed Cameron's demise as a blow to the economy. He'd built up the cattle industry and paid the men a decent wage. He'd given liberally to the fund to start a college; he gave money to the new hospital being built. He'd subscribed heavily to the society dedicated to bringing culture to the town, lecturers, theatrical troupes and musicians. Order had existed in the town, and Jack's death disrupted it. Certain people were enraged.

Hombre did not know any of this, struggling as he did to fight what pressed upon him in the dark, like a great hand pressing against his chest. Whenever Gil left him, a melancholy settled over him again, taking him back into the same old rounds.

"I wish I could walk out onto the land again," he said to Hippolyta, "without the darkness in my mind. It is not what you think,," he went on. "I rejoice in all I've done, in all you taught me. I am glad to die a man. But I think the shadows have said that I must die."

What could she do? As he hung suspended between life and

138

death, she grew increasingly fearful. She prayed and soughy divine help. It was more than the bullet that had struck him, given him his wound. He was innocent, she thought. That was how he'd lived. And even when she'd made a man of him and sent him into the excitements of the town, he carried that innocence with him. Not like Gil. His fate had been shaped out of an idea. Hombre had lived in the simple breath drawn in and out, and for his actions alone he would suffer.

During the days he sat in the garden, but he had no strength for work. Meanwhile the chapel walls were going up. When the roof was on, they would cover the walls with stucco and paint them.

"You have to think of this," Hippolyta said, as though an idea, a belief, might save him. "This is where the spirit comes. It is fire and fills the soul. It is the sun. It's what makes the earth rich and lives in all of us."

It was of no interest to him. He had grown indifferent to food, and though the wound appeared to be healing, a gray weariness settled over him. His face seemed gray. Something has possessed him, she thought. When you kill a man like Cameron, something hangs in the air you can't help breathing in. And for such as Hombre it was fatal. All this time she'd tried healing herbs, but now as a last resort, she tried to work a magic that would lift the spell from his mind. It all lies in potency, she reflected. If the mind bends, the body goes down with it.

It took potency to enter a woman and make a child. It took it to make a deed and it would take more to create a new world from what had perished. Old things rotted and tainted the new—it took all one's effort to begin again.

That day she picked special herbs from the corner of her garden and brewed a tea and let it sit in the sun. She added a certain powder distilled from a plant that came from Chihuahua, used by the Yaquis in their ceremonies. She brought out an egg with an unborn chicken to run over Hombre's body and feathers to sweep him with all these things she did with great care. Hombre drank the tea and a shudder went through him. For a time he yelled and sweated and gnashed his teeth.

"You'll feel better after this," she told him.

Gil had come and once again they both kept their vigil. Then the raging ceased and Hombre grew calm. To Hippolyta, he said, "It is a glory to be a man. If you hadn't come, I'd never have known either blood or spirit. In his gaze there was a remembered rapture. And then to Gil he turned a glowing face. "It was a great deed," he said. "Together we did it. How wonderful," he said, "to have a friend."

He looked at Gil with great fondness and took his hand. "It's all right now for me to die." He smiled. "Remember me," he said, and left them weeping.

X. Grief

It was over—the long vigil of hope clouded with fear. And now Gil knew but one more loss. He'd pushed away knowledge: Hombre couldn't die—it was impossible. His presence taken away, a gaping hole left in the world—impossible. He'd pushed himself beyond the moment, beyond the festering wound and Hombre's raving, beyond the tiredness that caved him in. He'd tried to lull himself with imagining fresh adventures: the world before them, open and free, gleaming with fresh promise; the shadow hanging over the town now defeated, dissolving into the illusion it had always been. And the forces fighting its presence, resisting, trying to break the deadlock, these, too, had dissipated. The town could now become whatever its citizens made of it, opening to the seeds in the wind. But to Gil, what did it mean, this dream Hombre could no longer be part of? Dust and ashes. He let out a howl, shook his fist, sank to his knees and rolled in the dust.

Hippolyta let him rage. Finally he would wear himself out, and, like any other man, succumb to exhaustion and sleep. Meanwhile she called in the neighbor women to help her lay out the body. After they had bathed and dressed Hombre in clean clothes and put on his boots, they laid him out in a room with candles burning at his head. They sent round the news so that those who knew him might come to pay their respects. Gil took no notice. He was a hollow mask. He couldn't hear what was said to him; he hardly knew where he was. But when they sent for the carpenter to take measurements for the pine box he would make, Gil told them he'd bury Hombre himself. They could have a funeral if they wanted, but he and Hombre wouldn't be on hand for it. No one argued, not even Ben Whittier, the blacksmith and sometime preacher, who'd come with a prayer book because someone had fetched him. He read his prayer, shook

Gil's hand and went back to the forge.

Although Gil was impatient to leave, to shake off the company that could give him no solace, they made him wait until the visitors had given Hombre his due. The next day they set up tables outside and ate the funeral meal, meat and chili, posole, tortillas and beans, and the funeral cake. Gil ate nothing.

Then the men carried the body out of the house, sewed it in canvas, and helped Gil lash it to a large mule he'd brought in. This done, he mounted his horse. In his saddle bags he carried a canteen and some of Hippolyta's tortillas and beans wrapped up in a clean cloth. He didn't know how far he was going or when he would return. Hippolyta took his hand, looked up into his face with eyes that mirrored his grief and said, "Come back soon. Remember, this is your home. You can't just desert us."

Had there been room for it, he might have taken a moment to let her expression enter him. But he was closed to everything except the need to put all distance between himself and the town. Near the stables and behind them where the chapel walls were going up, a crowd of people stood around him, mostly from the Hill, but others who had come to express their gratitude for what he and Hombre had done. They were not afraid to speak now of things the past had buried, those deeds fear had been kept unspoken or let abroad only in whispers. Now the secrets came forward, what this man and that had done at Jack's behest. While Cameron was alive, he was their shield, they said. No wonder their like was making noise, trying to call Jack's demise murder, squealing for justice.

It was as if those who came in gratitude did not want to let Hombre go, nor Gil either, till these hidden things had been exposed, all that had festered in the dark, like another great wound.

At long last Gil released himself from them, from the town, turned away down the Hill and took the road out of town. The rest of the inhabitants had long since followed the funeral carriage, drawn by black plumed horses, bearing Jack's remains to the cemetery, a barren stretch of ground to the south of town. They'd laid him out in his striped black suit, his ruffled shirt with the mother-of-pearl studs, his polished boots. And the mourners were suitably tricked out to make their moan, mostly for appearance sake. Gil knew who would be there. He wondered if the sheriff would make a showing. In all likelihood. No doubt he had fences to mend, depending on whatever side he stood.

Gil knew that among the mourners were those who had no kind thoughts for him. Jack was, for them, a prize too valuable to lose. Who would take his place? In *The Golden Era*, a black border enshrined his memory, with a long encomium that covered the front page. Apart from his being a man of enterprise, a great sportsman, a generous host known for his lavish entertainments, Jack Cameron had made a real contribution to the town's prosperity and culture, its prospects for its future. "The loss of one of the town's leading citizens, shot down in his prime, would not go unregarded. "A crime as heinous as ever the ones perpetrated by the well-known Billy the Kid." Gil had crumpled up the paper and tossed it away. Worse than sheep, this town of frightened, huddled citizenry. One moment ready to spit on the villain; in the next, to transform him into nobility. How fickle were the sentiments of the town, of those who had a stake in things as they were, no matter how unjust for those despoiled.

You've seen it happen. History is filled with such shifts, a running stream of ambiguities, a whole flood, to my way of thinking. The net is wide and what gets caught and what falls through owes much to chance. And all that gets mixed together—crime and error; accident and calculation, madness and misconception and sheer folly; good intentions and foul result—is enough to land any normal creature in confusion. Wonder has so filled me at times I could only stare into space. And where are you as you lie on a heap of conjectures?

Gil was too full of grief to let his mind be taken into all that muddy water and slippery muck. For himself, he'd bury Hombre, give him to the earth, with no one else to interfere. The bond that joined them had come from from their deepest core, what they'd evoked from one another. At first he thought of taking him back to where the cattle ranged, to the part of the ranch where he'd first been discovered. But it struck him that somehow even in death Hombre could not go back there again. Too much had happened since. But where did he belong? Some instinct told him he should bury him on Jack's land. He thought of the moment Hombre had agreed to the adventure, the smile that had suddenly emerged out of his resistance: *But we are friends.* Nothing mattered beyond that. And then the scene replayed in his mind of how the two of them had tracked their quarry through the lodge, dodging the bullets coming at them, how they'd cornered Jack and struck him down. Only the action wouldn't pause there, and the next instant came, too, the blow that brought Hombre to his death.

Would anyone remember how he, how Hombre more than he, had lived beyond anything they'd been?

It was a sullen day. Though it hadn't rained in the town, it had rained back in the hills; a cloudburst had swollen the creeks and filled the washes. At one point the waters roared down through an arroyo, a flash flood, and he had to pause until he could take his animals across. Beyond the ridge, the clouds still hung low with dark streaks beneath. They might hang there for the rest of the afternoon, or move his way and leave him drenched. He had to pick his way through the clayey mud until he reached the river, the cottonwoods and the pines beyond. On his way, he remembered their night under the big cottonwood, the stars sparkling all over the sky. And the fears that had set upon Hombre like a pack of dogs. He himself had been above fear then. All cocky with assurance until that instant when his own fear struck. Then it was Hombre who had brought him beyond it and freed him. That was how far Hombre had gone beyond himself. Known fear and risen above it... To risk everything. And die. And what was left to him now?

Death will crush me down. There's only death. The thought knelled in his brain. He plodded on, hardly seeing where he went. Then suddenly the great cottonwood, the tree under which they'd camped, was before him. He drew up and sat there numbly for some moments, but he knew, at least, what should be done. Here, Hombre should be buried—just beneath, in a space between the

144

biggest roots. He tethered horse and mule, and unloaded his tools. First loosening the dirt with a pick, then taking an ax to the smaller roots, he was finally able to dig out the dirt with a shovel. Several hours it took him in strenuous labor; for though the soil near the river was sandy and porous on the surface, it was filled with roots and rocks beneath. At last the grave was ready, deep enough that no wild animal would disturb it. After a pause to catch his breath, Gil unlashed the body and laid it on the ground; then, by the ropes around it, he lowered it into the grave. He went through these motions as numb, unseeing as the corpse itself. He shoveled in the dirt, found a stone to place at the head, then turned away exhausted. It was done. For a time, he sat staring at the river, tossing stones into the current.

Though weary, he knew there was no place of rest. He rose and packed up his tools, then stood, unable to move his mind. He couldn't go back to the town; he couldn't live there; he'd fallen into a hole deeper than any he had known. *I am living a death*. He had to make himself move. He mounted his horse and rode through the woods, hacking his way through brush and tree branches. For a little time, he lost himself in this struggle, hacking at anything confronting him, each swing of the axe making him want to swing it harder. He was riding in the direction of Jack's lodge, and at some point he recognized what he'd known all along—that he was going there. It was his now if he demanded it. Let them try to take it away from him. Sniveling cowards. Insects working in the dirt, feeding on their bits of dung. Now they'd be glad enough to go back to feast off the carcass he had given them.

He strode across the porch, then with his axe he knocked away the padlock the sheriff had put on the front door. His last entrance had been through a wondow Hombre had smashed with a huge rock—now boarded up. He saw that the door was handsomely carved with a scene of men herding cattle. Jack must have paid a pretty penny for it. In proper hands, the knife from some rancher's back could carve a door into a pageant. He threw it open, as though he were surprising a den of thieves, and stepped inside. *Well, here*

I am, Jack. At your invitation. You were going to show off your place and dazzle my eyes. Now I'll just show myself around, thank you . I'll take my own sweet time.

Now he was free to ferret out all Jack's secrets. *I'd like to tie you up and let you watch. That's what the Apaches did, tied up their captives and danced around them, built a fire under them, poked them with their spears, cut out their guts and let them die a slow death.* But all he wanted was to look into the heart of all that power. *It's gone now, Jack. But I'm still on hand.* Let him dig into its secrets there in the house that Jack built. And what would have happened if in that final moment when Jack had offered him everything for his life, he'd taken it? But he didn't have to make the bargain. He could take it now, hire all Jack's crew and more, set up his own stronghold. The new baron, handing round the bounty. That was what they wanted. And they'd crawl back to lick his boots.

Inside, he paused to survey his new domain. First the huge living room with the granite fireplace at the center of the back wall. Above it, the head of a mountain lion, conferring its majesty over all that passed beneath. And on either side, pelts of mountain lions and lobo wolves stretched along the wall. Though a great antlered elk dominated the sidewall and challenged all comers to the gun cabinets, and the pelt of a polar bear was white against dark wood, Jack had favored the mountain lion for the place of honor above the fireplace. The fierce heart of things.

Jack had hunted everywhere, for he had a good eye and a steady hand, not to mention a nerve that didn't flinch. So his trophies proved, heads and hides: deer, and antelope, even an eagle, stuffed, wings outspread, stood on the mantel, its yellow glass eyes ready to seize upon whatever prey happened along. Other bears adorned the floors, rugs spread about the room, the great heads fierce among the feet of those who stood on their pelts. Though Jack had gone up to Alaska three years in a row with his cronies from the East, and with a guide had taken a kodiak and a polar bear, it was the grizzly he most greatly prized. It was a story he was fond of telling, how he'd lost his footing and tumbled down a small hill, looked up and saw the bear coming straight at him. He'd grabbed up his gun, which he had cocked—it was a wonder it hadn't gone off and killed him—and hit the bear right square in the forehead. *Some aim you got there, Jack. And by god, nerves of steel.* One way or another you had to hand to him. He was a man who could kill anything. Gil could acknowledge it—he was himself a hunter. *Two of a kind, Jack.* It had been in his blood, man and boy, starting when he'd gone off to kill rabbits and quail. Though his mother hadn't been in favor of it. But there it was, his first gun. Jack had given him that too, and his mother hadn't been able to rise up and resist. Not if she was going to have a son who could stand up in the world. And those hands, when Jack came to visit, had taught him how to shoot, guiding his aim. He'd spent hours aiming at bottles, making targets for himself, then going after the living prey—the real challenge. The instinct to kill came early. And it made his blood beat until there was a red sun in front of his eyes. He couldn't wait till he could rush outside the agonies of the schoolroom, take off into the waiting land, narrow his eye and ear to their keenest attention, cock his gun and shoot. He felt alive then as though he'd reached down into an intensity that was smothered elsewhere. Stalking the game that was only trying to save its hide by outsmarting you. And the triumph of standing over what you'd deprived of life.

But Jack had crossed the line somewhere. *Why not humans too, Jack, to add to the décor? May as well have fixed their heads around the walls. Let them do homage to you. Or is that too savage a reminder?*

He walked over to the rack of guns lined up in the specially built cabinets. Rifles and shotguns. Against the back wall, a case with derringers and pistols. Fancy ones with mother of pearl handles, just for show. More guns than any one man could use. *Which ones did the business, Jack?* He opened the case and, one by one, turned the guns in his hand, got their feel, sighted along their barrels, opened the small closet just above the case and found it stacked with boxes of bullets. A whole arsenal. For his hunting parties. The sheriff had called upon Jack and his men a time or two when Indians had threatened the ranches. Some of the guns had fired on and shot down hostile Apaches. And which was the gun Jack favored when he'd had it in mind to do a piece of business on his own? How did it feel in the hand? And after a time, when the business was all in a day or night's work, when he didn't think more about it than to send one of his henchmen out to do away with a little interference for $300 a head—so the rumor went—had he pushed the matter aside with even less interest than a trip to the lawyer who'd see he'd get his parcel of land, from scaring off what widow or son or brother?

The other kind of hunting took his attention, after he'd crossed the line, settled matters, and become a gentleman—a sportsman. A use for leisure.

And what about me? He'd never thought before about killing a man until he'd done it. A rush of darkness with flashing lights dizzied him, brought a faintness that almost overcame him. He could hear the laughter rising up, coming after him. *You aren't really going to shoot that thing.* The curve of contempt shaped by Jack's mouth. He almost couldn't shoot. He'd had to get past that awful second; then the hatred had risen up like black bile, and he'd shot. It didn't take but that second. Afterwards his chest pounded—he couldn't keep it quiet, even though a deadly quiet lived inside him. He'd forgotten how it was. He'd pushed away all thought as Hombre lay wounded, dying. And now turned back onto himself, he recognized himself as one who'd killed a man. Dead, no longer a menace. And he, left to his triumph, whatever that triumph meant, was now come back for his revenge. Against the dead.

For a time he walked up and down through the rooms, hardly thinking, the rooms hollow with the echo of his boots. Nobody there. Deserted. *What does it mean now, all you pried away, hoarded up?* In the room that saw the violent end, he studied a surveyor's map that covered half a wall with all Jack's holdings, the spread of the land marked with mineral rights and water rights. Not just a cattle empire. Land rich in ore as well. Zinc, manganese, gold and silver. And quietly the mining operations had settled in, for Jack had got some big-time investors from back East. Quietly the equipment was brought in, and quietly men came out to work it. And in the drawers, put to order again by some deputy, surveyors' maps and a sheaf of assayers' reports. There were the mines: The Lucky Penny, the Silver Bullet, the Casey Bend, with reports on the percentages of ore and sales. And quietly the town got to watch: riches piled on riches.

In that room stood the safe no one yet had touched, the great iron box that held sources of Jack's power. Gil went for his pick and struck at the hinges until he broke them free, then pulled out the stacks of documents, the pouches and leather bags that lay within. Deeds and stock certificates, no doubt the deed to his own ranch among them. Stock certificates for mining operations, contracts, a pouch filled with gold nuggets, another with diamonds. He let them tumble out on the desk, where they lay in a little heap catching the light. He surveyed this chaos of ownership, all the treasure exposed, idly picked up one piece then another. Finally losing all interest, he left the spoils where they lay. He prowled through the dining room, gazed at the mahogany table that could hold sixteen people under the crystal chandeliers, and the sideboard proud with decanters of brandy and sherry. Behind it was the kitchen, where the cooks put their talents to serving up great roasts and fowl in rich juices for all the company gathered round. He gave it a cursory glance and left it for the music room with its piano and victrola and shelves of sheet music, its brocaded chairs set round for the music lovers. He surveyed the library, with stacked bookcases and shelves of books, with Navajo blankets and squash blossom necklaces laid out on display, and pottery and baskets from the pueblos in the north. All that Jack had hunted out and collected to cultivate his more civilized tastes. Books and music, good food and wine. The town could watch admiringly as the drovers carted up box and crate. Musical instruments, expensive furniture. How he loved good society! And the men he gathered around him were his chosen company. Raw power had been refined into good society.

As Gil made his survey, it was hard to add up the sum of things. *I'll give it to you, Jack, you knew better than anybody to stick it out down there in the hole of crude beginnings.* Then climbed out into a good library and the music that hath charms.

That took history, so I see it now; it took things buried back before time began and which time would never reveal except to guess and surmise. Even of things known it was too much for any man to conceive it all. The Pinta. the Nina and the Santa Maria were a mere thin line, only part of the all those countless human trajectories, some known, others lost forever. The discovery of the New World along with all those who'd pushed forward across the ocean and across the continent, and those who'd died of starvation and childbirth, disease and Indian attacks on the way. There were all those. And all the traders and slaves and gunfighters and cattlemen and explorers and hapless wives and their infants born in Conestoga wagons. They'd come to encounter all who'd wandered here from whatever piece of history they'd come from, living by their bows and arrows and wits, foraging around among bones of the continent: first the cliff dwellers, then all the various tribes, the Apaches among them, fiercely battling the invaders, and finally, down to the invaders becoming the victimizers even as they'd once been the victims themselves somewhere else. Plus all the local happenings.

All that history, so many layers of experience forming the texture of things and Jack entering into the middle of it, a combination of character and circumstance, little chinks for opportunity to enter into—it had taken all of that for Jack to get here to his showplace. His piece of civilization. So it came to Gil. *Only it doesn't stop there, Jack.* His own family had been lured there, too, to be part of destiny. Tom Weston, who'd built a hotel and got carried away in the flood. And left a widow with a son. It had taken the folly of that son, built on an old hatred of a man who'd come courting his mother, whose folly had taken him to loss and then to revenge. Hombre. It had taken all that, too, for this moment to arrive. So what was he going to do in that moment: what had to be taken forward and what could be let go? He didn't know. Nor what belonged to his grief and where it would lead him.. He could see no triumph. Jack was gone, but there was still his shadow hanging over. Things were stuck where they'd been. In two deaths. He'd have to decide, only it might take a goodly while, and he needed considerable help, of the sort only

Jack's imported whiskey could give him.

Back into the big living room he went for the cabinet that held the bottles of whiskey and brandy and Madeira and good Spanish port, took one of well-aged whiskeys and poured himself a glass nearly full. He stood against the wall, trying to think, but his brain was hollow and it would be an agony to force it to any conclusions. He'd have to sit and nurse his drink and then maybe he'd have an inspiration.

To ease his waiting, he picked out one of the pistols, loaded it up, went back into the dining room, pulled out the chair at the head of the table and took possession of an invisible company. He held up his glass, as if to offer a toast. *And now I'd like a goodnight kiss from all the ladies.* Jack had made such a request once, and they'd done it for the rogue, their husbands willing somehow to accept this gesture of gallantry. So it got around. He was the one for the ladies, that Jack.

"And now I'd like to make a little speech, in tribute to my host and yours. And all hat brought us here."

He drank, set down the glass and took up the gun, sighted one of the baguettes along the edge of the chandelier, picked it off and watched the little shower of splinters flake down over the surface of the table. He poured himself another drink, took it down, shuddered, and picked out one two three of the baguettes, causing little explosions. "And remember, friends," he declared, "in every moment lives a little barbarity."

He saw where the bullets whanging past the shattered crystals had embedded themselves here and there in the opposite wall, one having shattered the glass of a picture of a young woman meant to shed her allure over the company. He got up and went to look at her as she smiled down indiscriminantly at all who passed beneath her—now with a bullet implanted in the side of her forehead. "Sorry, ma'am, I didn't mean to assault a lady. Sometimes the innocent.." He sat back down again and took up his whiskey. He would sip it slow, take his time. First he held up a glass and toasted the young woman in the picture. "Like I say, ma'am, I meant no harm," he told her as she began to waver before his eyes. He shot one of the decanters and watched the liquid spill onto the Persian carpet. And another. "You see, I'm trying to figure out where to get to. Only there isn't a road, not even a donkey path." He stood up, took aim at the chains holding the chandelier and shot until it landed with a crash onto the table below. That wasn't any good either. A sudden spell of weeping came over him as he fell back down into the chair. He drank up the whiskey, then leaned on his elbows with his hands over his ears, as though the roar of a gathering crowd filled them.

When he looked up, they stood before him—all the animals Jack had shot. moving up to observe him, then loping back to one who stood in their midst. "Hombre! You've come back!" There he stood, one hand on the lion's head, the eagle hovering in the air. Gil tried to get up, but the chair had seized him and wouldn't let go. "Hombre!" A great force seemed to hold him back.

When he opened his eyes, the room was dark. He fumbled around until he could light a candle in one of the candle-holders on the sideboard and went back into the living room. There he lit a gaslight in one of sconces on the wall. The animals kept their guard around the walls. "But they weren't yours, Jack. They belonged to Hombre, because Hombre belonged to them. They have no business being trapped there on your walls. They should be free—to go back into the woods."

He wanted to go with them. The town could have all its civilized pieties. He took the knife from its holder in his belt and cut down from the two pelts of the mountain lions that hung there. He cut strips from the paws and slits in the pelt and tied them together. Then he pulled off his boots and threw them aside. Took off his Levis and shirt and slipped the pelt over his head. "Let it all be damned." Barefoot—that's how Hombre had walked the land. And naked. And now he'd let the animals go. He took out the matches he carried, poured the whiskey over the head of the lion and lit it. He went round the room to the heads of deer and antelope and elk, to the heads of the bears of the rugs on the floor. Each one he lit, until the walls were full of fire. Now the animals were free.

He left the lodge, threw away the pick and shovel, but kept the ax, turned the mule loose to wander back to its owner, mounted his horse and rode off into the woods. He turned to look back at the lodge to see whether it was burning, but it was not yet swept by fire. He didn't remain to watch. Let the whole thing to burn down, let the conflagration sweep over the land itself, burn everything to cinders. But it wouldn't change anything. Jack's presence still hung in the darkness. Nothing would erase his having lived. Or that Hombre would never walk through another doorway.

"Hombre! Why did you betray me? It was only a wound—you didn't have to die of it." He could never forgive him for dying of the wound created by history, which could only continue. He thought his battle had been against flesh and blood, something real. Now he was left to battle against shadows. . .ghosts. And what would he win from them? But that didn't change the fact he had to do it. Half crazed, he rode into the woods.

XI. Syd's Place

If he rode, if he slept, it made no difference, nor where he was being taken in that high country. Higher and colder. When he woke, he drank the whiskey he'd brought, courtesy of Jack, and let the horse go where it would. When the whiskey took over, he hung onto the saddle horn, the horse's mane, whatever he could cling to. When the horse stopped to graze, he got off and relieved himself, wrapped himself in his poncho and lay down and slept on the ground. They found water where they could in water hole and creek, and he filled his canteen, watered the horse. Then he climbed back on and rode till dark. He didn't notice the direction of the sun till it struck him in the face. It seemed they might be lost forever as they moved over the land, that if he went far enough he'd be nowhere, as far away from civilization as Hombre had been. Only let him get that far. One morning of the days he'd lost track of, his horse was gone. He wandered around trying to find him. Maybe he hadn't tied him up, he couldn't remember. The whiskey was gone, too, and it occurred to him he could stagger around until he, too, died. He didn't care. But then his horse ambled up to him from where it had been grazing along the creek!

They started off over the pine needles that carpeted the ridge. Then as he came down, he saw stretching there in front of him a road. He couldn't believe it. Hardly road, it was so rutted, so narrow, the wind and rain had played such havoc with it. Rocks, several boulders, even, had dropped down into it. It wound up so steeply in hairpin turns around the bluffs, it was a question whether any creature would actually want to go up or come down, but might instead think better of the idea and just sit there in the ruts. But it was a road, no doubt about it, and he figured there was a long shot he might find some whiskey at the end of it, and that was a powerful incentive. When he'd run out he couldn't exactly recall, except that the intervening hours had been even more hellish than those under its waning influence. Where he had come, he couldn't say. Nor what piece of territory he had crossed or what now lay before him. The horse would have done well to desert him, having somewhat more stake in its existence. Gil didn't care if he ever got back. And if there were a farther place where he might lose himself, he'd try for it. Beyond even the civilization claimed by this sorry road.

Plodding on, they came a few miles along to a spot once singled out for habitation in a place better abandoned. One ramshackle building displayed a still readable sign, *Saloon*, over one doorway, and *Hotel* over the other. Deer antlers and cow skulls had been nailed up along the walls for decoration, and from them came an odd suggestion of the theatrical, or even the rakish. From the foreheads of the cows' skulls came the gleam of amethyst or onyx beads. Another was festooned with red and blue ostrich feathers stuck into the eye sockets. Farther on, another building was marked, *Theatre*, perhaps the source of inspiration, but it was boarded up. And just beyond that was a store, though it looked quite as deserted as the theater.

As he approached, a calico cat got up from the wooden sidewalk where she'd been sitting and ambled over, meowing up to him, ready to receive his attention. Signs of life. She looked well fed. As she sat watching him, he dismounted, tied up his horse, and aimed himself at the doorway marked *Saloon*. "Anybody there?" he called out. No response. He went to the window, tried to peer inside. He couldn't see anything in the dim interior, just the length of the bar and a glimmer of light in the mirror behind the bottles. A voice, a woman's, called out. "Who is it?—Joe? Clyde? Vern? If it's Vern, don't let me see your face. I'll have your hide, you slinking varmint!"

"It ain't Vern," he said into the dimness. Then the woman herself appeared, opened the door a crack, took his measure and slammed it shut. "Murderer!" she cried.

"What do you mean?" he yelled. Murderer. What did she see? Her catching him out in that way filled him with rage. "Open up, he yelled, "or I'll take an ax to the door."

The door opened then and the woman, hands on her hips, stood her ground in the the opening. "Just what the hell do you want?"

It would take some doing to get past her, but he wasn't going to take anything from her. "You called me a murderer."

She looked him up and down. 'You sure as hell look like you could've throttled somebody. But if you're not going to kill me, come on in." And she stood aside to let him enter. Gil's eyes having adjusted to the light, they both stood planted in mutual astonishment. In front of him was a big-hipped, full-breasted woman, whose reddish hair curled along her forehead, fell down her back with loose abandon, heedless where it might go after that. She was dressed in a blouse with a satin sheen, flounces of lace around the collar, and a full long skirt festooned with more flounces, emphasized with ribbons and lace, as though to be prepared for whatever might offer by way of business or pleasure. But her outfit, which might once have taken her into a dance hall routine, now looked soiled and in at least one place was gaping at the seams.

She was the first to speak out of this new encounter, "Well, ain't you something. Not every day I see a man knocking around, wearing the hide of some puma. You look about as bad off as you must have left him."

Gil looked down at the skins covering him. It hadn't occurred to him he was wearing them, that his feet were bare.

"Where do you come from anyway?"

"Damned if I know," he said with a shrug. "Been wandering through the woods God knows how long. Right now I need a drink."

"A shave and some clean duds wouldn't do you any harm either," she said, moving behind the bar. "But I can fix you up either way and throw in a few other things to boot. Hair of the dog, eh?" She caught hold of the chain, pulled down the oil lamp behind the bar and lit it. Then chose a bottle from among those ranged in front of the mirror, took a glass and poured him a slug. "We haven't exactly been rushing for business here lately. I get tired of talking to the livestock." She gave a pet to the calico, which had followed them inside and leapt up onto the bar.

He gulped down the whiskey, shuddered, and held out his glass for another.

" Hold on," she said. "When's the last time you had food in your gullet? You'll make yourself sick. And I don't like cleaning up the mess afterwards."

"Another one," he demanded, "and then I'll be on my way."

"Listen, friend," she said, "none of my business to be butting in, only it looks like you're not in the best way to go traipsing about. There's mountain lions around here that'll come looking for those skins. And grizzlies and other kind of wildlife. I can rustle you up some food, good grub, if you don't mind my saying. And there's nobody in the hotel. You can grab yourself some shut-eye. Do you a world of good, I'm telling you. I've seen them miners and cowhands come along, plumb wore out like nobody's ever seen, from being out in their shacks months at a time, not seen a plate of decent grub nor a woman in a month of coyotes."

Her voice had a strange quality to it, raucous but spellbinding, and though he couldn't fasten onto the words, they worked a strange fascination on him. He hesitated with the glass, listening as though trying to make out some hidden message both beguiling and fatal.

Meanwhile she'd been looking at him, with a mouthful of questions. What was a man like him doing wandering around like a stray dog. coming to a place like this? A tall, thick man of the kind she admired and whose belly she wouldn't mind running a hand over, playing with the little soft hairs. Looking so much worse for the wear. Scratch-bearded, hair full of burrs and leaf bits, hanging around in smelly skins, feet bare and sore-looking. Wonder he hadn't perished out there in the bush. Must be strong as a longhorn bull. Just needed some feeding and some calming down to be turned back into something halfway human . . . She'd had experience with a wide range of types, whoever had landed out there in the wilderness, and here was a challenge for her, maybe to pull back a man at the edge of his wits before he tumbled over the cliff altogether and wasted what many a good woman had a hankering for.

She removed the glass from his hand and led him into her room at the back. He did not resist. "Now you sit right here," she said, pulling a chair out from the table, while I cook up some bacon and biscuits and some eggs from the chickens I keep. That'll do for a start."

But before she could put herself in motion, she saw his eyelids drooping, his head falling forward.

"Come on," she said. "I figured you were wore out, and I see I'm not wide of the mark." And she led him through a doorway, down a hall and into a room. She guided him over to a bed, helped him to lie down and covered him up. "You just rest yourself," she said. "And we'll think up a few things in the meanwhile."

When he woke, the sun was a bright stripe across his eyes, and his nostrils took in the smell of coffee from somewhere, the warm smell of bread baking, the sounds of someone bustling around. His eyes moved with slow astonishment around the room. He didn't know this place, hadn't the slightest idea where he was. He was lying on a mattress stuffed with husks and he could feel them rustle under him when he moved, and for a long time he contemplated a framed document on the wall, with yellow edges and large handwritten characters that struck him as somehow significant, like a message he was unable to decipher. The dingy roses of the wallpaper with their trail of leaves were of no help either, but abandoned him at nothing more satisfactory after repeated promises that got him only from one space of seeing to another just like it. He turned his eyes to a bureau marred and scratched from use, but with soap and towel placed on the top. For him, perhaps. He got up, went out into the yard to the privy and then to the pump, threw some cold water into his face and felt somewhat revived. His head still didn't quite belong to him, and his belly was hollow.

Behind the building was a stable and a couple of pens, chickens in one, goats in another, with a space for them to wander. A big yellow cat he hadn't seen before came and rubbed up against him as he stood surveying the surroundings. A couple of dogs tied up gave him a friendly bark. Beyond the little settlement, the land fell away steeply into a cascade of hills, and the mountains towered up beyond them. He could look down into a valley, where from miles away he caught an indistinct outline that could have been a rock formation or another settlement, a spread of buildings along what appeared to be the main street, a town larger than this one. Behind him a door clattered, and the woman who appeared on the steps looked familiar, though he was certain he'd never seen her before.

"Breakfast's ready," she said. "Come and get it while it's hot."

He regarded the fiery glints the sun gave to her red hair and the almost greenish tinge it gave her pale, freckled skin, as if she'd no business out-of-doors. Though she seemed to know him, everything was a puzzle to his mind. But for the first time in days he felt hunger gnawing at him, and the lure of coffee caught him as something familiar and even welcome. Then he was in her kitchen, which, going one way connected to a dining room in the hotel, and in another, to the bar. A big iron stove sat in the front part, with skillets and pans hanging on the walls, and on another, a table, a flour-covered breadboard and rolling pin showing signs of recent use. A large blue enameled coffee pot sat on the stove, giving out its steam, and the heavy bitter smell of boiled coffee, and skillets of eggs and bacon were cooking. The table in the middle of the room was set with plates and mugs. She put a cloth around the handle of the pot and brought it over to the table, poured coffee for him.

"Much obliged," he said, as he lifted up the mug. "But I can't remember our meeting."

"No," she said, with a peal of laughter. She filled a plate with eggs and bacon and put out a little plate with biscuits, "I doubt you could, considering the shape you were in. Name's Sadie, but they call me Syd, and this here is Syd's Place, meaning mine."

He ruminated over this information for a brief space, then said. "And where might that be?"

"Place called Gypsy, home of the Gypsy Mine. Only the ore petered out, and the folks moved on, and I'm just about the only one left, except for a few prospectors in the hills, and the miners. Not much business at the moment. Comes in spurts. Sometimes folks wander over from Picayune when they've done their business at the feed store and such. They know me over there."

"And you're here all alone?"

She shrugged. "I manage. You get used to it one day to the next, just get by without a man to help you out. Oh, I get a little help now and then," she said. "Isn't like there's nobody at all. I get a little fixin' done by them that wants to do me a favor. I get by all right."

He nodded. He could see she not only got by but then some. She had green eyes, he noticed.

"What took you out to those parts, friend? I don't even know your name."

"Doesn't matter any," he told her. "I don't think I have a name anymore. You get so far down there isn't any name that can hold your life."

She looked at him. "Glory," she said, "that's pretty far down all right. Had a few choice names myself along the way, but I can't say they ran out." She served herdelf a plate of eggs and biscuits and bacon, then poured a cup of coffee for herself, and sat down opposite him. What's happened to you?"

"I lost a friend."

She considered. "You come all this way on account of that?"

"I just came," he said. "Just stumbled around till I got here."

"Where'd you lose him?"

"He died of a gunshot wound."

"Well, he ain't gonna come here, that's for certain." She gave a little chuckle. "That is, unless you're headed for some place I don't know about."

He shrugged. "I can't go back now," he said. "I don't know where I'm headed." Then he added, "For some place different," he said. "Where I can find out something I don't know now."

"Sounds like a pretty far country. My own opinion is there are some things best left alone." She looked at him closely.

"Come on now, eat that food before it gets cold. I didn't put all that effort into it to throw it to the dogs."

He picked up his fork, and took a bite of egg, then tried the bacon. Tasting the food increased his hunger, and he tore into his breakfast. She watched him as though amused.

"Where's this place located anyway?" he said, when he plate was clean. "Is it on the map?"

She took his plate and filled it once again, replenished his coffee.

"Can't say I've looked recently. I figure if I know where I am, that's all that counts."

"No towns around? I thought I made one out down there below." He began to eat, slowly now.

"That's no town," she said, as though it were dangerous to mention it, and moved on. "There's the abandoned silver mine going up north of here. That's where the road's headed. Then the vein they struck farther on. You'll see them carting out the ore in wagons. That's where I get most of my trade. When the vein petered out up here, they found another one farther on."

"But the town below," Gil insisted.

"Ghost town," she said. She leaned over. "Full of ghosts of the worst kind. You don't want any truck with them." It was clear that was all she was going to say.

"And how did you get here?" Gil asked her.

"Quite a story," she said. She got up for the coffee pot again. "Came from the East almost twenty years ago."

"Homesteading?"

"Not exactly. Married me a preacher. Ain't that a laugh?" She looked to see how he was taking it in. "But the family thought him a fine young man, and he was all piping hot from his theological studies, eager to come West and bring the Word. So I figured it was better than sitting home embroidering pillowcases. There was a little town south of Albuquerque wanted a preacher and he was all fired up to go, got the call right before he came courting. Gave him the incentive." She gave a little hitch to her shoulder. "He needed a wife to help with the hymn-singing and the piety and the socials and what-all, and that was me."

He was gazing at her in her fullness, in the weight she carried so well, in the glory of her red hair. And he appreciated the way she was telling her story, as her amusement played over it. She told him how they'd joined a convoy of wagons headed out of Independence,

Missouri, and crossed the plains, how rough the journey was, their fear of being attacked by the Indians. One night they'd been set upon by a bunch of cowboys who'd scared her husband nearly out of his mind. When they found out they were newly married and on their honeymoon, they wanted to give them a chivaree. "They did up a regular celebration," she said, "hollering around the wagon and shooting off their pistols like you never saw. Fit to kill. They offered us some of their whiskey. Imagine that. And my man was all in a terror they were going to carry me off. But I tell you, I wouldn't have put in an objection. Or at least to join them for a drink myself after riding across all that rough country. Finally he worked up his nerve and came out and got them to promise to listen to one of his sermons, the next day being Sunday." She paused for a laugh.

"Did they come?" Gil wanted to know.

"Well, most of them had rode off into the Sunday silence, still whooping it up, but some came nice as you please, and he figured he'd got his triumph out of it. Poor fellow," she said, shaking her head. "It was about the only triumph he ever had."

Gil, having finished eating his breakfast, pulled back his chair and sat watching her as she cleared away the dishes.

When done, she came and stood in front of him. "We finally got to the town after well nigh freezing to death. Got caught in a snowfall and wandered for hours till a Mexican sheepherder found us and took us onto a ranch. The folks wanted us to take a drop of brandy to warm up the blood, and he was finally persuaded, though it went against him to take any spirits. I was young and innocent," she said with her deep laugh. "Hard to believe this tough old bird was ever a tender chick."

She walked past him to fiddle with something at the stove, running her hand along his neck en route, giving him a pat on the shoulder.

"Umm," she said, "you got a good arm on you. Have another biscuit or two. That's real good apple butter." She passed him the plate and once again sat down across from him. "I thought maybe my man would work down under all that layer of piety and find

162

something to romp with underneath. I like a man who can romp with a woman," she said, looking at him directly. "But that partook of the evils of the flesh." She paused, looking down into her coffee mug. "I figured there's lots of evils worse than that. And there've been times I wouldn't have survived without them."

"What happened to your preacher?" Gil said, carried along by his increasing curiosity.

"Got done in by a boy, Indian, don't know what tribe. Maybe twelve or thirteen. They'd captured him, and Obadiah got the notion to convert him, take him into the house and civilize him into a Christian. Only one night the boy took a knife and slit his throat then took off into the wilds. Wonder he didn't take care of me while he was about it." She paused to think on it. "I've had four husbands since, she said, responding to his unasked question. "One got his brains dashed out in a bar room brawl; the next was ambushed by a claim jumper; number three got caught in a stampede and the last one fell down a mine shaft."

Gil looked at her in amazement. "What rotten luck," he said. "What goddam rotten luck." He pounded the table with his fist.

"Hey, take it easy." She gave another shrug and let out a sigh. "It's just the usual. I've knocked about," she said. "Hell, I've survived. Was with a trader to the Zunis for a while, had a good life. Then I went to the mining camps, cooked and did laundry and took care of the men. I had a little money, so I figured I'd open a tavern up here while things were still going good. No law against a harlot opening a tavern," she said. She got up and came over to him. "No law against a little playing either," she said, "with a man who needs a woman." She rubbed her knee against his.

He shook his head. "This carcass is hardly a man anymore," he said. "My heart is like a stone."

"It's no wonder," she said, "you wandering around in such a sorry mess. Look," she said. "Let me heat up the water and set out the tub. Soak that hide of yours and you'll feel like a different critter. And get you into some decent clothes. Come on," she said, caressing his cheek. "I can tell you need a little consoling."

It was too tempting to resist. She set various pots and kettles on the stove, brought out a copper tub and filled it with the heated water, soaped him up and sponged him down. Washed the dust and bits of chaff out of his hair and beard. Dried him off and set out shirt and Levis she'd been keeping in one of her closets. And by means of the thrill in her voice and the touch of her hands, she persuaded him into her bed. It was a long time since he'd had a woman, and the mood she put him into was the sudden freedom of a great weight lifted. Her arms, the softness of her body ... She took him into her, and he found himself in a soft land, rich and luscious, gracious to him. It took him, all of him, into forgetfulness, as though she were a drug to his senses. He was her captive, held in thrall. They made love long into the nights and lay rich and lazy with one another in the mornings. He found himself trapped on an island where past or future ceased to exist. So things went on till he lost all track of days.

He'd neglected his horse. Had hardly given it a thought. It, too, was enjoying an easy life. Syd fed it with the other livestock and left it out in the field with her own cow and horse. One day, annoyed with himself for reasons he couldn't define, he went out and curried it until its hide shone. The horse held up its head, pranced to the fence and neighed like a trumpet. For a moment Gils heart leapt with an old impulse. Then he turned inside and left it alone again!

So he lingered out the days in Syd's embrace, spent the long winter when nobody came. Got up to snow in the yard, saw his frosty breath in the air. She put him to work chopping lengths for the fire and nailing up things around the place that had come loose and needed a man's arm. In the spring the miners and prospectors would come through on their way to Picayune into the excitements of the town. No one to disturb them meanwhile in their cozy nest.

One morning as he lay in bed, a question came to him: what had happened to the old lion skins he'd worn there? Syd had already risen to feed the animals and put on the coffee. The old skins. He tried to dismiss the question, but it nagged at him. He turned over, covered up his head, but the question buzzed him like a fly. Quickly he got up, dressed and took the question to her. She shrugged for an answer and became suddenly evasive. They were around somewhere, she'd have to recollect. Though he couldn't say why, he was overtaken by the old part of himself he recognized--rage.

"You'd better find them wherever they are."

She looked at him in amazement. "What do you want those filthy old things for? I threw them out in the trash a long time ago. They're gone."

"Where are they?" he yelled and caught her by the wrist. "I want to know where they are."

Frightened, she said. "Maybe they're out in the shed--there's lots of stuff piled up. You can give a look."

He didn't find them there, though he took the place apart, and then turned on her in a fury.

"Maybe I took them over to the theater," she said. "I'll give a look--just be patient. Why you want them smelly hides is a mystery to me."

Somehow she managed to put him off. The next morning when he woke, he flew up out of bed. The smell of burning hair twisted his nostrils. Out in the yard she was throwing the skins into a fire. He rushed out and seized them from her hands, and when she fought him, he struck her across the face.

"What are you doing? Are you crazy?" she wept. "They're just old pieces of animal."

Animal. And he'd been one of the worst sort, lingering and pampering his hide. Even an animal hunted its food. In a single instant, he flung away the torpor that had bound him. Now the thought of Hombre maddened him more fiercely than ever--how he had betrayed him! He had to get out of there before another moment passed. He tore across the yard.

"Listen—wait!" Syd cried, grabbing at him, trying to stay him. She caught up, her voice a breathless flutter in his ear. "Listen, there are things I can give you, help you to . . ."

He paused. "I didn't mean you any harm," he said, thinking of what she'd done for him. "You've given me all you could, all I could ask for. It's me," he said. "It was wrong of me to lull myself."

"No, listen," she said, once they were inside. "This place has secrets. I know things." She paused and from lowered lids looked toward him. She'd snagged his curiosity, at least for a moment. She rushed on, taking the advantage. "This land around here... The reason I stay is because it's got a fortune in gold inside it. Tons of it. Rich veins for the right folks to come along and take it. Listen... Wait," she said. "I'll show you," and she began rummaging in the drawer of a cabinet. She came to him arm extended, three nuggets the size of walnuts in her open palm. "See that and there's more where they came from." In her other hand, she held a vial of gold dust. "If I told what I knew, this place would be swarming," she said. "They thought it was all petered out. But I know where the Lost Diggings are."

"The Lost Diggings?" he said, trying to recall what he knew about them. Jack, he remembered. "That's what you could offer me?"

"There's a mountain. I know the way there. It's got a woman's face painted on the side. And then it's easy to find the canyon. It's all yours."

"How come you haven't let on?" he said.

"You got to have somebody you can trust," she said. "Me a woman here alone. There's folks do just as soon put a bullet through you as look at you. I figured I'd wait till I got the right partner." She stroked his arm, tried to lure him into her gaze. "Think of what the two of us could do together," she said, taking his hand. "All the riches. You could have anything you wanted." She made little circles in the palm of his hand. "This place could be a roaring town again. Good times a-plenty. Everything brought back to life. Liquor flowing, music and dancing." Her mind was filled with visions. "I'd go back on the boards," she said. "I was never so happy as when I was in the theater, all the men throwing me flowers and buying me drinks. I'd dance till the wee hours."

He thought of the cows' skulls hanging on the walls with the feathers in the eye sockets.

"You see," she said, grabbing his arm. "It's a chance to start over —do it right. You'd have the money get anything you want. Live like a king. Why you could be president if you wanted." Her hands kept weaving her fantasies, trying to tempt him, for she could see it all, believed it all.

"And how many others," he said, "have you made promises to?" He flung her away from him, went off to his room and shut the door. Outside, she pleaded, while he shucked off the clothes he'd been wearing and put the skins over him. "Hombre," he said, looking into the mirror, as though he might find him there, "I'll never betray you again."

When he opened the door, he couldn't bear to look at her face, pale, full of tears. "Tell me . . . tell me what to do," she wept. "Haven't I been good to you? Haven't I satisfied you? Only tell me what you want."

"I've been here too long," he said, taking her hand. "I've forgotten my life." And with her following, he went out to the stable to saddle up his horse.

"Where are you going?" Syd cried. "Tell me where."

"Anywhere the horse will go. Down there," he said, pointing to the ghost town.

"You'll never make it out alive," she said. "Nobody that goes there ever comes back. There's a bunch of varmints like you'll never see. And they don't cotton to strangers."

"Who said I ever wanted to come back?" he said. "I don't have to look for ten more ways of being useless."

"Don't go," she pleaded. "Isn't there a good life here? Haven't I pleased you all the times I've taken you inside me. Where's heaven if it's not there? Where else are you gonna get it? All the good food and liquor I've fed you. Haven't you had your pleasure? I gave you all."

He turned and looked at her and for a moment there was the lure of the old tenderness. "You gave me everything," he said. "It was good what you gave."

"Your friend's dead, and there's nothing left but the few good things that take you from one day to the next." She pressed up against him, rubbed against his side. "You and me," she said. "Think about that. Think about the softest thing that comes from forgetting."

He had almost forgotten. And he was torn by the powerful lure of forgetting altogether. "I've got to go," he said. "I owe it to him."

"You don't owe anything to the dead. It's the living that matter. That's all there is."

He had no argument, only something sharp as an arrow that pointed him into the distance.

"I don't know," he said. "I don't understand what's pushing and pulling. Suddenly I can't hold on."

"Gil," she cried. "Gil. Don't give your bones to the vultures."

He turned away, started to lead his horse out of the stable.

"You can't take him," she said. "He's not yours anymore."

"What do you mean?" he said.

"It's what you owe me for taking care of your miserable carcass." Her eyes were two fires, as though, if she couldn't have him, she meant to destroy him.

"All right," he said, as he started to walk out of the stable. "He's all yours."

"Go on then. Go kill yourself. I hope you die of thirst with the vultures picking over your bones." When she saw that he was determined to be on his way, she cried out, "Oh, take the miserable creature. I don't want him or you. But wait at least till I can give you some food to take with you. You've not even filled your canteen. All the water you'll find down there is full of alkali. Make you sick, and your horse. Best water him good before you go. "

Suddenly she was bustling about, alive with activity, seeing everything was done properly. And when, finally, she'd seen to it he had what he needed and was mounted on the horse's back, she looked at him as though he made her proud. "Well, you're the one," she said. "Guess your likes won't be passing this way again."

He gave her his thanks, turned and started on his way.

"Don't turn into the canyon on your left," she cautioned. "That's sure death."

XII. El Dorado Part 1

He passed through the settlement and took an old wagon route that stuttered into the bush and gave out. Like a ghost trail, it began fading into its downward curve past the red and yellow mine tailings, the mines carved out of the hills, one more testimony to abandoned effort. When he looked back, he saw only the outline of the buildings on the edge of the bluff. Then these, too, were gone, the nothing at his back equal to the nothing ahead of him. He may as well have lost sight and hearing, as he, loosed from where he came from, was swallowed into the wherever he might be going.

An inhospitable land had been chucked out ahead of him, mountains hurled up around him. The vegetation was sparse, a few patches in a flat barren stretch. Alkali desert. Disturbed with mine tailings and broken machinery strewn about: a history of things started and let go in this land where finally nothing having flourished, everything was left to rust and weather under the blazing sun.

He plodded on for hours without seeing a hawk or a rabbit, and then as it grew rocky underfoot, the sun-cracked land a web of hard metallic glints. The rocks he wove through were great heaps of slag, whitish yellow, pocked and cratered; then finally the low hills he entered, reddish from the iron in them, had been eroded into thick ropes, into monstrous claws.

I have come to a land of lostness.

The thought augured its way into the blankness of his mind— destitute of purpose, bleached of all but a harsh white light. What desperation must have beckoned anyone into these parts. He couldn't believe anything human had ever ventured here, even to look for gold, let alone a new beginning—that they'd prospected and sunk their shafts, struck up their tin-roofed shacks. Illusion— its blind machinery. And they'd offered their bones to it, to whiten in the sun. Wracked and broken. If anything was worse than death, this was it. Or was this what came to be when the veil of illusion was ripped from the eyes?

In the blank sky of his mind dream corpses floated, bony skeletons beckoned, wraiths and shapes that moaned and twisted themselves into the dust devils the wind picked up. Terror shook him. It leapt up at their grinning falseness, their luring one to this place, to the dry heaves of anguish.

"Hombre!" The cry was the sound of all lost illusions. And then it too died. Only this—when he might have been lying in Syd's arms, surrounded with welcome.

If only he might turn back to where she beckoned, to lose himself in her. This is what she'd tried to keep him from. This knowledge. Her effort to keep him dying into her soft flesh every day, moaning with pleasure. To think how he had swooned into that all-consuming luxury, dying to Hombre, to himself. What Hombre had brought to him, had made him into, had been broken into fragments. Syd, luring him into forgetfulness, had left him more hollow, more broken than before. He wanted to tear his hair, rend his flesh. If he could have known what lay in front of him . . . But he knew as the wind swirled round him, filled his mouth with dust, swept up his tracks, there was no going back. And there was nowhere to go except to wander this land of lostness.

Let me die, he pleaded, *since there is only death.*

He could only hunch up his shoulders and surrender to the wind. Whatever he tried to think back to was no longer real: he and Hombre together, a single force and purpose. Thrown against the violence that kept life from moving. Now, Hombre dead and purpose shattered, all the painted shapes evaporated. He was one more wraith among the skeletons that kept reaching toward him. His horse was frightened too, he could tell. And he felt a sudden pity for it—it hadn't asked to come, but only to lead the steady horse life it had been given. Did it wonder, too, if it was still among the living?

He dropped into fitful dozing as the horse plodded on, then woke as the land slid into nightmare: scaling white stone, huge

170

chunks of volcanic rock tilted after whole sides of mountains had split, heaved up and left chasms and jutting edges. Boulders thrown in chaos everywhere. And where once the water from sporadic rains had coursed through and down in falls and flashes, wearing away rocks, tearing away the land, it had left it all now to speak of one more mindless force. It was impossible even to believe in the notion of water. He had never passed through such sickening dryness. When he wet his lips from the canteen, the air drank up the moisture, thirsty too.

They passed through great shapes thrust up as though at the hand of some imagination heaving itself into myriad forms without knowing its own force. Some rose like reclining goddesses, forming the mountains around them. And others suggested camels and elephants and huge bison, massive sphinxes and reptiles, as though they were the remains of what once had been on the land. He moved among these and saw what looked like the ruins of ancient temples and fortresses from defunct civilizations. And to the bare horizon of his mind came barren words:

All dreams are blighted here where civilization falls on its knees. Nothing, nothing could ever live here. "Hombre!" he cried out again. The surrounding cliffs gave back the echo.

The heat made fiery arrows before his eyes. A red wavering band, dizzying. He shook his head, the pain in his flesh knifing him like the cruelty of stones; in his ears, a siren raising its pitch.

You're crazy. Even as he acknowledged the possibility, it began to unwind him. Time, bound in itself, would not move. As his horse plodded on wearily, he saw them—the shadows flitting along the ground. Whose ghosts? Shadows, circling shadows. Then he looked up and saw the vultures wheeling overhead. That's where he first knew them, in their shadows. Then there were more of them, drawn by the smell of death. What could their presence mean but that? The message had gone out to summon them. *They are the knowers. Death and evil they recognize, the scent you give out. Following always.*

The vultures wheeled above them for a time, keeping their

distance. Then they swooped down in casual circles as though to inspect horse and rider, to decide how much longer they had to wait for dinner. They were patient—it would come; first a line had to be crossed into their domain. He saw their hooded lids, their red eyes, their waiting beaks. They would dip those beaks into his eyes, long past seeing, into the eyes of his poor horse—what comes to those who think they can bend the world to their own shape. He could see it in the stricken sky of his mind now riddled with vultures.

Child. That's what a woman's arms are for—to hold you against all this. Now see what the mind can do,

"Let everything come." He yelled out to the insinuating voice.

Shapes swam in front of his eyes, in the heaving scape of his mind. He saw them, swam among them, the shapes of the mountains, goddesses and dinosaurs, the sun boring into him, the animals taking up battle with tusks and horns, their battle cries lost in the clash. It was all shadow and fire. He was filled with the dust of all dust and dryness, and his stomach heaved. He would stop and surrender, give his meat to the vultures. He reined up in the shelter of one of the white crumbling cliffs, where the shadow could at least give him shade and sank into sleep. There was no peace.

No place for pause or respite among the barren hills. No lizard moved, nor fly; no instinct, nor the gleam of prophecy. Only blind machinery working over the land, huge spidery arms reaching out and plucking up mountains, rearranging stars, lifting hot molten lead from the center of the earth. Tentacles shaping great forts in the desert, sucking up the dust, while ore trains roared across the land—some flying out into space. When he woke it was blank and silent. Perhaps the stillness woke him, for even the wind had died. No sound anywhere.

This is where I watched him come. Perhaps I knew all along, even before I set out to discover where his life had taken him. Sitting there in the town with only the banality of the ordinary, its curse. I followed him here into the torment, the way it took him farther and deeper. This was the experience he was taking me into, though I resisted with all my claws. Yet all the time he was leading

172

me there, I knew I couldn't avoid it. Into the blind machine. It is the despair of having no experience of your own that forces you to go: it's being set adrift in your own century, being mocked and teased by what you don't have that takes you there. To that point of the deepest dark. When you, in spite of yourself, have awakened from the common dream.

He had to shake himself awake. He must have slept, he realized, and now just as he stepped back into waking, sparks, bits of color danced before his eyes. Rays of intermingling lights, shifting colors, becoming . . . He couldn't believe what he was seeing: trees full of fruit—jewels, gleaming red, purple, yellow—all in a green space filled with game. He saw a game trail that led up the canyon where the elk and deer moved up to water at a pool created above them by a falls. He saw wild turkey and quail and mountain goats. A land where the desert stopped suddenly and the grass was never so tall and lush, and in its midst, streams of water flowed; cedars and pines sprang up alongside. And beyond the canyons and into the valley, a city of red-tiled roofs and handsome adobe dwellings, with peacocks wandering through, opening their eye–decorated fans. In all directions tilled fields, the presence of wheat and barley. He turned toward the pool to refresh himself and his horse, but was held back, and the vision disappeared.

You can't go there; it's not time yet.

Then the wind was back and the dust was in his eyes.

You find yourself alive, he thought, and you have to live, even in a land of death. It was absurd, and he had to laugh. "You might as well laugh too," he told the horse. "Nothing like a good horse laugh." He patted the creature on the neck. It was a good beast, there not by any choice of its own, making the best of things. They were together, he in his skins, the horse in his hide—two animals joined together. He got back on his horse, and as he rode, he saw the vultures leave him one by one. Dead or alive—and where was he?

Before he recognized it, it was there in front of him, the town he'd seen from Syd's place. A ramshackle affair, partly adobe and

173

partly timber. The stuccoed buildings were dingy, streaked yellow from the wash of rain, and in some places the outer layer had broken through to reveal the straw-flecked bricks beneath. The wooden buildings had weathered silver. As he rode into town, a sign nearly blown over by the wind announced that he was entering *El Dorado*. Though no life appeared in any of the other buildings, the air was full of noise ripping out from the *Centennial Saloon*. Light flowed out over the swinging doors, and the piano was going full tilt, drowning the roar of voices in its rhythm. He pulled up the reins, sat for a moment, trying to put himself together and gather his sanity from the din, then got off his horse, and staggered inside. The music stopped suddenly, the voices fell to silence, and those gathered looked at him, a stranger, a wild man in animal skins, while he looked at the strangest company he'd seen in a long time. A gang of ruffians was his first thought. A murmur rose around him, "How come he's here?" "Some loco..." "Who let him come?"

A slight movement above him and he looked up to see two men hanging from the ceiling, ropes around their necks.

Someone laughed. "Impressed by the decor, ain't you?"

"Oh, don't mind Bill," another said. "Bragging all the time he was a Roosian count—till we got sick of him. Hanged one for a horse thief, the other for being a plain, damned nuisance."

"We keep them up there for entertainment."

Bill tried to bend his neck toward him, "My poor mother," he said. "Grieving over me. At least it's better up here than down there. I can watch anything that's going on—the whole shebang. A little excitement now and then."

"Let's hang him up, too," a voice at the back called out. "He's got no business here," another added. "Don't you know better than to come poking round where you don't belong?". . . "How d-d-did he get here anyway?" a short stocky fellow said, as he leaned against the bar.

"Beats me," said the bartender. "Ain't nobody can pass though that desert."

"Well, he's done it, by gee and by golly," a deep-voiced fellow sang out. "By dumb luck, the dumb cluck. May as well buy him a drink."

There was a murmur of agreement among two or three. Gil's eyes went from one to the other, as he tried to figure out his chances at least for getting a drink in this strange, mostly hostile company.

"Come on, fellow, name your poison—the General here, name of Crook, is going to stand you one. But all we got is whiskey. Three grades but it all comes from the same barrel."

Gil tried to locate his benefactor and settled on a tall, broad-shouldered man, built like himself, with a handsome beard, much more presentable than most of the others. The General looked his way, gave him a brief smile.

A small gnome-like fellow, bent over, with a beard that reached past his knees, cocked an eye up at him and said. "Must be you're plumb wore out getting here across them salt flats. Betcha you need a little help getting your tongue unstuck from the roof of your mouth. I've known some thirsty times myself. A little hospitality . . .

"I'll get the next round." He called to the bartender, who, assailed on all sides for drinks, ignored him.

"Shake a leg. Come on—a little entertainment," one of the men back by the piano yelled. "Let's have some music, I say. This place is going dead."

Everybody laughed. "Where you been for the last century?" A roar of laughter.

"Here's your poison," the bartender said to Gil, pouring him a generous slug, then adjusting his wig.

The General came up alongside him. "The best we can offer. I've drunk better in my time, believe me. It's going to be a long night."

Gil took his drink, his eye following a long scar that began at the jaw and continued down the bartender's neck like a fork of lightning. The bartender noticed his stare.

"Indians—them's what got me. Stabbed me with hunting knives and scalped me." He lifted his wig. "See—bald as a egg. The General here, he was the one defeated the varmits."

"That'll teach you," somebody yelled, "getting caught by them

175

red devils. I wouldn't take no Indian's scalp. I'd take his head—nail it up there on the wall. See that over there. "

He pointed to a painting that hung across the room. "General Custer hisself. All that yellow hair—the handsomest man alive. Killed him right after Independence Day." That general stood at the center of the picture, holding his hand to his chest, as though he were to deliver a speech to the viewer. A ring of Indians, teeth bared, faces lit in the flare of torches, danced around him.

"A fine thing for this nation," a red-faced man shouted out. "A bunch of them savages..."

"Kill 'em all," someone yelled.

The General, who was putting out money for their drinks, gave him a little wry smile. "Yes, I fought them. My duty. But I knew them too, wanted to..."

He was interrupted by the fellow standing on the other side of Gil. "You ever think you're going to accomplish anything in this life? Look at this." He opened his collar to show Gil a bullet wound just over the heart. "I was trying to bring a little law and order to a piece of Montana. Only for some folks that don't fit into the scheme of things. Ever try to give a fair deal to the Indians?"

A chorus of voices rose: "Bring on the entertainment."

The woman at the piano, a bare-armed woman in a gown of crushed purple velvet, yelled out hoarsely, "All this damned commotion! What d'ya think I'm doing here, milking the cow?"

"Might as well be, considering that noise you're pounding out."

"Doesn't sound any better than a cow neither."

She seized hold the lamp illuminating her music and threatened to throw it in the direction of the offending voice.

Gil took a sip of the whiskey, the inside of his mouth burning, and then his throat as it went down. He wondered if they'd distilled the alkali. Maybe that's what you needed to be in the place.

"Come on, Madge, can't you take a little joke?"

"Where are the gals? We want the gals."

"Upstairs primping."

Again a chorus. "Bring on the whiskey and the women. Bring on the whiskey and . . . Bring them on." The men were pounding the counter of the bar. "Bring on . . . Bring on the women."

"Who wants to drink this rotgut?" a voice yelled out.

The chorus grew louder, more insistent. "Bring them on, bring oh bring on the... on the whiskey and the women."

"They know better than to come down when you're here, Hank Magruder," Madge said.

"Yeah, well they need a man to let 'em know what a good time is. None of your pissant little . . ."

"How'd you like a taste of my fist?" A man with a red nose and rheumy eyes held up a large fist.

The air was thick with cigar smoke, the atmosphere choked with old grudges and accusations, very likely excited by the whiskey. Gil looked around. If these beings were dead, they'd certainly carried their past with them. Perhaps that's why they could still drink whiskey. Not knowing what he should do, he looked over at his companion, who took his arm and guided him toward a table in a corner at the back. "Maybe you'd like a little distance from the uproar," the General said. They'd forgotten all about him, it seemed—which was something of a relief. He preferred not to be in the middle of the fight he felt brewing.

"Don't worry," his companion said. "This is all they are; what we were is all we can be. We gather a little excitement from it." He indicated a couple of men who were engaged in a shouting match.

"You lowdown rustler—slitting the tongues of the calves you stole. What could they do but die there out on the range?"

"And what did you do but cheat the Indians, sell 'em booze and set 'em on the warpath." Both drew guns and shot, while the others went on with their drinking. The two fell to the floor, were pulled outside by their feet.

"Another drink? How about another round?" The General signaled the bartender.

"Coming Round the Mountain," a voice yelled. "Play that one, Madge," someone else suggested. "C'mon, Madge, be a sport."

"All right, quiet down." Madge yelled as she replaced the lamp, she'd been holding, seated herself with an elaborate shifting of skirts and launched into the tune. A chorus of voices sodden with drink began to sing along.

The tune swirled in Gil's head, the chorus sung by the cow skulls on the wall at Syd's place. "Who's coming round the mountain?" Gil demanded, pushing back his chair and going back to the bar. He began to thump the glass on the bar for another drink.

"Careful, young fellow," an old man cautioned him. "You're here by our sufferance. We don't take kindly to strangers. And if I was you, wouldn't get too big for your britches."

"Ain't nobody coming round the mountains, friend," an insinuating voice murmured in his ear. "But it's right nice to think of some golden gal—like her."

Soft Voice extended his arm, pointing toward the back wall, and Gil found himself confronted by a large gilt-framed painting that had escaped his notice. A woman who reminded him a little of Syd lay naked on a bear rug, beckoning to a man. Her coral lips were parted, the corners lifted in a little half-mocking smile, as though she knew she possessed what her admirer couldn't resist. And the parrot in the cage where her fingers lightly touched the wires also knew, and so did the little pug dog wagging its tail at her feet. They were all in on it. The parrot viewed the scene from its perch as though it sat far above the unfolding folly. For the man nothing else existed. His eyes were riveted on the woman, as if he were in a trance.

"I lost my voice when they hanged me," Soft Voice said. "Now I can speak to a woman like that one up there, all the words to lure them to my bed. I've learned the trick of it."

"You got no more come-hither than a railroad spike, Tim Moore. Did you think your gold would buy a woman? You never got enough for that."

"Nor you neither, Rabbit-face." The two men launched into an argument about their relative means and talents in the drama of seduction. "She's for sale like everybody else. Only things worth having are the ones you can buy. And that goes for the female of the species."

"See you like our art work," the bartender said, pouring Gil another whiskey.

"Adam and Eve in the garden," Rabbit-face said.

"All grown up in weeds," the bartender responded.

"Only maybe it never existed," Gil said.

"This here is out in the world," Rabbit-face said. "And she knows she's got him where she wants him."

"Bring on the entertainment," somebody yelled over the noise of the piano.

He saw Madge rise up again as if she were on a spring. And he had the impression that everything that was happening kept on happening in an endless repetition. He put a hand to his throbbing head.

"If I'd been able to work my claim, I'd have had me a woman like that," Soft Voice said.

"You're dreaming," the bartender told him, leaning on the bar. "You'd drink it all up in whiskey first."

Soft Voice turned his back to Gil. "Look-it here," he said. "You see them two bullet holes. A couple of snakes in the grass followed me out to my claim and shot me on my way back to town. That's what they done. I took a different route every time, only my partner—he was the one. Betrayed me. That's him grinning over there. He got his too. I'd found them too, the Lost Diggings."

"Listen to him, shot and hanged both. Naw—often shot, but never hung," the bartender said.

We'll all go to meet her when she comes.

A tall rangy cowhand gave Soft Voice a poke in the ribs. "Everybody's found the Lost Diggings, every flea-bitten, starve-bellied, son of a whore who can let out a fart has claimed 'em. Pretty soon old McConeghy himself will come romping in."

As though he had prior knowledge, the door flew open and a man buck naked half fell into the room, clutching a leather bag to his chest. "Hey this ain't no sight for the ladies. Cover him up."

"That whore? Hell, she ain't no lady. Nobody's wife neither."

Before the lady in question could clout someone with her lamp, somebody found a horse blanket for the naked one to wrap himself in.

"It's only McConeghy," someone said.

"Let's get on with the entertainment. Here they come."

There was a roar and a clap of hands as the girls came down the stairs singing,

We'll be coming round the mountain when we come.

They pulled up their skirts, flounced them back and forth, revealing their legs among their lacy petticoats and descended the stairs, mingling with the men, clinging to them, their arms around their shoulders, demanding drinks. The bartender entered into a sudden flurry of activity, a dozen hands reaching in his direction. The drinks were served, the air made boozy, filled with noise and raucous laughter. McConeghy was forgotten as he sat shivering in his blanket, his hair falling over his face.

"Who is this fellow?" Gil said.

"C'mon," Soft Voice said, drawing Gil to the table where the fellow sat, still clutching his bag.

"Where you been, McConeghy?"

McConeghy looked wildly around him. "Gold," he said. "More than you'll ever see—even in your wildest dreams."

"Where'd you find it?"

You gotta go by the mountain with the woman's face painted on it. Then you follow the game trail up into the canyon. I got there," he said breathlessly. "I got the gold, all what's in this bag." He looked around wildly. "They came after me. "

"What happened, McConeghy?"

"It was the Injuns. Cochise and his devils. They set upon me, sent their arrows streaming after me. I hid under a boulder. Then the storm broke—lightning all around, like to kill a man. I snuck up the canyon. But see, this is where they hit me in the foot with a lance."

"You're dreaming again, McConeghy."

"I got to get back. It's the Lost Diggings. I found them, dagonnit."

"Everybody's found them and lost them again. Snively's diggings and the Nigger diggings—yes, a slave they put in the army—he found them, too. Everybody's found them. Even the Indians got some of them nuggets. They knew where it was."

"Glad to kill anybody they could trap there. Come on now, show us what's in that bag."

"You'll steal my gold."

"Nobody's gonna steal it."

"It's a fortune right here."

McConeghy opened the sack and poured out the contents, but Gil could see nothing. "What is this place?" Gil demanded.

"It's the place where everybody died of their life," the bartender said. "Lured by the dream. Saying a man could get whatever he wanted. Cross the ocean, cross the continent and you'll find it. Never mind all who got struck down on the way—lost, lost to the dream. Never mind any of them."

"And Hombre? Where's he? I've come all across this land looking for him."

"He hasn't come this way, friend. No sign of him, whoever he is."

"Where would I find him then?"

"It wouldn't do any good. You got to go back where you came from."

"I'll never leave this place till I find him," Gil cried, pounding the table.

There was a sudden silence, as the voices stilled and the notes from the piano fumbled to a halt.

"You got to leave, friend. This isn't your place. You got flesh on your bones. We're suffering you to stay for a drink or two, maybe sleep the night, but then you got to vamoose."

"No, I won't leave."

"You'd better call Tom. Otherwise there'll be hell to pay. . . . Why'd we ever let him in. Call Tom."

"Nah, just throw him out—we're missing the entertainment."

"Never should have let him in."

"It's against the rules. Against nature. Call Tom—it's an emergency."

"What kind of ingrate are you?" the bartended challenged Gil. "Do you a favor and you want to hog the show."

"Look fellow, I was a soldier at Glorieta. The fight at Glorietta Pass. Just an ordinary foot soldier—mustered out at twelve dollars a month. I'd rather shoe horses all my life than carouse every night in this hell hole. Better go get Tom—he'll set things straight."

The air was full of dull, angry muttering. And Gil found it full of threat.

Then a figure strode through the door who took everyone's attention. Gil stared at him, his heart taken in a strange grip of anguish. "So you've come, his father said, "come all this long way. So far for so little."

XII. El Dorado Part 2

His father: and he was that small boy watching him being sucked into the flood, the piano, his chosen hearse bobbing away in the distance. And now his grown man's terror whelmed like the waters, heaved and swelled, and lived in him again. He fell to his knees, unstrung. A murmur rose around him that bore more of consternation than sympathy, with inter-weavings o f conjecture: "What's a matter, can't the damned fool hold his liquor?". . . "That boy's got no more moxy than a tin can if he can't hold it better'n that . . ." "It's Tom's coming on him so sudden what's unsettled him. He's got a face that would terrorize an Apache..." "All from his being English, I'll warrant . . ." "But the Scots are devils the worse. Prob'ly from all the oatmeal and haggis they eat. Enough to terrorize any man."

His father there before him, who did not exist except in a memory that had followed him all down the years, more compelling in its reality as the one who inspired it became more unreal. There now to complete his loss, the father of loss. And what was he now, this figure who stood beyond life, this face struck from out of the void, this voice speaking? The bartender broke the spell: "Tom, give this boy a drink. You've done given him the wheemies."

"Come on, lad, it's not that I don't mind seeing you," Tom Weston said, helping his son to his feet. "But you don't know what you've come to."

"What place is this?" Gil said, looking to his father for answers. "Who are all these?"

"Come off a little way then," his father said, "if your curiosity has got the better of you. Let's sit over here now we're together, get acquainted in this little space we have allotted to us."

Those gathered, now increased by a flood of new arrivals, the level of noise and laughter filling out the corners, stood aside and made a little path for them through the crowd. They took their drinks and went to sit quietly at a table in the corner, where they were soon ignored. Madge at the piano took up where she'd left off and launched into a bawdy song,

There once was an Indian maid
Who said she wasn't afraid
To lie on her back in a tumbledown shack
And let some cowboy . . .

the men finishing the line in raucous chorus. The revelry continued .

"Tell me now," Gil said, "where I've come to."

"It's all like they said. No more or less. We're brought here by whatever fancy led us by the nose."

"You too?"

"Afraid so," He gave a wry smile, "but only a few of us can see it." He revolved his glass in his hands. "I was brought by a piano. Now I'm something of an official—here they so appreciated the joke, they put me in charge. 'We got a piano here too,' they boasted—'you'll feel right at home.' It fits my deserts, if you don't mind my saying so. Lured by one of the grander Illusions. Going to make my little mark on the wilderness." He looked at Gil as though he was trying to read something from his face. "Entering a whole new era. When I went back East for the Exposition of '93—crossed the country by rail— you could still see a few Indians roaming, look out at them from the windows. In Chicago, I saw such mighty things. Whole corridors of sewing machines, and reapers and grand equipment. From the factories springing up all around. And there I was—on the outposts of the frontier, to make way for it all. Bringer of hospitality. Good food and wine. The blandishments of music. Mozart in the dining room. Public lectures and uplifting experiences for a town of wild men and run-down whores. That piano was the acme of everything I dreamed of, there in Weston House. Ah yes." He tapped the table with his glass. "Without the sense to save my hide. All swept away in the flood. Like everything else," he said, with a snap of the fingers. "Everything you put up, thinking it's going to last . . . At least I've left you behind to carry on."

184

Gil shook his head. "I've had enough. People robbing and cheating the Indians and each other, murdering to get what they can seize. The law worse than those breaking it."

"See that man over there, sitting alone, just under *Custer's Last Stand?*"

Gil turned to look at his former companion, now a solitary figure brooding over his glass.

"You'll see him there every night. The General did his duty, old Gray Wolf—the Indians respected him too. But he got no thanks for it—ended up being betrayed by everybody. By Washington and by Geronimo. Yes, they sent all the Apaches off to die, even the Indian scouts who'd helped the General. Civilization for you. He spent his last days pleading their cause."

Gil observed him closely. "It sounds like I belong here too, with Hombre. How come he's not here?"

His father grew formal. "I'm afraid I'm not at liberty to discuss the rules governing this place. Don't know or understand them all myself. They put me in charge here, an honor, if you can it call that. But it's more trouble than it's worth."

"But you've got to satisfy me. I've come all this way. I've killed a man and it's my fault my friend is dead."

"Hold on," his father protested. "I don't know what you're asking for—it's beyond my sphere. But tell me about this fellow you killed. We got some rumors out here. Some Cameron fellow. Sent a bunch of homesteaders this way. One or two at a time, grieving over the injustice."

"I killed him. He was a threat to the town—to my mother."

"Well, so that's what you undertook? Did him in, eh? Can't say I blame you. We're always the last to get the news. Slower than by mule back in these parts. And then you can't always trust it."

Gil thought his father was trying to distract him and regarded him narrowly during his silence.

"So that's what you took on," he said, still considering it. "Well?"

"I was full of justification." He had to pause. "Only one who was innocent died too—I can say his death is on my hands."

"A great pity. I've heard such stories," Tom Weston said. "At least you took something on. I speak for myself. It is less than nothing to die in a flood. Used to be a flood was a big thing. A whole pile of animals saved on an ark, the waters covering up the mountains— while God tried to make up his mind whether or not to destroy the whole works. Would have left a big emptiness. Lonely. No one around. No eye to meet the mountains or the first star of the evening. Something would be missing. So it was a new beginning— the rainbow in the sky. Go forth and all that." His father gave a wave of the hand. "Only now, what are men and gods?" He shrugged. "But at least you are a son after my own heart."

"Death is the only doorway left for me. Nothing else is real."

"Don't be a fool—just look around. What's real in any of this? From this place Death gives nothing back."

Gil said nothing.

"Death enters so that life can come through—as through a doorway. You think it's only about death. But there was already a dying in the things that stood."

"Don't try to slick things over," Gil said testily, "with your philosophizing." I'm tired of ideas dreamt up by those who haven't anything better to do. What can you offer me? Even the liquor here is rot-gut. Hombre was blameless—it's my fault he's gone. What about that? Why isn't he here? I've come a long way. So now give that grief an answer, something more than memory to wed it to the flesh, a loss . . . . Bring him back."

"Another drink!" his father, half standing, yelled to the bartender

What was his father trying to do but squeeze something out of his despair, his boredom?—his words were like wood. Gil glared at him—this shadow. One more in the whole collection. Whereas Cameron Jack hung over his life and left his shadow behind like a weight, his father was the shadow of an emptiness. And Hombre was a hole where life had been.

"We feel things in the organs of our pain," his father said, as though it was all he could come up with, "—the heart breaking so that we can be consecrated to memory, even as you remember me, put fragments of my name back together. So I live in you—"

"I want more than that," Gil protested, his voice rising. "If that's all there is, I want to stay here."

"It's not allowed. It's a piece of error you got here in the first place. Things muddling along. Worse than England. The living aren't supposed to consort with the dead. There are rules about these things."

"So what am I supposed to do, if you can't give me back what I lost. Here, then take this knife . . ." He rose up.

"Be on your way," his father ordered, rising up as well. "I'm just trying to do right by you, give you a little fatherly wisdom and advice. I didn't have the chance before, and now I'm out of practice. But you'll goad me beyond all patience. Sons are supposed to listen to their elders. What's the world coming to? Who do you think you are, throwing yourself against the world, trying to storm your way through? Turning the world on its ear just to satisfy your suffering— as if you were the only one."

"Please," Gil said. "Just put me out of my misery."

And now once again the company paused in its pursuit of pleasure and began to take an interest in the altercation. A low commentary went round. 'Throw him out, I say. Nothing but trouble since he barged in . . ." "Tom's son, is he . . . ? Sucking up and demanding favors . . ." "I hate them kind of shenanigans—using your kin to get you someplace. . . ."

"Bring him up here," the hanged horse thief roared once more. "We could do with a little company." "What's so damned wonderful about being here anyhow?" the Russian countered

Madge had left the piano and come over to Tom's side. "Do something for him, Tom," she said, taking his hand. "He's your own and he's come such a long way—" Her gaze went to Gil, as his father stood in his impatience.

"Believe me, if he'd been around when I was in my prime . . ."

"You got yours, didn't you, Mag?" Soft Voice said, jutting his face toward hers. "Bet you had all such likely young fellows squeezing your—"

"Hold your tongue, you scum. You got no respect and no decency." She sent the speaker reeling before she turned back to Tom Weston. "Don't send him away empty-handed."

"Since when have you become such sugar? If you're so sweet on him . . ." She gave his father a winning look.

"Well since you're so set on it . . . You know I can't refuse you anything. " Turning to Gil— "Tell you what, if you can outlast me in a drinking competition, you can stay."

"How about that?" said the horse thief strung up on the ceiling.

"You mean something interesting's gonna happen?..."

"What'd you want to bet?" someone said.

"How about my place up here?" the hanged man said. "You get to see everything . . . ?" "Wait a minute. It's my turn to come down," his partner, Bill, objected.

"I'll warn you though," Tom Weston said, "nobody's beaten me yet. Some have been all hot to take me on the moment they arrive. They insist on it. And all they have to show for it is the rottenest hangover you can imagine."

Meanwhile various bets were being placed all around. "Bring out the glasses. This'll be the champion drinking bout . . ." "Ain't never had a son pitted against a father before—that should add a little piss and vinegar to the competition."

"I'm setting up the first round," the bartender announced. A stocky man in flannel shirt and suspenders laid several silver dollars on the bar and drew further comment from the ceiling: "Look at that, will you. Never thought I'd see the day . . ." "Well, you old tight fist. Must be something if you're going to put out."

Interest kept rising. "Always wanted to see somebody drink old Weston under the table . . ." "That one can hold it, I'll bet. Can't even tell he's been drinking." "Bring out the red eye. Bring on the poison. C'mon everybody."

The bartender poured out the first round and everybody took down a slug. "Ever tell you about the time I get drunk in Dodge City," a man in a battered Stetson, torn by a bullet hole, said. "Me and Nelson took up a bunch of cattle and decided to shoot up the town . . ."

"He's told that one a hundred times," Bill yelled down. No one paid attention.

"We came roaring in fit to kill, guns a-blazing. And there was a little fat gal on the street. First she just backed up against the wall, then when we come back along the main street, she seen a empty barrel and jumped right in, her legs kicking in the air. I tell you it was a sight."

"I'll bet you made that up. You were too drunk to...," Bill's partner yelled down.

"Only then she couldn't get out—they had to break open the barrel. "

"I don't believe a word of it."

"Only she was sweet, that gal. I went up to her and said, 'Ma'am it waren't my aim to frighten you all to pieces. Me and the boys was just having a little fun.' Well, I took her over to the dance hall and she was as light as a feather on her feet... And the sweetest kisser. I've never known anybody could kiss that sweet..."

"I don't believe a word of it, Sam Abernathy. You lie like a snake. And crawl like one too. Anybody ever put a pistol in your face, you'd piss your pants."

Gil drank down his whiskey, and he and his father signaled for another. His head seemed to be detaching from his body one moment and his arm reaching as far as the wall in another. He seemed to be looking inside himself, to be seeing his various organs and veins and arteries; to be seeing inside his head, to be looking into his own eye.

Do you want to know what history is?" a voice hissed in his ear. "It's the narrow curve of the quotidian, shaped by your understanding I. All the stuff in it. And you're standing in the middle of it all. So you want to reach back into the whirl of atoms, do you? Haul out a new universe? Get past the snake in the garden?

Gil hardly knew if the voice was in his head or somewhere beyond him.

"Drunkenness has saved a man or two," someone broke in behind him. "Saved me from being sober—that's something."

"Come on, raise your glass. Things are lagging. How many is that? Serve up another round."

"I tell you, drunkenness saved me and my partner."

"Spill it out. Here comes another stretcher."

"We was out working our diggings, and it was getting colder'n a bear's ass. So we took our jug and warmed us up a little. Sang a ditty or two and took another round. Then all on a sudden, we was looking straight into the eyes of Victorio and some of his braves. They'd rode right up when we waren't looking. Well, his braves had their tomahawks out and was headed right for us. But Victorio said, "No leave 'em be. Drunkenness is the scourge of the white man."

"They left you alive?—ain't that something now. Left you alone to do yourselves in. What a joke."

"They might as well have taken my scalp. Not two days later, that ornery son-of-a-bitch I trusted for my partner took a knife to my back. He was going to have all the paystreak from those diggings."

The words began to din in Gil's ears as he watched his father take down another glass. *You want to know what history is?* the voice teased him again.

Jack reaching up out of the urges of his flesh to make his fate. And you trying to reach beyond into the unseen, the whirling matter of light and stars. Making your fate from an idea. What else is the vision of heaven and hell? Dividing things in two. Entering Chaos that—"

"What's the matter, you hearing too many voices?"

His father's face seemed to be melting before his eyes. "What's happening?" . . .

"It's too much for one mortal brain—all the voices from here to eternity. All the human sounds filling up the ether, all that's ever been spoken, still vibrating in the air—if your ear were tuned fine enough to hear it. I had an interest in science myself when the blood was beating in my veins. My ears are tuned differently now, and I listen for the faintest sounds . . ."

"I can hardly hear you," Gil said, in a panic. "What's happening to me?"

His father looked at him compassionately. "We've reached the shank of the evening, son. When you come again, perhaps you'll listen too, trying for other sounds than these. Sounds to ravish the ear. The ancients spoke of the music of the spheres, a higher harmony. Nights I go out to one of those mountains the Indians call sacred and give my ear to any ghostly sound that might strike a ghostly ear." He signaled to the bartender. "I think another round might do it—I'm just getting into my stride."

Gil, not to be outdone, took his down immediately. "Another one," he said.

"The boy's got stamina, I'll grant you. You sired a good 'un, Tom. Drink to that. They don't make 'em that way very often. A rare privilege having you in our midst, " Madge told him.

The bartender poured everyone a round. "A toast," Madge said. "May you survive. Oh, I can see you .. " she said, wiping away a tear.

"Going all blubbery on us? Sing us one of your songs, a tender ballad," came from the ceiling.

Madge moved to where all could see her:

Cursed be all your silver
And cursed be all your gold
Cursed be the men whose love's untrue
And love that's bought and sold

"Can't say that's exactly tender."

"Tender as I'm gonna get, roughneck. Come on, hon,"she said, going back up to Gil, taking his arm. "I hate to let go of the likes of you. A man I could fix my admiration on—that's what." And from around her neck she undid the ribbon of the cameo she was wearing and tied it to one of the thongs of Gil's puma skin. "My parting gift," she said with a rush of sentiment. "Belonged to my mother."

"Wait, Gil said, turning back toward his father, who wavered and swam before his eyes. "Another drink—he's getting ahead of me."

"You've done your best," she said, sadly. "Only 'tisn't in the nature of things. Life is all a father can give you. The rest you have to scrape for on your own."

"It wasn't fair," Gil cried. "It wasn't a fair contest. And Hombre's gone and . . ."

"Nothing's fair," she said, brushing back a stray lock of hair from his forehead, "But you'll do all right. Your horse is waiting for you."

"Hold on," he insisted. "There s nowhere I can go. Let me have another drink."

"You lose," a chorus of voices sang out. "The competition's over."

He didn't know what happened then. Smoke filled the air, acrid and choking, as if ore had been smelted, and his head came to pieces. He staggered out the door of the saloon and fell into oblivion. When he woke again on a spot of ground in the middle of nowhere, it was broad daylight. Great clouds sailed over him. High mountains surrounded him. His horse was standing patiently beside him.

XIII. Onward

Nothing. Nothing but cactus and joshua trees, clumps of mesquite and scrub cedar covering the land between himself and the mountains. In all directions, nothing. The town, the saloon had vanished as surely as if they'd never been—a mirage—and he was left there, his horse beside him, pulling at the thin grass. "It's you and me, pal," he said, "and not much of either of us after what we've been through." His eye was caught by the brooch Madge had given him, the cameo from which a woman looked out tenderly. He clasped it in his hand, wondering how this token had come with him. But as he looked at it, it dissolved with a little poof before his eyes.

He took out his poncho and put it on, for though the sun shone direct and clear, the air was chill. He climbed onto the horse. Where to now? All four directions looked to be alike. He prompted the horse simply to go ahead, and they plodded off across the land. "Poor old beast," he told the animal. "I've not done well by you. If a grizzly doesn't get us, thirst will. Two carcasses for the buzzards to pick at."

He could barely stay awake as they moved through the brush, what with the sun beating down, the hangover from the night's debauch, and the sheer confusion of his mind. They moved into the distance that receded like a mirage itself until he began to perceive a clearer outline of the mountains on the horizon. He tried to focus on the images his muddled brain kept sending his way. Unreal. Hombre—Cameron Jack—his mother, who'd wept over him—Hyppolyta and Syd, in whose arms he had taken refuge. And now his father, who had been an absence. These visited and tormented him—all ghosts, whether they'd been in the world or not What were they? He tried to bring them back with whatever he could summon of love or hate. For a little while, atop the motion of the trotting horse, he thought hate might prove the stronger, with all its mad obsessions.

His mind kept delivering up the man he'd killed. The more he tried to resist, the more some new image presented itself. But the parts wouldn't come together to make a single human being. The one Jack kept fracturing into a dozen men, or else he kept slipping away like smoke. All the Jacks: more than the jacks in a deck of cards and all the jokers thrown in. The jack of all deals and trades. Jackpot Jack. He'd have to spend the rest of his life killing him, it seemed, and the rest trying to bring Hombre back to life. Nothing to hold onto—what was his experience? It seemed to exist only when those in question were there to summon it.

Then his father, who could offer him only tired platitudes. Yet powerful enough to deal him the final blow of defeat. They should have let him stay in the saloon, to carry on the competition for all eternity. Lose themselves in it. Better than wandering on his long-suffering horse, still without means or purpose.

Now his only thought became the thirst that overtook him. He wanted to laugh. He'd be joining the rest of them soon enough, once the sun had parched him dry.

He moistened his lips with the last drops from the canteen, found a bit of biscuit Syd had packed for him in the saddlebag but didn't eat it. It would dry out his mouth. The day slipped away as they began to climb into the hilly country they had reached, gradually ascending into the mountains. The late afternoon grew gauzy with pink clouds, and began to dim around them as they came into high pine country. He started looking for a place to spend the night before darkness overtook them. And when he paused, he could hear the sound of water traveling over rocks. His horse pricked up its ears and strained forward to a creek where both could drink. He filled his canteen.

After they'd had their fill, he tied up his horse where it might graze while he set about making himself a shelter for the night. Back among the trees, he piled up pine needles to put between himself and ground, then threw his saddle blanket over them. He was in the midst of chopping some branches from a fallen tree, both for his shelter and for his fire that night, when a scream came from his horse. Axe in hand he ran to it, saw that a mountain lion had seized its throat, taken it to the ground. The lion turned on him as soon as it saw the threat to its prey. Gil smashed it across the head with his ax as it leapt. It was dazed, but before it could leap again, he struck it on the head. And again.

A little life still flickered in the horse. Gil went for his gun and put him out of his misery. "You've been unfortunate, my friend," he said, with a sense of its sacrifice and his betrayal. "You should have had a better fate." Tears sprang to his eyes.

The horse, he realized ruefully, had saved him from his hunger— it might have come to that if he wanted to live—killing his horse for food. The thought appalled him. But now he cut out pieces of the haunches to roast over the fire. Then he left it, moving out of the range of other animals that might be attracted to the carcass. It was dark by the time he'd made shelter for himself and built a fire. That night his belly was full.

He sank into sleep like a stone. Weary to the bone marrow, he slept without thought and could not remember dreaming. Towards morning it began to snow, the cold finally waking him. When he woke, he walked back to the carcass, found it stripped down to the hide. He cut pieces of the hide to wrap around his feet and dried them by the fire. With his knife he made thongs to put through slits and tied them around his feet. Awkward moccasins, but better than the snow and the bare ground. Then he threw the saddle blanket over his shoulders, took his saddle bags and axe and worked his way through the woods, looking for a cave in the rocks where he could take refuge. When finally he found one, entering carefully to make sure no bear would come at him, he gathered wood and built a fire.

He did not move except to gather wood, fill his canteen and relieve himself. There was nowhere to go, and if he rationed it out, he had meat to eat. Most of the time he slept, woke, and drank a little water. One day flowed one into the next, and he didn't keep track of how long he slept. One morning when he left the cave to search for wood, he found new tracks in the snow that did not belong to deer, bear, mountain lion or coyote. A man's footprints.

Despite all the distance he had traveled to this wild remote place, yet someone had gotten there ahead of him. Perhaps he should not have been surprised. Here, too, civilization had come, pushing into where only animals had been. A single set of footprints, and some disturbance of the snow suggested that game had been trapped there. Someone struggling alone like himself? How many more settlers did the tracks point toward? For him, they formed a crossroads. His food was gone. Gray-bellied clouds hung over, promising more snow. If he didn't follow the tracks, he would be forced to lie down in his own.

He cursed himself for the pull of his own flesh, for its fresh vigor that urged him to struggle against cold and hunger and whatever waited in the future. But his uncertainly was brief. Taking his axe, saddle bags and canteen, he followed the tracks through the woods and down toward a valley. The snow had drifted deeper here, and the cold entered his bones. He went on until his legs would no longer move and half-frozen, he sank beneath his exhaustion, to the ground.

He woke to the sensation of warmth, to the feel of blankets against his body, skins beneath him. His eyes opened to a roof above him—the inside of a cabin. He felt the warmth of a fire burning in a corner of the room, and he saw a woman tending to a cooking pot, an Indian woman, he guessed, though strangely disfigured. The end of her nose was gone, as if cut off. And a man with grizzled hair and beard, dressed in buckskins, sat at a rough table mending a boot.

"Well, fella, I see you're awake. Looks like you had to walk the blade of a knife to get here."

He tried to sit up, but trudging in the snow had used him up.

"Good thing I found you when I did; you'd have frozen to the ground by now." He could hear the grimness in the tone. "If I thought you'd tracked me here to do harm, I'd have left you there to die."

"It's all a toss of the dice to me," Gil said feebly. "I hear freezing to death is not a bad way to go. Anyway, I owe you my life, such as it is."

The woman came to sit beside him and feed him a soup with venison in it. But he could take only a few spoonfuls before an overwhelming weariness overtook him. He lay back and slept. Sleep engulfed him, and his waking seemed also a part of sleep. Woven through it was the voice of the man who had taken him in, and whose story unwound, threading together sleep and wakefulness— as though the voice had not spoken for a long time. Where it had begun, Gil had forgotten. Somehow a story had come in response to his curiosity: who were these people and how had they found their way to this remote and isolated place? He had aroused the same curiosity in them.

"We came away as far as we could," the voice told him. "Jesse Grimes is the name and my woman here is Circling Light. A holy man found her name in one of his journeys and gave it to her—that's what they told her. But for her and me, there's nowhere else for us to belong."

The idea of belonging somewhere . . . The voice seemed part of a dream as it went on. "I'm not hiding from the law and don't owe anything to any man. I've trapped in these woods come ten years now or maybe a dozen—I've made notches on the post, but one year flows into the next, and I lose track."

Trapping beaver and martin, taking in the hides and selling them, bringing back flour and beans and bacon and corn meal and coffee—that was his life. He'd built a shed for the mule and tack, set up a place for skinning the beavers. He hunted the meat they ate— deer and antelope, wild turkey and bear. Gil could see him there in the woods as the dream continued.

Over the next few days, as he strength renewed, he began to tell Jesse something of his own origins and wanderings.

"I have no idea where I've come," Gil said, "but I wonder there's anybody living so far away from anything. How did you come here, if it's not a secret and you don't mind the telling?"

197

Jesse told him how his folks had come up from the South after the land had been burnt during Sherman's march to the sea. They'd come west to the Territory to homestead after the War was over, when times were so bad for the land being ruined for farming. "They tried to homestead here. Only one day when I was off getting water, the Apaches came up through the woods on a raid for our horses and cattle."

He'd tried to hide in the bushes, but they'd tracked him down, captured him, fled with him and the stock and took him to their camp. "Apaches—I became one of them."

As the story wove through his dreaming, he saw how the Indians taught the captive along with their own boys how to ride and shoot a bow and arrow, throw a lance and hunt with the best. He saw how the boy settled in with them, speaking their lingo, all but forgetting his own.

He could see this life unfolding: "They gave me over to their medicine man, and he taught me to know all the herbs for healing and for ceremony and sent me out to gather them. Taught me their songs and chants."

The telling seemed to agitate Jesse with old memories. He took out a pipe, filled it with tobacco and began to smoke. "That's when the evil thing happened."

Waking and sleeping, time falling away into the alternation of light and dark, Gil could hardly sleep enough. The woman cared for him, giving him meat and drink when she could. He was dimly aware of her as the story went on.

Then he was awake, somehow restored. He sat up, took in his surroundings as if for the first time, looked into the faces of those who had taken him in. When Jesse picked up the story again, they were standing at the edge of the evil thing.

Was memory a dream too?

"I was out gathering herbs when cavalry spotted me on their way to attacking the camp. When they captured me, I went wild yelling and fighting. I was Indian and that's where I belonged. But they took me back and gave me to my folks. Only they weren't my folks any more. They were white strangers speaking a language that wasn'r mine. I grew up silent and surly; I wasn't one of them. But neither could I go back to the Indians. Not after a dozen years of having to be a white man. And some of the Indians used me pretty rough—a joke, a paleface slave. No, once I was away, I couldn't go back and just live among 'em. And then all the killing on both sides... Who was I supposed to kill?"

The two men sat silently, both looking at the burning coals of the fire. So they had both emerged from their experiences, left with all their questions. Even when you thought you knew the answer, Gil could have told him, it was not the one you wanted or anything you expected.

The next day a blizzard whirled round the cabin. The wind was a wild thing, like an animal raging to enter. They piled wood on the fire and tried to keep away from the drafts. They went back to the story. "If you don't mind my asking," Gil said, "Circling Light, as she's called—how did she get here with you?"

"I saw her when I came to the reservation to trade—I could speak their lingo. My woman here is Mexican and Indian. Captured when the Apaches made one of their raids south of the border, and she grew up away from her people just like me."

"Not an easy life. I was treated pretty well, but some captives weren't. The other girls and women pulled her hair and called her names, treated her with spite because she had a pretty face and a different light in her eyes, and the men looked in her direction."

Circling Light came and sat with them, and took up the story herself. "The hardest chores they gave to me. One day they marry me to a man, not the one I liked and who liked me. He had no spirit. Weak and lazy. After, the women make trouble—say I sneak out and go to the man I liked. It was not true, but my husband made a fight with me and said it was true. . . . I try to run away but they catch me and cut my nose. Such pain I never knew. And after, I was dirt."

Gil had been looking at her as she fed him, washed his face, helped him sit up. He had come to see the beauty in her face.

"I saw her when I came to camp to trade, and she was a sorry sight," Jesse said. "They laughed at me when I told them I would take her for my wife. But she was the one I wanted. We're fit for each other and not for anybody else."

And so their stories came together into one strand—they had made a life together.

The day after the weather grew calm again, though it was bitter cold, Jesse went out to hunt. Circling Light spent her day splitting wood and tending the fire and sewing. Gil was hardly equipped to venture outside, what with the rags he wore and his bare feet, from which the swelling had finally gone down. She had sewed him a pair of moccasins she'd cut from deer hide that she'd hung and dried. And when she finished those, she cut out a shirt from the softer part of the leather, and breeches as well. There was nothing for him to do except help tend the fire and wait until his clothes were finished.

"Tell me something I can listen to," he said. "Tell me one of your stories."

She could tell him, she said, how the world began, if that was the kind of story he wanted to hear.

"A true story?" He'd heard one too, a long time ago. Perhaps they were all true. "Let me hear it then," he said.

She told him how once in the womb of the earth it was dark and there were only the dark gods who grew weary of themselves. *Let us make a creature that will give us praise and do deeds of honor in our name,* they said. And they assembled bits of mud and made a creature, but it would not hold together and kept falling apart into little pieces. They were greatly disappointed, though the bits and pieces turned into animals and birds. One of the gods took a bird and whirled it around until the bird grew dizzy. It could see eagles and hawks and all kinds of other birds. And these came into the world too. Then he whirled it in the other direction, and it saw all the things that come in dreams. And then he let it go. And it flew upward into the air.

They tried again, the dark gods. It was a great struggle, this time to fashion a creature out of wood, carving away pieces until it looked

200

like something they hadn't seen before. But when they'd done, it was still wood, and though it could multiply and there were little manikins in the world below, it had no memory of who created it, and could not offer praise or anything sensible. It had no heart; it had no mind to think with. Dreams did not come to it. Again they were disappointed and wept in their frustration until the tears became a flood and carried away all the manikins. And jaguars came to rip their bodies and left them in splinters.

All the time she sewed she recounted the difficulties of making man and the strange shapes he came in as the gods tried experiments that ended up as failures. For each man came in the shape of error.

"Isn't that always true?" Gil asked her.

She looked at him for a moment. and left him with an enigmatic smile. "You will have to decide," she said and went on with her sewing and her story. "The gods looked at the other creatures they had made—the mountain lion with its strength and courage and the wily jaguar and the monkeys and parrots with all their tricks and the sharp-eyed lynx and the clever fox, and they tried again to make a creature that had all of these qualities but who could remember and feel gratitude and give praise. They shaped him and his mate, and this time they were certain they had done everything right. "

She let him take that in and then continued. "But the darkness was so deep they could not see, and even in the dim place the animals and birds had climbed to, nothing was clear. Surely there was a good place for all the dreams the bird had seen when it was whirled around. Some that made their home in the dark, like the bat and the owl, moles and others that hunted their food at night were content. But for others, it was a place to lurk and slink in the dark—to hide their deeds."

"I've known a few like that," Gil said. He watched her as she sewed the skins and wove her story, watched the light from the fire touch her face and ruined nose. He wondered where her story came from, what languages it flowed through on the way to a tongue she'd not been born knowing. It sounded as though she'd had to take the rough sounds and shape them for her own.

"Once when the gods weren't looking, a tribe of rattlesnakes mated with the women; and their children came into the world. Since they didn't look different from any of the others, there was no telling them apart. They mixed with the rest."

But underneath the surface, she told him, they seethed with jealousy and spite, for they knew their fathers were snakes. At first they slunk down and refused to go where there was light. 'Till the people wondered. For they were eager to move out of the darkness. The birds had discovered the way and all the rest were climbing out of the dark womb deep in the earth and into the upper air. And finally the Snake Children didn't want to be down in the dark alone. They carried their jealousy and hatred into the upper world, knowing it would make a power for them, and they watched how it rose and took shape and followed them everywhere they went." The low tones of her voice carried him along, pulling him into darker territory.

"You haven't told about death," he said. "—how that got here."

She did not answer then. For the trapper entered the cabin, after tromping the snow from his boots and shaking off the snow from his clothes. He came home with a pair of beavers he'd trapped. He skinned them and hung up their hides, and Circling Lignt roasted the meat over the fire for their supper.

The next day after Jesse left, Circling Light asked him how he had come to be wandering in those woods without boots and with only the pelts of mountain lions covering him. "It is a story," Gil told her, "that has taken all the marrow from my bones, all the juice and joy. He told her about Hombre and how they came together. Then about Jack and his hold on the territory and how they set out to kill him. And then he told her about the wound that wouldn't be cured and about Hombre's death and the grief and guilt that had sent him on his wanderings. As he told it, it seemed to have happened to somebody removed from him, to a stranger even. The distance left him strangely vacant, as though in some sense it ceased to belong to him any more, but was only a story..

"It was not only that I lost Hombre," he told her, "but that our deed was an empty deed. The very thing you want to destroy," he said, "destroys something else. And leaves its shadow behind. And though I have wandered far and into strange realms where I met my father, who has been dead since I was a boy, and others who perished and now live in the realm of ghosts and shadows, they could offer no solace or advice. And finally they abandoned me in disgust. I have gone as far as I can go. And perhaps that's why I feel only emptiness."

"You have been away long enough," she said, "and now it is time to go back."

"Why?" he demanded. "What is there left?"

"You don't know what lies ahead or where the story will go. Perhaps you've spent too much time looking at shadows."

He said to her, "I don't know how to go back. There is no story. I want only to be forgotten."

"There is always a story," she said, "that your life weaves. Even when it sinks back into the earth, into the dark womb. From there it is born again in someone's mind."

"And what difference did it make? I see only a darkness behind me and a darkness in front. I don't know how to find a story I can belong to—where I can enter and go forward. Tell me a story I can enter."

"That's not so easy," she said, as she worked on his clothes. "It is much easier to make a shirt. I have stories in my head, some my grandmother told me, some from the women of the Apaches and other stories people brought from other tribes. And when I am sitting in front of the fire, I think of this one and that one. Sometimes when I'm alone I make up stories out of all the pieces and threads. Things I hear and what others tell me. Nothing stays the same, and so it is with me. It would be different if I lived with my people. There are those who tell the stories the same way over and over, for they are always true. But now they are gone from me, and my life is here. I can listen to whatever comes into my head. But everyone has to weave his own story."

"I have fought with shadows," he said. "That is my fate."

"I will tell you about the Shadowmaker," she said, "but I do not know if it is your story or if you can enter it."

"Yes, tell me," he said, "it will be something to listen to, and I will put more wood on the fire."

She waited until he had done this and settled back down on one of the bearskins to watch the flames.

"When the world was made," she began, "and men climbed out into the light, some of the gods created the thunder and the mountains and sky. But one stayed in the darkness, the Shadowmaker. It is he who brings all the things that visit the world of dreams and the one who gives everything its shadow. To all the things that live in the light. And all that happens in time. For each thing has its shadow—all the things a man does. Part comes into the light and the rest falls into the darkness and lives there. But we do not see what falls away from our lives—or else only a long time afterwards. And there are many shadows—all the things men do and have done before."

"All the ugly things," he said.

She shook her head. "It is all mixed up. Hard to tell one from another. Ugly things, deformed things, unknown things. Even in the things with sun on them—all those things that look real and good. They come and go like shadows. And the things that fall away, some of them are full of seeds."

"Jack is among the shadows," he said, "And Hombre as well. Something remains of both. But one smells of rot, the other smells of earth."

"There were men," she continued, "who came to this land from the Old World—men who had grown tired in their experience, for whom all things were sick and rotting. They longed to cast away from them all the shadows that had come down to them and to find the beginning of things all fresh and new. And gold. For there were great cities full of gold. They found people who lived in the land the way their ancestors did, men dark-skinned like the earth. Some who made wars and others who lived in peace. Some who had gold, and others who never saw it. But for those who came, those they found had to be conquered—they took up the land. The killing has gone everywhere—great killing, And all those with a hunger for land came to get it."

"The man I knew had such a lust. . . . He killed many men to get a vast territory. That was the man I killed."

"There was a man," she continued without comment, "who wanted to be rid of shadows, to live in a world where there was only light. He wanted true things, the spirits that lived in them. Otherwise he could not be content. He did not to have a wife or children. He ate only a little food; he did not care to hunt and take part in the festivals. For these were empty things to him. Finally after many prayers and much suffering—maybe he was like you—he entered the world of shadows, going to the doorway of death, where living things have cast off their flesh and bones, but are not done with life. And the man went there and saw there all the things he had not lived. Hunting and fighting and bearing children and the dances and festivals. He couldn't stay—there was nothing for him. *Let me go on*, he said. *These are not true things.*

"The farther he went the more he cast off all he knew, all that belonged to the world above. The spirits allowed him to visit their home. And there he saw he cast no shadow at all. And he rejoiced. But neither could he join the spirits—he was only an emptiness."

There was a silence as he waited for her to go on. "That is all the story," she said and left off and went for jerky to cook into a stew.

"But wait," he insisted. "What happened then?"

She said she had told him all she knew. That day she finished sewing for him the shirt he would wear and the breeches.

"You've got the better of me," he said. "You're a clever woman— you slip out and leave things without an ending."

"There is no ending," she said.

The story had left him unsatisfied, as restless and angry as he had felt before. He couldn't sit still and did not know what to do with himself. It was time for him to leave, but first he had a debt to pay. "Tomorrow," he said, "I will put on the clothes you've made for me and go out and hunt."

"Yes," she said. "It will be a long winter. And the meat will not last."

They had given him their food, their meat and bread and coffee. He had to restore what he'd taken from them, it was only fair. The next day the two men rose before dawn, ate bread and coffee and prepared to go out for the day. For the hunt, Jesse gave him a shirt and a pair of breeches and his spare boots. Gil put on his poncho, and the two men went out hoping to track a deer that had come out to forage, made hungry by the storm. Gil took the rifle Circling Light used to hunt, for she was a good shot, Jesse said, and had brought down more than one deer.

The snow was deep, and had drifted here and there among the trees, but the sky was clear and brilliant blue. They breathed in the cold and their breath steamed in the air. They had to move slowly. They found fresh tracks down by the creek and followed them through the woods. Jesse and Gil spotted a buck just as it got wind of them and both fired, one after the other. The deer dashed away but they found its blood darkening the snow, and they followed the wounded animal. Through a stand of thick pines they made their way. They saw where the animal had paused in the hope it had lost them, then sheered off deeper into the woods. The trail of blood marked the way over a hillside blanketed with snow, down into a low valley. Early in the afternoon, they came upon the fallen animal, a young buck, panting and bleeding in the snow, spent with the chase.

They shot the deer, then Jesse cut open the animal from the gullet to the anus, lifted out the entrails, skinned the deer, cut up the meat and wrapped it in the hide. He lifted out the liver and cut it into pieces. "Eat some of this," he said to Gil. "It will give strength to your blood." They ate it warm and still steaming in the cold air.

XIV. Return

He was glad to return to the cabin to take shelter from the cold that had sent his blood racing, The fire felt good. All was quiet in the cabin as the fire played on the walls. His senses, sharpened to the keenness of the hunt, were shaped by hunger as he breathed in the smell of cooking meat and burning wood. he felt a contentment, at first purely physical, that left his mind behind, then finally invited it in. He knew he would sink into sleep and sleep deeply.

They would not let him leave just yet. The next day he and Jesse went out and cut saplings that they made into a frame held together with thongs in a space where a pit had been dug. Circling Light then covered the frame with blankets and hides while Gil and Jesse gathered wood for the fire Jesse then built in the pit. They fed it and waited for it to burn down into coals, then brought over rocks from the pile Jesse had collected and placed at the side of the cabin. With an offering of corn meal, Circling Light prayed to the spirits of the four directions. Gil and Jesse each placed a feather as an offering at the entrance, then stripped down to the cloths they had wrapped around, their loins, crept through the opening and sat on hides Circling Light had put inside. With tongs made of deer antlers, Jesse took the first round of rocks from Circling Light's hands and set them carefully in the fire at the bottom of the pit. Circling Light handed him a bucket of water with a dipper to pour it over the rocks. Gil and Jesse sat amicably sweating in the heat and steam until sweat poured down their bodies. Jesse took the pipe he had brought from the cabin, recited the prayers he had learned from the Apaches and passing the pipe, invited Gil to pray to the spirits for what he needed. Something to go back to—he prayed for that.

After they had gone for the four rounds, Jesse opened the entrance flap, and the two of them crawled out, raced into an open space and, giving a yell, rolled in the snow. When Gil had dried off and they were back in the cabin, Circling Light gave him the clothes she had sewed for him.

The next morning he and Jesse prepared for his departure. Jesse would guide him part of the way. After their breakfast together, he expressed his thanks to Circling Light for the care she had given him, for the clothes she had sewed for him, and for her stories. He and Jesse made their way to a trail Jesse had blazed that wound through the mountains. Jesse gave him a rough map to help him past the caprices of the weather. and directions to take him to the town he had nearly forgotten. Indeed it had begun to snow again, on top of the snow that already lay on the ground. The distant peaks were veiled, merging with the sky, and the boughs of the evergreens tipped beneath the downfall.

Gil carried with him a parcel of dried deer meat and Indian bread to last him for the days it would take to get through the Mogollons. He was wearing the pair of boots Jesse had given him. It would be slow going through the snow and moccasins would not suffice.

Jesse walked ahead, and Gil kept his eye on him as he tried to keep his orientation. He kept thinking of how much he owed to the two people who had saved his life and cared for him without any thought of their advantage. Two strangers. He felt a gratitude that was new to him that began to take in those who had given him much of themselves in the past and had suffered at his hands.

Their last evening, Circling Light had roasted venison over the fire, and they had feasted on meat and bread and roasted corn, while the light from the fire played with the shadows on the walls. He tried to hold onto that scene of warmth and celebration.

Jesse had described for him the way back, how to go and what signs to look for. He would descend to the river, follow it until it forked, then go south through a pass in the mountains. He would be back in the outer reaches of Jack's old domain, back into territory he was familiar with. But it was hard for him to visualize. He still stood inside a kind of dimness—he had not entirely left the realm of shadows. Nothing of substance down there, only the bloodless

208

semblance of the life above. He'd come back, it was true, with an emptiness he still had to fill. It was hunger that had helped restore his sense of vitality. And he thought of how he and Jesse had paused there in the snow and the cold, eating the liver of the deer as the Indians did.

He and Jesse plodded through the snow-laden trees as he glanced now and then at the white sky, the mountains dissolved in whiteness.

Jesse waited until Gil caught up with him. "This is where I leave you, friend," he said. "See there, along that ridge is where you go. Even with the snow, you'll be able to make your way. About halfway down is the abandoned miner's shack I told you about. I left some wood there, for when I want to spend the night there after a day's hunting."

He didn't want Jesse to leave him. Everything was covered, hidden under the snow. And he felt something like terror at the thought of going back. But he could ask no more. He shook Jesse's hand, expressed his thanks and let him go. He continued along the trail. It was indeed slow-going. A wind had kicked up, the flakes stinging his face. He had to give all his attention to the task, make his way alone. He was glad to reach the abandoned shack where he started a fire and spent the night wrapped in his poncho. He slept until the light summoned him through the cracks.

He woke with a strange dream in his head. He dreamt that the snow had melted and left behind thick mud, a swamp stretching before him that he had to make his way through. He worked from hummock to hummock, careful not to slip. The muddy water was full of snakes, some dark and rotting, but others in brilliant colors, yellow, red, green, all entwined in shining curves and arcs, like flames rising and falling. Fire snakes. He marveled at them, the way they rose up, submerged and rose again—dozens of them. The image stayed with him.

He ate a breakfast of Indian bread and jerky and continued on his way. The sky was clear now and the sun glinted on the snow. He breathed deeply, filling his lungs. Sleep had refreshed him and he was eager to be on his way again. The sharp air drove its keen edge into him, excited him, made his scalp tingle. His step seemed lighter, and he grew warm with exertion. The landscape began to take his notice, things discovering themselves to him. He could see trees emerging from the whiteness that had enclosed them, and faces of the rocky landscape broken now by lines and shapes. His spirits rose as the world came back, discovering itself again.

It was familiar country, but it was as though he was seeing it with new eyes. He had ridden through it how many times during his youth and young manhood. It was the same, yet different. He began to take notice of the way the hills curved away into the peaks, some luminous with bony outcroppings, others worn away with runnels caused by the erosion from wind and rain. He regarded the slopes that moved down into canyons. And then the stretches of the tree-lined river, which flowed in a narrow channel down the center, the rest crusted with ice. The cottonwoods moved in and out of the light, becoming what they were given to be, with their thick deeply grooved trunks and tall branches, their many shapes and facets. The pines and pinon trees, each with its own shape. The light did it all, playing with cloud and shadow and the color of the sky. The rocks moved up into the daylight with their various planes and angles, as they had done from the very beginning,

As the shifting light played with them, deepening colors, arranging shadows, they brought a series of images to his mind. Whole cities emerged and castles and strongholds that might have held the histories of civilizations rising and falling. But they went beyond human invention—they held the history of the earth.

There were faces in the rocks. He saw them looking out. Faces, robed figures, whole processions of them—men and women who seemed to have taken into themselves the experience of the past and now stood like hieratic figures. Their faces were crags, sharp, and not quite molded into the human, though they suggested it, for they stood beyond the moment, enigmatic—silent and regarding. He could see how the forms had been created by wind and weather.

His father and Hombre, even Jack, belonged now to that procession of the past. Gone now. He was the one to carry their memory forward. There was nowhere else to take his grief. All, busy at their labors, would have put it aside. He continued on; the closer he came, the more his mind filled with familiar things, of what the town looked like and how new dwellings kept being built. He thought of his mother, whom he'd abandoned. Had she been mourning for him, her only son? Very likely, since that's what mothers do, but she had not kept him back from whatever awaited him. She had let him go to his destiny, generous as always not to hold him down, and now she would see him return.

Pieces of the story came and went. He'd have to remember how it had unfolded, for he knew how things keep moving, changing, until you couldn't distinguish one from another, each reborn from the alloy, some things lost, others found, taking form.

He passed through Jack's domain, continued down along the river to where Hombre was buried underneath the great cottonwood. He paused there, stood silent at the grave for a moment while other images rose around him, he and Hombre as they went out on the land to hunt, as they camped beneath the tree, with their fears and bursts of courage, as they closed in on Jack. Hombre lying wounded—the man who'd been part of him since they'd wrestled one another and broken into laughter.

As he stood there, visited by all that had passed and left its mark, he felt something live and moving at his side, a nuzzling at his hand and looked down to see a dog. What dog had wandered out here in the woods? His dog? He couldn't believe it might be, he'd given her up so long ago. Yet there was no mistaking her, though she'd lost a paw since he'd seen her last. And then he knew. She'd been caught in a trap somewhere, a big trap that had taken part of her leg.

"Is it you?" he said, still incredulous. "How did you survive?" He bent down and sank his hands into her fur. He tried to imagine her fending for herself there in the woods, somehow keeping herself alive. Waiting for him perhaps.

He said his farewell to Hombre lying under the great tree and set off with his dog loping at his side on three legs instead of four. When his thought went to his return, did he wonder if anyone cared to remember him? Hippolyta? He could see her as he left, her face turned up to him, her eyes filled with the promise of whatever she might offer. Would she be there to give him welcome? Had she finished building her chapel? Had she discovered the gods she might worship—or had they been discovered yet? Perhaps he began to wonder why she had set herself such a task, what his might be, what, if anything, might lie there in the shadows waiting to be born.

This is where I followed him and where I now take my leave. He is the one who descended into the abyss. And I have gone to stand beside him there. I, too, had to wonder what I was and where I'd been. For I have been him and all the rest, as I've become their stories, trying to create from memory and motive. We're always put to that task, to imagine the unimaginable. For it is always there, waiting to be encountered. Though everything dies, the experience remains, breaking through the seal of memory, playing out in dreams, making its claims, bitter and sweet, unfinished—something to take forward, emerging from shadow into light.

Afterword

Though my first discoveries of the epic, especially the *Iliad* and the *Odyssey*, revealed to me a rich and fascinating world, it didn't occur to me until I read Robert Warshow's intriguing essay, "The Westerner," that we had anything like the epic here on our native ground. Indeed, the Western is, in his view, our national epic. Much less did it occur to me that I would attempt to enter that particular territory.

With a random comment, my husband, Richard, set me on the track. At the time, we were teaching the epic of Gilgamesh in a Great Books course. "You know," he said, "Gilgamesh would make a great story in a Western setting." I don't remember now how long it was before I took up the challenge—at least a couple of years—but the idea must have been working underground. I'm not sure now quite how it all got started. I do remember that on a visit to Silver City, where I grew up, I spent several days poking around in the files of the museum there, thinking I might find some interesting material. I was not even looking for anything specific. I made copies of various incidents I still haven't used. Whatever the case, I began to pick up all sorts of cues. I read in detail about gold and silver being discovered in the area and the emergence of the town: the flood that wiped out the main street; the land baron who, through murder and intimidation, acquired extensive holdings; the prostitute who, denied admittance to the church, built her own chapel; a man who had been running wild in the Gila Wilderness. (Later, in one of J. Frank Dobie's books, I read a brief description of a man who ran with cattle.) These incidents seized my imagination. From them I have woven my tale, which, though inspired by the great Sumerian epic, is a story I hope will stand on its own and speak to our time.

Gladys Swan has published two novels, *Carnival for the Gods*, (Vintage Contemporaries Series), and *Ghost Dance: A Play of Voices*, (LSU Press, nominated for the PEN/Faulkner Award), as well as seven collections of short fiction. Her poetry and essays, and short stories have appeared in many literary magazines and anthologies. Much of her work is set in New Mexico, where she grew up. Though she has spent most of her career as a writer, she has devoted much of her time during the last two decades to painting and exploring the creative process. She was the first writer since the inception of the Vermont Studio Center to receive a fellowship for a residency in painting. She also received a fellowship from the Lilly Endowment for a year's study of Inuit art and mythology and a Fulbright Award as a writer-in-residence in Yugoslavia. Her paintings have appeared as the cover art for various literary magazines and books, including the most recently published, *The Tiger's Eye: New & Selected Stories*. She has twice been a Guest Writer at the Vermont Studio Center and has held residencies at Yaddo, the Chateau de Lavigny in Switzerland. the Fimdacion Valparaiso in Spain and others. She has taught literature and creative writing at various colleges and universities, notably, in the MFA Program at the Vermont College of the Arts, and at the University of Missouri-Columbia. She received an Honorary Doctorate of Humane Letters from Western New Mexico University and gave the commencement address. *The Carnival Quintet*, an outgrowth of her first novel, is being published by Kiwai Media in Paris. The first volume, *Carnival for the Gods*, appeared in September, 2014. She has done the cover paintings for the series.

I would like to acknowledge and express my gratitude, first of all, to Walter Cummins for his encouragement, enthusiasm, and tireless efforts in bringing the book to light. My thanks also to Philip & Shirley Parotti, Sudie Kennedy & Carl Ruhne, Bonnie & Librado Madonado, Monte Nevin, and Kathy Bower for their interest in and support for my work.